# LADY LA

*Lynna Banning*

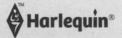

## Harlequin®

TORONTO  NEW YORK  LONDON
AMSTERDAM  PARIS  SYDNEY  HAMBURG
STOCKHOLM  ATHENS  TOKYO  MILAN  MADRID
PRAGUE  WARSAW  BUDAPEST  AUCKLAND

ISBN-13: 978-0-373-29627-9

LADY LAVENDER

# The warm air smelled of horses and fresh straw. And lavender.

Wash half turned to her. "You all right?"

She nodded, and he climbed down and began to unhook the rig. She thought a smile touched his mouth. He was pleased, then, with their day's work? Or was he pleased that his precious railroad could now roll its iron tracks over her farm?

Jeanne was weary, but not so much that she couldn't feel the inexplicable pull toward the man who was now lifting her sleeping daughter into his arms. He paused at the door to her room while she unlocked it. Light spilled from the doorway, illuminating where she and Manette slept.

He entered as if expecting to be ambushed, then gently deposited Manette on the big double bed. When he straightened Jeanne laid her hand on his muscled forearm. He flinched the tiniest bit, and somehow she guessed he was weighing his reticence about her against his masculine need. That pleased her.

"You have been very kind," she said. "You are a good man, Monsieur Wash."

The oddest expression crossed his face, and in his gray eyes she suddenly saw both wariness and raw desire.

\* \* \*

*Lady Lavender*
**Harlequin® Historical #1027—February 2011**

*Available from Harlequin® Historical and*
*LYNNA BANNING*

**Look for another romantic ride
into the West from
Lynna Banning
in
*Happily Ever After in the West*
Coming May 2011**

For my dear friend Susan Renison.

With thanks to Tricia Adams, Suzanne Barrett,
Kathleen Dougherty, Karyn Witmer-Gow,
Shirley Marcus, Brenda Preston, and David Woolston

# *Chapter One*

*Smoke River, Oregon 1867*

When Wash Halliday came home from the war, Smoke River gave him a hero's welcome. The tattered remains of the marching band gathered in the town square wearing their faded green uniforms and once-gold buttons and blared "Hail the Conquering Hero" only slightly off-key.

His ears rang with the noise, and he felt it all the way down to his feet. He glanced down at the leather boots in which, a year ago, he had marched from the Union prison at Richmond all the way to Fort Kearney. Now, he was back in Smoke River.

Midsummer sunlight glanced off the tuba and Wash stifled an urge to duck; the flash of light looked exactly like an exploding mortar.

Thad McAllister, the graying band leader, pumped

his skinny arms rhythmically up and down, up and down, but now Wash could hear nothing. A roaring noise bloomed in his head, rolled and echoed like thunder, and then a high-pitched scream began. He pressed both hands over his ears.

*Stop. Stop.* Behind his closed eyes the red-gold explosions began again.

"Havin' one of yer spells, are ya?" his grizzled companion queried softly.

"What? No…no. Just can't stop remembering."

The sun-blackened half-Comanche furrowed his salt-and-pepper eyebrows. "Let's get away from this headache powwow and have a drink. Saloon's just across the street."

Rooney was usually thirsty for some Red Eye about this time of day. Wash usually wasn't. But today it was the other way around.

He waved his thanks at the bandleader and the two men marched through the crowd across the main street of hard-packed dirt. The hot afternoon breeze rustled the leaves of maple and poplar trees, already turning gold even though it was only August.

The buildings were sparse but well-kept. Livery stable, sheriff's office, mercantile and two saloons. "Damn small town for a railway station," Rooney muttered.

"It'll grow," Wash said with conviction. "When the railroad comes through it'll be the biggest town in Jefferson County."

Rooney shot him a look and spat tobacco juice from one side of his mouth. "Railroad ain't comin' if you don't get the surveyin' done and get yer clearing crews out here."

Wash didn't answer. He had plenty of time. Grant Sykes of the Oregon Central Railroad wouldn't expect a route plotted for another week; that gave him four days to inspect the area and get the survey crew started.

He resettled his Stetson and gestured at the rickety-looking two-story building with a fancy gold-lettered sign out front. "Golden Partridge. Jupiter! Oregon settlers sure have a knack for fancied-up names."

"Name don't mean nothin'," Rooney said in a dry tone. "It's the whiskey that counts."

Wash gritted his teeth. "Names always mean something. Just look at George Washington Halliday here and tell me you don't see the gold braid and spit-polished boots Pop thought went with the name."

Rooney grunted. "Get over it, Wash. Your pa named you, but it was you went off to be a big hero in the War. You said your momma like to die when she seen you all bony and crippled up after Gettysburg. Anyway, that was back then, and the Golden Partridge is in the sweet here and now."

Wash tramped up the board sidewalk, glanced at the horse he'd tied up at the hitching rail and pushed through the double doors of the saloon. Rooney puffed through the entrance behind him.

"Howdy, gents," the grinning barkeep called. "Beer?"

Wash planted both elbows on the polished wood bar. "Whiskey."

The place smelled of sour chicken mash and off in a

dim corner a black man was playing a twangy-sounding piano. "Oh, Suzanna." Rooney, already humming the tune, held up two fingers and the barkeep nodded.

"Welcome home, Colonel," the barkeep murmured while the whiskey gurgled out of the bottle. "War kept you busy, I hear. Sorry about your leg."

Wash swallowed hard. That wasn't the worst of it, getting his hip half shot off with a minié ball. The worst was that Laura had gone off and married someone else before he'd even left for the War. His chest had ached for weeks. The years after Laura had been pretty damn dark. Still were, he acknowledged.

The barkeep, short and round with a swatch of red hair and a mustache to match, swiped a rag across the counter. "What'll you do now?"

"Now I'm working for the railroad."

"Heard it was coming. Good thing, too. Where you plan to route it?"

"My boss had a choice between Scarecrow Hill and Green Valley. He's choosing the valley."

"Not this valley he won't." The barkeep recorked the whiskey and set the bottle at his elbow.

Wash's gut tightened. "Oh? Why's that?"

"The widow Nicolet, that's why. She owns land in the valley. Small farm, but you can't get into town without running an eyelash away from her place."

"So?"

"Hell's haystacks, Colonel, a narrow trail alongside her fields is one thing, but a railroad right-of-way? That's a different breed of bull."

Wash set his empty shot glass on the bar and caught

the man's eyes. "The railroad owns the land, not the lady."

"Maybe. But Miz Nicolet thinks it's hers." He pronounced the name with a long *a* at the end. Nicolay.

"You know that for a sure thing?"

The barkeep shrugged. "She hasn't given in on one single thing in the four years since she settled here. Real stubborn woman. Frenchie, you know. Worst kinda female on the face of the planet."

Wash quirked an eyebrow. "Why's that? Because she's French?"

"Because she's female. A woman don't belong out here, farmin' on her own. Plus that woman don't allow nothin' anywhere near her place, not even Fourth of July picnics."

Wash shifted, hooking his boot onto the bar rail. "That's a railroad right-of-way her farm's sitting on. Railroad wants to use it."

"Huh!" the barkeep spluttered. "Railroad got a few hundred soldiers to back you up?"

"Nope. They got something better—me. I'm a lawyer, and I'm overseeing the railroad crews."

The red-haired man again swiped his cloth over the bar. "No fancy law-spoutin' Back-East lawyer's gonna make a dent in that woman's spine."

"I'm not a fancy Back-East lawyer," Wash said quietly. "And it's not her spine that interests me. It's her fence posts."

All Wash knew about France was that Napoleon was a big overgrown bully and the wine had bubbles in it. Didn't seem to him that a woman, even if she was

French, could be too big an obstacle. If she was halfway intelligent he'd simply point out the advantages the rail line would bring to Smoke River.

And if she wasn't intelligent, well, then he'd have to maneuver her into relinquishing the land the railroad owned. At his left, Rooney downed a second shot and when he could draw breath, smacked his lips. "Damn good stuff, Wash. Thanks."

"Don't know how you could tell, it went down so fast." He rolled three two-bit pieces down the shiny wood bar and together the two men stepped out into the fading sunlight.

Wash grabbed the reins of the black gelding and swung up into the saddle. "Gonna ride out and take a look at the narrow end of the valley."

Rooney chortled. "You mean take a look at the lady farmer at the narrow end of the valley."

"Just reconnoitering the enemy. You coming?"

The stocky man turned back toward the saloon. "Nope. Rather stir up a poker game 'stead of a hornet's nest. That's your department."

Yeah. Hornet's nests were his specialty. That's what he'd dealt with in the War and later with the Sioux at Fort Kearney. And that's what Grant Sykes paid him for now. He reined away from the hitching rail and headed the horse past the whispering maple trees toward Green Valley.

When he got to the overhanging cliff, Wash reined in. Below him stretched an undulating sea of lavender, washing up the surrounding hills like a purple tide. The little farmhouse nestled at the neck of the valley, a long, slim island of green surrounded by hills as brown and dry as old tea leaves. A peaceful place.

He guessed few travelers passed by and those who did kept their horses on the narrow pathway to avoid trampling the purple-topped bushes next to the lane. Wash had to chuckle. Patches of bright green mint grew along the edge, so if a horse strayed off the path, the sharp minty scent alerted the rider. Miz Nicolet must be one canny farmer.

He wondered for the twentieth time why Sykes's railroad had purchased a right-of-way through this narrow valley. He guessed back then it was the only land the Oregon Central could acquire at a favorable price; the government had set aside the rest for homesteading.

Below him, a movement caught his attention, a flutter of blue swirling across the ocean of purple, a woman running, her apron crushed into one hand, bare legs flashing. She slowed and pointed up at him, then began wading through the field, shouting something.

He spurred the horse, stumbled down the steep edge through crumbling shale that shelved off under the mare's searching hooves. He shifted his weight to help the animal balance, and when they reached the level valley floor he bent forward, his eyes narrowing.

The tall patch of lavender just outside the weathered split rail fence twitched. His horse tensed and stood still, neck quivering. Wash laid a reassuring hand on the mare's warm hide. "What is it, General? You smell something?"

The black stood motionless, then took a cautious step

forward. Something scrabbled inside the little stand of lavender, and the bushy fronds waved back and forth.

"Jackrabbit, maybe," Wash murmured. He drew the Colt from his waistband. Too close for a rifle; it'd make mincemeat instead of supper.

Another wriggle and Wash fingered the hard metal trigger. "Okay, girl, let's flush it—" On the word *out,* he kneed the mare forward and aimed just left of the jiggling patch. If he guessed right, the critter would exit just in front of General's front hoof.

He waited. The horse settled a leg on the dark earth and a high, thin cry came from the bushes.

"What the devil…"

A small girl popped up, a little sprite of a thing, with two red-gold braids and a grimy white pinafore. "I am not a jackrabbit," she announced. "I am an anteater." She stuck out a tiny hand and unfolded it to reveal a smear of squashy-looking black stuff on her palm.

"You eat ants?" Wash asked.

The small hand closed up tight. "They taste like peppermint. I eat grasshoppers, too, but they wriggle. Do you like ants?"

He studied her. Bits of dry grass were stuck in her hair, and her sunburned nose tilted up as she gazed at him. "You gonna shoot me?"

"No, I never shoot little girls. Only jackrabbits." He started to stuff the Colt back in his holster when a blur of blue hurtled over the fence and plunged through the lavender patch. The spicy scent wafted on the still afternoon air.

The woman planted herself in front of General, breathing hard, and the horse shied.

"Don't touch her!" she screamed. She grabbed the child and shoved her behind her skirts.

"He wasn't gonna touch me, *Maman*," came the high voice from behind the blue skirt. "He was gonna shoot me."

The woman's face went dead white.

"Oh, no, ma'am, I wasn't going to—"

"He was, too, *Maman*. He was going to shoot me and eat me for supper!"

*"Mon dieu!"*

"I was not," Wash protested. "See, I thought she was a jackrab—"

"Do not bother to explain, *monsieur.* Just turn your horse around and go."

"Now, wait a minute. Let me ex—"

"Go!" She made shooing motions with the blue apron, her cheeks blazing crimson and her eyes...

Her eyes snapped. Magnificent eyes. Like two shards of teal stone flecked with gray. Eyes that made his heart stutter.

He studied the rest of her as she stood panting before him. Slim. Small waist. Couldn't tell about her hips under all those petticoats, but her breasts, rising and falling as she struggled for breath, looked lush and rounded. His mouth went dry. It had been a long, long time since he'd admired a woman's breasts.

He wrenched his gaze from her bosom. Her face had a smattering of freckles over a sun-browned nose and a soft-looking mouth the color of ripe raspberries. A wide-brimmed straw hat hung down her back, the blue ribbon ties knotted about her throat.

Wash cleared his throat. "You Miz Nicolet?"

"That is none of your business," she snapped. "Leave my land this instant!"

"Ma'am? Just listen a min—"

"And do not come back!"

Wash figured if he stayed until sundown, he'd never get to complete a sentence. "Well, now, I can't exactly promise—"

The woman spun, scooped her daughter into her arms and tramped away toward the house, taking long strides that kicked up her petticoats to reveal mud-caked black leather work boots. Over her retreating shoulder the little girl grinned at him and waved an ant-stained hand.

"Goodbye, *monsieur!* I hope you find something to eat."

Something to eat sounded like the balm his shaken confidence needed. Better yet, something to drink. He guessed Rooney would still be dealing cards at the Golden Partridge; maybe he could rustle up a steak and some beans before they figured out his partner was cheating.

"Come on, General." He headed the gelding down the narrow wagon trail toward town. "Wouldn't be the first time a woman hasn't liked what she saw of me right off," he muttered to his horse. "But sure as hell's the first time a woman's ever plain run me off. Not good for a man's spirit."

## Chapter Two

From the double swinging door of the Golden Partridge saloon, Wash took in the cobwebby walls, then the expanse of tobacco-sticky plank floor. Cowpunchers crowded three-deep around the poker table, but the barroom was so smoky he didn't see Rooney right off. When he did spot him, Wash wished he hadn't.

Hell's holy hobnails, Rooney was gambling again. The place reeked of whiskey and sweat, and underneath the sour smell lay a tension so thick it clogged his lungs.

His gray-haired sidekick was absorbed in a game of blackjack with five other men. Three were obviously ranch hands—hair slicked down, fresh-shaved, clean shirts and polished boots. The other two were older men with paunches and gray in their beards. Ranch owners, maybe. After all, it was Saturday night. He hoped they were all drunk enough that they wouldn't watch Rooney too closely.

Too late. A fresh-faced kid leaped to his feet, revolver drawn. "You're cheatin', mister! That card came from your sleeve."

Wash saw the kid's trigger finger tighten. He put a bullet through the kid's hat and the other men at the table swiftly rose, hands in the air, knocking chairs over backward.

"Pay up, Rooney," he ordered in a quiet voice. "Now. Before you get yourself killed."

"Hey!" the barkeep yelled. "Thought you was a lawyer-man."

"That's right," Wash replied evenly. "But even lawyers can shoot straight." He holstered his Colt. "Come on, Rooney, you're holding up my supper."

With a scowl, Rooney began to divvy up his pot.

Wash had to laugh. After the war, when he'd soldiered at Fort Kearney, he'd picked up Rooney Cloudman as his part-Indian army scout. It was Rooney who had helped him give up serious drinking. He was a good man except that he'd never been able to walk past a poker table with a card game going.

Every man had his weakness, Wash supposed; when he was younger he'd had the same hunger for whiskey and taking chances, for "riding close to the cliff" his father had said.

He no longer had the carefree heart he'd had at twenty-one; it had taken him three years of prison in Richmond and another year chasing the Sioux before he'd realized he was as close to self-destruction as a man could get. Even now, some days, he felt like a walking corpse. He didn't seek human interaction beyond keeping his poker-playing partner out of trouble, didn't want to dance with any of the ladies at the hoedown every other Saturday. And he didn't want to feel anything except pleasure over his breakfast coffee and bacon.

Dried up as a sun-parched cornstalk, Rooney said.

Rooney was right. The heart he carried around in his chest was dead. Pretty, blue-eyed Laura Gannon had been his first love, the kind that hurt the most. She'd also been his last. He'd never loved anyone like he'd loved Laura, but she'd jilted him the night before he'd left for the War. For damn sure he'd never risk wanting a woman again.

With shaking fingers, Jeanne Nicolet crammed a cartridge into the rifle and propped it with a satisfying *thunk* on the wooden gun rests over the front door of her tiny cabin.

"Are you going to shoot someone, *Maman?*" Manette craned her neck to inspect the rifle.

"*Non, ma petite.* Not unless I have to," Jeanne said between clenched teeth. Not unless another strange man trespassed in her lavender fields. No one from town ever rode out to pay a call, friendly or otherwise, not since she'd shot the sheriff's hat off when he'd questioned her right to the land. She had darted into the cabin, dug the deed out of the Bible on her nightstand, then returned to unfold it under the man's large nose.

He'd stepped forward, saying he wanted to look closer at the document, and that's when she'd pulled the derringer from her apron pocket and fired. Since then, no one had ventured past her gate.

Until now. She did not know what to think about the tall man who had come. What did he want? All she knew was that she did not trust him, especially since he was not only tall but had a nicely chiseled face and attractive, unruly dark hair.

When Henri had been killed, she'd wanted to get as far away from New Orleans as possible. The men who had survived the War were uncouth and pushy, particularly when they learned she was a widow. It had not been difficult to leave, even though she was completely on her own, the only one to provide for herself and her daughter.

Sometimes she felt so frightened she wanted to crawl into her bed and pull the quilt over her head. But she could not. She must have courage. She must move on with her life, no matter how difficult.

The climate in Oregon was perfect for growing lavender and, thanks to the New Orleans War Widows fund, she had scraped together enough money to buy the narrow strip of land that ran the length of the small valley and the abandoned prospector's cabin that had come with it. She had known no one; half the time she was scared to death of people, especially the men, but she had managed.

And she had the deed to prove it, now safe in the bank vault in Smoke River. Once each week she saddled up the mare and rode into town to trade for supplies; and once each week she stopped by the Smoke River Bank and smoothed her hand over the strong box where her precious document rested.

Green Valley was the only land she'd been able to afford, and nobody, *nobody,* was going to stop her from growing her lavender. French lavender. English lavender, Spanish lavender. Her family had grown lavender back in France; she knew more about lavender than she knew about ladies' fashions.

Her lavender field was the only source of income for herself and Manette. She reached up and patted the rusty barrel of the rifle mounted over the door. She would fight to protect what was hers, even if she had to shoot the first man since Henri who had made her heart jump. All the more reason not to trust him.


The following morning, Wash and Rooney rode out to Green Valley, drawing rein at the rise overlooking the valley. Beside him on his frisky strawberry roan, Rooney grunted. "You see what I see down there?"

"Yeah, I see it. Damn cabin built on railroad land. Who'd expect to find a squatter way out here?"

Rooney patted the neck of his mount and surveyed Wash with narrowing black eyes. "A better question is what're you gonna do about it?"

Wash blew out a long breath. "If I knew the answer to that, maybe I would have slept some last night."

Sykes had ruled out Scarecrow Hill because the railroad owned no right-of-way there. Wash had to get Green Valley surveyed, then get Miz Nicolet off that land before the clearing crew arrived. Problem was, she'd set to farming on land she didn't own. Most likely she *thought* she owned it; probably paid that cabin owner $2.50 an acre and he gave her a ginned-up deed and skedaddled before the law caught up with him. It had happened before.

He watched gray smoke puff lazily from the stone chimney into the summer air. Poor misguided woman. Her entire crop of whatever that purple stuff was would have to be ripped out. It looked like a nice, neat little farm. Pretty spot, too, with walnut and sugar maple trees covering both sides of the steep hills that enclosed the valley, and the sun bathing her crop in a glow of golden light.

His belly tightened. He hated to see things destroyed, whether it was Reb trains or ammunition dumps or Georgia plantations. Or little farms, like this one.

He'd try not to think about it.

Rooney nudged Wash's elbow and pointed. The French woman was out beside the cabin, hanging up laundry on a sagging clothesline: four white flounced petticoats and three girl's pinafores and…

He sucked in a breath. Leaping lizards…underwear! Lacy chemises and ruffled white underdrawers so small he could bunch up a dozen and stuff them in his pocket.

He shut his eyes to block out the sight, steeling his mind against the sensual tug of those delicate lace-trimmed garments and the woman he imagined wearing them. His groin heated anyway. Gritting his teeth he worked to squash the feelings he'd kept buried all these years.

Abruptly he wheeled the black gelding away. "Come on, Rooney, let's ride back into town and get some whiskey. The railroad can wait."

But the railroad couldn't wait, and Wash knew it. All the way back to town he cursed the problem unfolding before him.

"Ain't 'xactly her fault," Rooney observed when they had settled themselves at the Golden Partridge's polished wood bar.

"Widow lady on her own, speakin' a foreign language. Coulda been took by a swindler easy."

Wash snorted and sipped his whiskey. "Maybe you should mind your own business."

Rooney paused long enough to empty his own glass. "Or maybe *you* should mind your business and get that lady off the railroad land before the sheriff arrests her for trespassin'."

"I don't think the sheriff would do that."

"Somebody's gotta do it. That's why Sykes's railroad company is payin' your salary. Think about it. Why else would they hire a lawyer with courtroom smarts to supervise railroad crews?"

God knew he didn't want to think about it. He especially didn't want to think about those slim bare legs flashing through that purple field.

Late afternoon shadows stippled the trail as Wash guided General back to Green Valley. He didn't fancy returning, but Rooney was right: he had his orders.

When the path narrowed and began to slope

downward, he fought off an attack of belly butterflies. Pretty ironic, to have lived through Laura's betrayal and then the War, the Yankee prison in Richmond and Sioux-Cheyenne skirmishes near Fort Kearney only to find his entire frame laced up with nerves over one lone woman. A woman who had no legal claim to the land she sat on.

Now on a level with the thick, waist-high field of bushy growth, he reined General to a stop and dismounted. It had to be done; he'd best get it over with.

Dropping the reins where he stood, Wash patted the animal's neck and made his way toward the small cabin at the far end of the valley. The greenery on either side of him was so close to the uneven footpath his elbows brushed against the purple fronds. A pleasant spice-like scent rose. Lavender! That's what she was growing. Looked damn nice in the hazy sunlight, like an ocean of blue and purple waves.

He raised his head and glimpsed a movement on the cabin porch. Miz Nicolet had seen him.

He didn't slow his pace until he was maybe twenty yards away, and then suddenly she pulled a rifle from behind her skirt and aimed it at his heart.

Wash put his hands in the air. "It's me, ma'am. The jackrabbit hunter, remember?"

She said not a word, and he kept walking toward her, the slight hitch in his gait more noticeable now. When he was close enough to see the dark curls escaping the blue kerchief tied over her hair, he stopped.

"You do remember me, don't you?"

Her mouth opened. *"Oui,"* she snapped. "I remember you. What do you want?" She moved the gun barrel an inch to the right. If she pulled the trigger at such close range, she couldn't miss. His heart would be splattered all over the path.

"I'd like to talk to you, ma'am. About your farm-land."

The teal-green eyes narrowed. "I own this land. It is not for sale."

"Oh, I don't want to buy it…well, yes, I do, in a way, but let me explain. You see—"

"You are *trespassion*—trespassing," she corrected. "I ask you to leave."

"I can't do that, ma'am. See, I've been ordered to—"

"Go away," she interrupted. "Or I will shoot."

Frantically Wash racked his brain for some words in French. *Bonjour?* No, that didn't fit. *Au revoir?* Not yet. Not until she had heard him out. *Comment ça va?* That would do.

He pushed his stiff lips into a smile, but it was dicey with that rifle trained on his shirt buttons. *"Comment ça va?"*

Her gaze widened. "I am quite well," she replied, her voice tightening. "But I am not patient. Go!"

He waited three heartbeats. "My name's Washington Halliday, ma'am."

He took another halting step forward, and then another, until the toes of his boots stubbed the bottom step. At each step she adjusted the angle of the gun to accommodate his position. He was so close now he could see those odd flecks of gray in her eyes.

Wash drew in a long breath and began to recite the first French words that came to mind. *"O, claire de la lune…"* Damn. He wished he hadn't switched his long-ago college language class to Latin.

She frowned and tilted her head, obviously puzzled.

*"Mon ami…"* On the word *ami* he charged straight up the single step toward her and knocked the gun barrel upward. It went off with a crack, the shot skimming off into the trees where a chatter of birds broke the quiet.

She gave a little cry and Wash grabbed the gun out of her frozen grasp and checked the chamber. She backed away from him until he clunked the rifle flat on the porch beside her, and then she stopped, one hand covering her mouth.

"Sorry I had to do that, ma'am. But it's hard to talk sense if you're dead."

Her throat convulsed in a swallow.

"Talk about what?" Her face was white as limestone.

"Ma'am, you got any whiskey? I think you need a shot."

*"Non.* No whiskey."

"How about tea? Coffee?"

All at once her legs gave out and she sat down hard on the porch, her skirts fluffing up around her. "Café," she said. Her voice sounded shaky. "Inside. *Mais, je*—I cannot…"

He strode past her into the tiny cabin and headed for the potbellied stove. The place was as neat as his mother's parlor, he noted. Nothing out of place except for a child's exercise book on the kitchen table, propped between a sugar bowl on one side and a white ceramic cream pitcher on the other.

"Coffee," he muttered. His own hands were shaking by the time he found the coffee mill and a small bag of coffee beans. He chunked up the fire, brewed the coffee extra strong and found two patterned china cups. He grabbed the bubbling pot off the stove and carried it through the doorway.

She was still sitting where he'd left her. Trying to control her trembling hands, she reached for the cup, then quickly set it down on the porch and blew on her fingers. "Hot," she explained.

"Couldn't find any saucers," he said more calmly than he felt. He settled himself not too close beside her.

"There are no saucers. They were broken when I came in the wagon from New Orleans."

"Drink it black?" He had a hard time getting the words out; being this close to her made his heart beat in an odd, ragged rhythm.

Her forehead wrinkled. *"Pardon?"*

"Do you want milk or sugar? *Du lait? Sucre?*"

Her frown lifted. "Ah, *non.*"

A long, awkward silence fell. He let her drink her coffee while he gazed over the purple fields and tried to gather his thoughts. *She's sure not gonna like what I'm going to tell her.*

A heavenly scent invaded his nostrils—probably the lavender. He leaned imperceptibly toward her and drew in another breath. No, it was her. Soap and something spicy.

Wash gulped his coffee and tried to think of how to tell her about the railroad.

# Chapter Three

Jeanne could scarcely swallow the hot coffee the tall man had poured into her grandmother's china cup, but it was not because it burned her tongue or tasted like scorched peppercorns. Her throat was so tight she could not even swallow her own saliva.

He'd come to talk about her farm, the only mainstay she'd found in five years of widowhood, outside of her daughter. And outside of her handed-down family knowledge about growing lavender. How precarious her life seemed at times. Whether she and Manette managed in this untamed, rough land depended solely upon her skill as a farmer. Their survival hung by a thin stalk of lavender.

Gingerly she lifted her cup from the porch and tried again to sip it, mostly just to gain some time. It was lukewarm now, but still the tightness closed her throat. Strange, but he seemed as ill at ease as she did. Three times his mouth opened to form a word, and three times his jaw snapped shut with a decisive click. *Mon Dieu,* what did he wish to say?

Once more his lips opened and this time she couldn't help but notice how nicely shaped they were—not too full but… She calmed an odd flutter in her chest… sensual.

This time some of his words tumbled out. "I'm sure glad you didn't shoot me, ma'am."

"I meant to," she said in a quiet voice. "I do not like strangers."

"How long have you been farming out here, Miz Nicolet?"

She looked up sharply. "How is it you know my name?"

"I asked around in town."

For an instant she forgot to breathe. "Why?"

He hesitated. "Well, because it seems like…" He smiled at her, his teeth white against his tanned skin. "Seems like you've settled on land you don't own."

"But I do own it, *monsieur.* I have the deed to prove it."

He slurped down a mouthful of coffee. "Problem is, Miz Nicolet, you've been swindled."

"Swindled? What is that?"

"Hoodwinked. Gulled."

"Hood—?"

"To put it straight, ma'am, you've been cheated."

"Ah, *non.* I paid all my money for this land, and Monsieur Lavery shook my hand and brought the deed to show me."

"I'm sure he did."

The man's usually rich voice sounded odd. Did he not believe her? "Yes," she reiterated, "he did."

The man chuffed out a long breath and stared out over her lavender fields. "I don't exactly know how to tell you this, Miz Nicolet, but—"

"Then do not." Her hand shaking, she lowered her half-empty cup onto the porch beside her. "Please, do not say anything that will make me feel sad about what I did. Please, *Monsieur...*?"

"Halliday. Wash. Short for Washington, but just call me Wash."

Jeanne followed his gaze as it skimmed over her lavender crop. "It is beautiful in the afternoon light, is it not?"

He nodded without lifting his eyes from the fields.

"This valley, it reminds me of the land near Narbonne, where I grew up. My mother grew lavender to sell at the market. And now I do, as well."

"I can see that, ma'am. You have a fine crop here."

"I let it grow as it will, and each summer the ground is covered in purple. I leave some of the stalks uncut until they go to seed."

The air was sharp with the spicy fragrance. Each year her lilac-tinted sea had pushed farther and farther up the canyon sides. "It makes a small income for Manette and me. I feel safe here." Up until now.

For an instant Wash closed his eyes. He sure understood safe. "It's almost dusk, ma'am. I've got to get back to town, but before I go, could you show me your deed for the place?"

She could not answer.

"Ma'am?"

"I can show you, yes. But not today. The deed is at the bank in Smoke River."

He turned his face toward her. His eyes were nice, gray like her grandfather Rougalle's, with fine sun lines crinkling the corners. Her heart stuttered at the expression in their depths. Such sadness. She did not like that look.

*Liar! You like it very much, even if it is sad.*

Something about this man's eyes made her chest hurt. She wished he would smile once more.

"How about meeting me at the bank tomorrow morning?"

She looked at him so long he wondered if she'd heard him.

She turned her head and looked into his eyes, saying nothing for a good two minutes. At last she dipped her kerchief-swathed head in the slightest of nods.

"Very well. Tomorrow."

Wash unfolded his long legs, stood up and stepped down off the porch. "Eleven o'clock." He touched the brim of his brown Stetson, then turned away and strode toward General where he patiently waited at the end of the footpath. His hip hurt like hell from squatting on the porch, but he worked to keep his gait smooth.

The eleven o'clock sunlight on a midsummer morning in Smoke River revealed a number of town folk briskly crisscrossing the dusty main street on their way to buy feed or pick up their mail. The grocer, Carl Ness, was sweeping the board walkway in front of his displayed bushel baskets of ripe peaches and bloodred tomatoes. He hummed a tune as he worked his broom down as far as the barbershop where he stopped abruptly, leaving an obvious contrast between the barber's dirty, leaf-strewn frontage and the grocer's clean expanse of walkway.

To the left of the grocer's sat the Golden Partridge, quiet at this hour but not empty. The minute Carl stashed his broom, he ambled toward the saloon where Wash knew he'd sit nursing a beer and glowering at Whitey Kincaid.

Whitey Kincaid was the barber. Watching Carl from the sheriff's office across the street, Wash laughed out loud. What was known as the "Boardwalk Battle" had been waged since he'd been a boy attending the one-room schoolhouse twenty-some years ago.

The struggle between the two men had started years ago, when Whitey's prize mare had stumbled into Carl's carefully stacked boxes of potatoes and fresh-picked corn and broken its leg. Whitey had put the horse out of its misery and then come gunning for the grocer. The sheriff arrested both of them, Wash recalled, and three days in the same cell at the jerry-rigged jailhouse had fanned the animosity into an unspoken war both were determined to win.

Wash gazed at the saloon and ran his tongue over his dry lips. No time for a drink; Miz Nicolet should be riding into town any minute and he had to keep his head clear. He sure didn't relish telling the French lady how easy it was to get the wool pulled over a foreigner's eyes out here in the West.

The sound of hooves pulled his attention to the far end of the street; sure enough, it was the lavender lady herself. Her young daughter rode in front, holding a sheaf of dried lavender fronds on her lap.

The woman rode astride, her sky-blue skirt rucked up revealing black leather boots, an expanse of ruffled white petticoat, and the flash of one bare calf. His mouth went dry as a dustbin.

He strode up the street to meet her. "Morning, Miz Nicolet."

"*Bon jour,* Monsieur Washington." She drew the skinny mare up in front of the redbrick bank building next to the hotel.

Wash plucked Manette off the horse and carefully set her on the ground, then reached up for her mother. No stirrup, he noted. How the hell did she mount, anyway?

He closed his hands around her waist and felt a jolt of heat dance up both arms. When she laid her hands lightly on his shoulders, the warmth swirled into his chest. He lifted her down and found he couldn't bring himself to release her. Her high-collared white shirtwaist swelled over her breasts and nipped into the waistband of her skirt.

She glanced at him from under the wide brim of a straw hat banded with a blue ribbon. He didn't see her eyes for more than a half second, but her mouth had gone white and tense.

"Manette, take the lavender over to Monsieur Ness."

But Manette was absorbed by a scraggly dandelion

poking up between the wood planks of the boardwalk and the grasshopper clinging to the flower head.

"I'll take it," Wash volunteered. He needed to be away from her to regain his equilibrium. "Meet you at the bank."

Jeanne scarcely stammered out her thanks before he had gathered up the sheaf, bound in twine, and started for Ness's Mercantile & Sundries.

She turned to her daughter. "Manette?" But just now Manette was looking for bugs under the walkway. She would probably eat one or two, as she was insatiable in her curiosity, and very often hungry, as well. She squinted at something cradled in her tiny palm, a grasshopper. And then whoop! It was gone.

Like life, Jeanne thought. Like youth. You blinked and it was over.

Inside the bank the air was cool, the light dim. Jeanne stepped up to the teller's window. "I wish to see my safe box, if you please."

The blond youth behind the iron grate glanced up at her, then focused on Wash, who was suddenly standing at her shoulder. "Sure thing, Mrs. Nicolet. Just step this way."

Manette settled herself on a bench to wait, and Wash followed Jeanne through the grille and toward a private room.

"I heard all about you, Colonel Halliday," the boy said as he led the way. "About gettin' shot and being in prison and—"

"Take my advice, Will. Don't join the army."

"Pa wouldn't let me anyway. Says I have to be a banker, like him."

"Not a bad life," Wash said.

"Not very much excitement, bein' stuck in a bank all day."

Wash grinned. "Excitement is highly overrated."

Jeanne's breath stopped. When he smiled, the perpetual frown on his face lifted. He was not so frightening, now. *Alors,* he was almost handsome. Or would be if his smile ever reached his eyes. Surreptitiously she studied his profile while the boy returned and plunked the small steel box onto the polished desktop.

"*Merci,* William."

The boy unlocked the box. At the click, she leaned forward, plunged her hand inside the receptacle and drew out a rolled-up parchment tied with ribbon.

"Here is my deed," she said with a note of triumph. "See for yourself."

Wash unrolled the document and scanned the words. He'd known it all along, but his heart sank anyway. "It's like I said, ma'am. You've been swindled. This deed is fake."

Her face turned white as cheese. "How do you know this?"

"Well, look here, ma'am." She stepped up beside him and studied the document he held out.

"There's supposed to be two signatures, buyer and seller. Only got one here. Yours. Doesn't prove a thing."

She stared up at him. "You mean it is false?"

"'Fraid so, ma'am." He breathed in her scent and his fists clenched.

Her whole body went rigid. "You mean I do not own my farm? My lavender?"

Wash wished he could drop through the floor. "The Oregon Central Railroad owns it."

"But I paid money to Monsieur Lavery. I paid him all the money I had!"

"I'm real sorry, Miz Nicolet. You're not the first person to get taken in like this, but I know that doesn't help much."

"You mean I have nothing? Nowhere to live? No land? No lavender to sell to Monsieur Ness at the mercantile?"

He nodded.

Tears shimmered in her eyes. "But what will I do? I must care for Manette."

His fists opened and closed. "Maybe I could get your money back. I work for the railroad, see, and—" He broke off at the look on her face.

Her tears overflowed, spilling down her pale cheeks like fat droplets of dew. Wash's throat ached. Dammit, watching her cry ripped up his insides. He closed his hand about her elbow.

"Come on, Miz Nicolet. You need some coffee." He folded the deed into her hand and ushered her out past the teller's window. Manette scrambled off the bench where she'd been waiting, took one look at her mother's face and flung her small arms around her skirts.

"Don't cry, *Maman*. Please don't cry. It makes me feel bumpy inside."

Absently Jeanne smoothed her hand over her daughter's red-gold hair. *"C'est rien, chou-chou."* The words sounded choked.

Manette tipped her head up and pinned him with a furious look. "Did you hurt my mother?"

Wash flinched at the question. Of course he'd hurt her mother. He'd yanked every bit of security out from under this woman in less than three minutes. He released Jeanne's elbow and knelt before the girl.

"If I did hurt your mama, it was not on purpose."

"Make her stop crying, then."

"I would if I could, honey. I think maybe some coffee might help." He gestured toward the hotel across the street. "Do you think that's a good idea?"

"Yes. And some ice cream, too?" She was out the door like a nectar-hungry bee.

Wash rose to his feet with a grimace, fighting the urge to wrap the sobbing woman in his arms. Gently he took Jeanne's elbow. Her entire body trembled like wind-whipped aspen leaves.

"Oh, hell, I'm sorry." He grasped Jeanne's upper arm and guided her out onto the boardwalk and across the street to the hotel dining room.

She gave no sign that she had heard his words.

# Chapter Four

A plump older woman in a checked apron glanced up as Wash and Jeanne entered the River Hotel dining room with Manette dancing after them.

"Morning, Rita. Got any coffee?" The woman's face darkened at the sight of Jeanne. "Always got coffee for you, Colonel. Made fresh, too."

The waitress shot another look at Jeanne, instantly dug a handkerchief out of her pocket and pressed it into her hand. "Here, dearie. You just cry it all out of your system."

Wash settled Jeanne at a corner table and lifted Manette onto the chair between them. The girl leaned toward him. "Why is *Maman* crying?" she whispered.

Wash flinched. "Because…well, because she's just had some bad news."

"Can you make it go away?"

"I wish I could." Never in his life had he felt this helpless. He didn't like the feeling one bit.

The waitress sailed off to the kitchen and returned with two delicate cups of steaming coffee. One she placed before Jeanne; the other she brought around the table to Wash and leaned in close to his ear.

"What'd you do to her, anyway?" she muttered.

"Railroad wants her land," he explained, keeping his voice low.

"And I hear you're workin' for the railroad." Rita sent a speculative glance at Jeanne. "A man's always at the root of a woman's troubles," she sniffed.

Wash waited until Rita had retreated into the kitchen. "It's almost noon. Are you hungry?"

She shook her head, blotting at her eyes with the damp handkerchief.

"She is hungry," Manette whispered. "She let me eat all of her breakfast."

"Well, then, perhaps you both would join me for lunch?"

"Oh, *non*," Jeanne protested.

"Oh, yes! Manette's bright-eyed grin made Wash chuckle. He'd order a steak—two steaks—and a big bowl of chocolate ice cream; maybe it would ease the sick, guilty feeling in his gut.

Jeanne spoke not one word during the meal, but he noticed she ate every ounce of her steak, right down to the bits of gristle. Wash cut up half his meat for Manette, but found he couldn't swallow even his own portion.

After a tense quarter of an hour, Jeanne quietly laid her fork across the empty plate and looked up at him. "I came from a small village in France to marry my husband," she said, her voice near a whisper. "It was a mistake."

Wash blinked. "You mean he was the wrong man?"

"I mean he was killed in the War when Manette was a year old. He had no family and no land. I could not survive in New Orleans, so I left. I came out to Oregon to buy a farm where I could grow lavender. It is all Manette and I have."

"Your husband was a Southerner, then? Confederate Army?"

She nodded, then lifted her china coffee cup and cradled it in her hands.

"I fought for the North," Wash said. "Union Army. I grew up out here in Smoke River but I'd gone back East to school when the War broke out. I volunteered right before Manassas."

Again she nodded. The rivulets of tears had stopped, he noted with relief. Talking seemed to help.

"When my father died," he continued, "Ma couldn't wait to get back to Connecticut. Some women aren't cut out for life on the frontier."

She held his eyes in a long, questioning look. "What is required for a life on the frontier?"

He blew out his breath. "Horse sense, for one. Hide like a tanned buffalo. Temperament like a rattlesnake. And grit."

"Grit? What is 'grit'?"

He studied her work-worn hands, the sunburned patch on her nose, and the unwavering look of resolve in her eyes.

"Grit is being strong when the going gets tough. It's what you had when you packed up your things and came out here on your own and started your farm."

She pursed her lips and his groin tightened. Lord, but she got to him easy. Was it because her body swelled in and out in just the right places? Or because he'd been without a woman for so long he'd forgotten the pleasures female company brought?

Or was it because he just plain liked her?

That thought sent a cold thread of fear coiling up his spine.

"I know this has been a hard thing to come to grips with, Miz Nicolet, but do you have any idea what you plan to do?"

She folded her napkin and laid it over the wadded-up handkerchief next to her plate. "Do?"

She reached up to straighten her hat, and tried to smile.

"I will go home to my farm. I will feed my chickens and I will harvest my lavender when it is ready."

"I mean what're you gonna do about the land the railroad owns?"

Her smile faded and her eyes suddenly looked distant. "About the land and the railroad I will do nothing."

"Nothing! You've gotta do something, ma'am. My survey crew will be here day after tomorrow."

She stood up slowly. "That may be, Monsieur Washington. But no matter who comes, I do not intend to leave."

Wash shot out of his chair. "Wait a minute! You can't just—"

"But yes," she interrupted in a soft but determined voice. "Yes, I can. Come, Manette. We will go home now."

Five minutes later he watched the woman and her daughter clop back down the street atop the scrawny gray mare. Sure was a sorry excuse for a horse.

*Sure is one stubborn woman!*

And maybe he was a sorry excuse for a railroad lawyer. He'd ended up doing the wrong thing for the right reason and his insides felt like they were splitting in two. One half of him wanted to bundle Jeanne and her daughter up and drag them off that scanty plot she called a farm. The other half wanted to help her fight off the railroad, like David and Goliath.

There was a third part somewhere in there, too—a part of him that wanted to hold her close and smell her hair.

The horse disappeared in a puff of gray dust and Wash headed for the Golden Partridge. He had a headache that felt like the town blacksmith was hammering on his temples.

Rooney stood, his back to the bar, his boots casually crossed at the ankle. "Been waitin' for ya, Wash."

"Yeah?" Wash positioned himself next to his friend and hooked one heel over the bar rail.

"One reason is that French lady. That's a mighty weak-looking horse for carrying all her household baggage out of that canyon."

"It's all she's got. What's the other reason?"

Rooney turned around so they stood shoulder to shoulder and hunkered over the shiny mahogany bar top. "Don't rush me, Wash. I'm thinkin' how to say what I got to say."

Wash dropped his forehead onto his hand. "I'm dead tired, Rooney. Just spit it out."

Rooney lowered his voice. "You see those gents over there by the window?"

Wash turned his head to glance at the men. Mean-looking types. One was paunchy, with a ragged canvas shirt and shifty black eyes; the other was well-built, dark-skinned and silent. He had a crescent-shaped scar under one eye. Both wore double holsters.

A third man sat near the other two. This one looked young and fresh-faced, with a hat so new it didn't yet have creases in it.

"That kid looks so clean he'd squeak," Wash said under his breath. "The other two look like a couple of hired guns."

"Looks can be deceiving," Rooney muttered.

"Yeah?"

"Yeah." Rooney raised his thick, salt-and-pepper eyebrows. "That's your new railroad survey crew."

Wash's hand froze around his shot glass. Those grungy-looking men would be hanging around Miz Nicolet's farm all day? Watching her feed her chickens? Watching her hang up her laund—

"Oh, God," he murmured.

Rooney nodded. "That's what I thought, too."

## Chapter Five

The next morning Wash and Rooney escorted the rough-looking survey crew out to Green Valley. The three men unpacked their equipment and set to work at the far end of the valley. Under Wash's watchful eye, they worked their way toward the far end of the valley. The closer they got to the cabin, the more uneasy Wash felt.

He didn't want Miz Nicolet's rifle to stop his crew. He also didn't want the men getting too near the pretty French woman. He didn't usually carry a weapon, but today he'd strapped on his Colt and dropped a handful of extra bullets into his leather vest pocket.

No matter how unsavory the men looked, now that they were on the job, the crew seemed to know what it was doing. Handy, the paunchy man, set up his leveling gauge and peered through the sight. Dark-haired, unshaven Joe Montez—the one Rooney had pegged as a hired gun—marched off paces through the lavender field with the measuring chain. The blond kid, Lacey, held the ranging pole while the paunchy one at the leveling gauge sent hand signals, waving the other two farther up the hillside.

The men gradually worked their way closer to the Nicolet cabin. Wash squinted at the structure. Hell and damn, it sat smack in the center of what would soon be a steel railroad track.

The spiral of blue smoke from the stone chimney told him Jeanne was at home, even though he'd not seen her all morning. He left Rooney in charge of the crew and walked his horse through the lavender field, dismounted and tramped up the path toward the cabin. It was close to noon. The sun poured down on the lush purple fields and his elbows brushed the spikes as he moved through the tall plants. Be kinda nice to smell like lavender when he saw her instead of horse and sweat. In the next instant he wondered why it mattered.

Manette burst out of the open cabin door and flew across the porch to clasp her arms around his knees. "Oh, Mr. Washington," she cried. "Did you come to see my spider box?"

"Manette," a voice called from inside the cabin. "We have not finished your lesson."

Wash reached to gently tug one of her braids, tied at the end with a crisp red bow. "You can call me Wash, if you like. What's a spider box?"

"Manette!" came the voice again.

The girl tipped her head up and grinned. "My spider box is where I keep my spiders. Want to see?"

"Manette, where are you?"

"Here, *Maman*. On the porch." She tossed the words over her shoulder and peered up at him again. "Don't you want to see it?"

Jeanne Nicolet stepped through the doorway, wiping her hands on a huck towel. "See what?"

Wash straightened and their eyes met. A queer little zing went up the back of his neck. Lord but she stopped his breath! Her lustrous dark hair was caught with a ribbon in a fall down her back; she wore a faded blue gingham skirt and a matching body-hugging shirtwaist. From her head to the tips of her black boots, which brushed up a foam of white petticoat ruffles, she didn't look like any farm wife he'd ever laid eyes on.

She stuffed the huck towel under her apron. "Monsieur Washington."

He lifted Manette's thin arms away from his knees. "Morning, Miz Nicolet."

She inclined her head and pinned him with an unflinching look.

"I'm going to show Mr. Wash my spider box," Manette announced.

Jeanne's gray-green eyes widened. "What spider box?"

"I keep it under my pillow, *Maman*. I have all kinds of spiders, even a big yellow one."

Jeanne shuddered. "*Mon Dieu,* I do not wish to see spiders of any color. Especially not under your pillow."

Manette skipped away into the cabin as her mother

spoke. When she disappeared, Jeanne turned her attention to Wash.

He brought two fingers to his hat brim in a salute and smiled. "I see you have no gun today, ma'am."

She narrowed her eyes at his gun belt with its holstered weapon hanging low on his hips. "And I see that you do."

"The survey crew for the railroad is here. Thought I better warn you that those three fellas climbing up and down the hillside work for me." He gestured over his shoulder just as Handy, halfway down the hill, came to a dead stop and pointed.

"Joe! Hey, Montez! You ever seen a prettier gal?"

Montez's dark gaze followed Handy's pointing forefinger and his mouth dropped open. "Holy—"

Wash spoke quickly to cover the profanity. "They won't bother you, ma'am. They're just doing their job."

"And what job is that?" she inquired through pinched lips.

"The survey. You remember, I told you about it yesterday?"

"*Oui,* I have forgot. How long will they work?"

"Just today and tomorrow."

She made an involuntary motion and then studied the men more closely. "They trample my lavender."

"With all due respect, ma'am, what does that matter? In a couple of days it'll all be gone."

"Gone?" Her voice wobbled.

"'Fraid so, ma'am. The clearing crew will come through in a few days and mow down—"

"*Non!* I will not permit it."

Wash took a step closer, catching the elusive scent of that spicy soap she used. He brought his head up and inhaled deeply. Damn, she smelled good.

"Miz Nicolet…Jeanne…you can't stop the railroad. I've sent a request for your money to be returned, but the legal right to this land belongs—"

"So you have said," she snapped.

*Would she ever let him finish one single sentence?*

"If you know that, ma'am, you also know you've got to leave."

She turned away. "Excuse me, Monsieur Washington…I have the bread rising."

Before he knew what he was doing, he snaked out his hand and captured her forearm. Under the thin gingham her flesh was warm and alive. And so soft he didn't want to let go.

"Jeanne, you are the most stubborn woman I've ever encountered. Even my mother wasn't as prickly as you! Now, you've got to listen to me."

Jeanne wrenched her arm out of his grasp. "I will listen." She watched his lips thin. Very fine, those lips. While she stared at them, his mouth opened.

"I think it would be wise not to, uh, do any laundry while the survey crew is here."

"Oh? And why is that?"

"Well…" He swallowed. "It could rile a man up seeing your…um…you know, small clothes, drying on your clothesline."

She cocked her head. "What means 'rile up'?"

"Ah. It means to, well, to upset a man. Make him want something."

Jeanne laughed at his embarrassment. "In France, men are much less—what is the word? Suggestible?"

He groaned, grabbed her by the shoulders and pulled her up so close her chin almost brushed his shirt. She looked up into his angry face and her heart began to pound.

"You know damn well what a man wants," he growled at her. "So don't go flying your lacy underdrawers under the noses of my crew. We've got a railroad to think about, not..." He did not finish the thought.

"I know little of men except for my husband, Henri. And even him I did not understand." After Henri had lured her to New Orleans with all his lies, she had sworn she would never trust another man.

He glared down at her.

Well! She did not get the smile she had hoped for. What she got instead was an unsettling reminder of what *this* man wanted—a railroad through her lavender field. She wanted to scream.

But in the next instant she looked into the hard gray eyes in that tanned face and wanted something else entirely. She liked this man, even if he was with the railroad. She liked him so much she hoped he would smile at her again. A man had not looked at her in that way since her husband had been killed.

Late in the afternoon the survey crew finished, packed up their equipment and mounted their horses. Wash led the way back to town on General, remembering that puzzling look on Jeanne's face—half fear, half pleasure.

Something had shown in the green depths of her eyes he hadn't seen before. It was when he'd grabbed her shoulders and she'd looked up at him with uncertainty and…something else. He'd wanted to kiss her. To pull her close enough to feel her breasts against his chest and capture her soft mouth under his.

He was glad he hadn't; he was afraid he wouldn't have been able to let her go. It was a funny thing, being without a woman for so long. Like the sweet flavor of his first spoonful of chocolate ice cream, he hungered for another taste.

He thought he'd had enough of women since Laura. The day he'd ridden off to the War, he'd told himself that women were fickle and demanding, fainthearted and selfish.

Most women, that is. Jeanne was different. Or at least he thought she was different. But he still didn't trust her completely; maybe he never would. She had one big strike against her, and that was that he liked being near her. That in itself was a danger sign. She aroused feelings in him he'd long since put aside as the yearnings of a younger man, not some burned-out ex-colonel with a gimpy leg and a heart crusted over like an overcooked flapjack.

He felt an odd protectiveness toward Jeanne Nicolet. Maybe because she was a foreigner, struggling for a livelihood on the rough western frontier, as his mother had. Maybe because she was so delicate she couldn't hold up a rifle for more than four minutes. Maybe just because she was a woman. Whatever it was, he couldn't get the feeling out of his head: she liked him. And he liked her. She was all woman, and he was a man.

Damn, that did soothe a broken man's sense of worth.

Rooney was waiting on the board walkway outside the Golden Partridge when Wash got there, his thumbs stuffed into his denim pockets. The early evening light glowed through the larch trees, turning them into shimmering gold torches. He sure liked these long days, but his stomach told him it was suppertime. Plenty of time to enjoy his steak and beans and linger with Rooney over his coffee. Ever since that Yankee prison at Richmond he'd hated eating in the dark.

He heaved a sigh of satisfaction. He'd survived the War and the Indian skirmishes on the plains, and now he held a good job with the Oregon Central Railroad. The railway fed some hunger inside himself he was only now beginning to recognize.

After the chaos and destruction he'd seen, he longed for order. As the iron tracks spread from town to town across the western frontier he recognized at long last some peaceful purpose in life. Washtubs for farm wives; bolts of calico and denim for their sons and daughters; sacks of seed for the ranchers. It felt good to be part of something growing, even something as inanimate as an iron railroad track. He was building something instead of blasting it to smithereens.

He figured he was a lucky man; he had a satisfying job. And his life was…well, it was satisfying, too. Except for Jeanne Nicolet. He wished he could get her off that land. *He wished he could get her out of his mind.*

"How come you workin' the crew so late?" Rooney swung the hinged saloon door open and Wash dismounted, tied General to the hitching rail and hauled off his saddle. He strode inside and dropped his burden just inside the door.

"Not working late. The crew finished early. I let 'em go around sunset."

"Well, they ain't back yet. The blond kid rode in 'bout an hour ago, but Handy and that tall Spaniard weren't with them."

An icicle clunked into Wash's belly. Dammit, were they loitering out in Green Valley? Near Jeanne's farm?

Wash pushed the swinging door back open and peered down the street. A puff of dust signaled a rider about half a mile from town. "That's probably them now," he muttered.

Handy clopped into town on his sorrel, headed straight for the saloon, and tied up his mount next to General.

"Where's Montez?" Wash yelled.

"Dunno," the big-bellied man replied. "Went back for somethin'."

Wash's heart dropped into his boots. "For what?"

Handy jerked his head up at the steely tone of Wash's voice.

"Dunno, boss. Have to ask him when he gets in."

Wash had a pretty good idea what would keep Montez hanging around Green Valley. He hoisted his saddle onto one shoulder and bumped past Handy just as the burly man punched through the saloon doors.

Rooney poked his head out the door. "What about yer supper? Rita's savin' a big steak for ya."

Wash tossed the saddle over General's back and bent to tighten the cinch. "Tell Rita I'll eat it later." He mounted, turned the animal back toward the valley and dug in his spurs.

He rode as fast as he could, but it was full dark by the time he reached the lookout from where he could survey the farm. The entire valley was shrouded in black as thick as a velvet curtain save for a soft glow of light from inside the tiny cabin. He pulled up and listened for hoofbeats.

Nothing. He could hear chickens scrabbling in the crude shelter Jeanne had nailed together, and now and then a spurt of melody from an evening song sparrow somewhere in the maples. All seemed peaceful save for intermittent rustling among the lavender bushes. Rabbits, maybe?

But no Montez. He peered through the darkness at the trail that led down to the gate, but he could see nothing. He'd best pick his way down the hillside and check the—

A thin cry floated up to him from the direction of the cabin. Then another, this one sounding choked off.

He kicked General hard and let the gelding find its own footing through the blackness. At the bottom where the trail leveled off he didn't stop to dismount; he jumped the horse over the gate and pounded up the narrow path toward the cabin.

# Chapter Six

In the circle of light from the cabin Wash spied the back of a tall, dark-shirted man bent over something. A blue gingham ruffle poked from between his legs. A woman's choked cry stopped his breath, and then he heard the crack of a palm against flesh. The man twisted away, one hand pressed to his flaming cheek.

"Ow! You hellcat…"

Sounded like she'd lambasted him a good one. Wash couldn't help but congratulate her.

Montez lunged at her. "You think I am not good enough for you, is that it? Because my skin is not white, like yours?"

Wash sprinted onto the porch, caught the attacker's thick shoulder and spun the man toward him. Then he smashed his fist into the side of the Spaniard's jaw.

Montez dropped like a felled tree and rolled off the

porch. Wash peered over the edge at the crumpled form on the ground and tried not to smile. Out cold.

"Is… Is he killed?" Jeanne quavered from the cabin doorway.

"Naw." He turned toward her. She was trembling so violently the ruffles down the front of her gingham shirtwaist fluttered. She gazed at him blankly.

"Jeanne." He stepped in front of her to get her attention.

"Did he hurt you?"

"*Oui.* H-he take my wrist, so." She extended her arm. A crimson handprint bloomed on her skin.

"Manette? Is she safe?"

The ghost of a smile flitted across Jeanne's lips. "*Oui.* She hides in the ch-chicken house. I send her there when that m-man knocks on my door."

Wash stared at her. She might be shaken, but she'd showed admirable presence of mind in the face of danger. He'd seen army lieutenants fold up under less.

But her face was still white as chalk, and suddenly she sank onto the porch in a froth of white petticoats.

"Oh," she exclaimed. "Forgive me, but I c-cannot…"

Wash extended his hand. He pulled her up so close to him he could smell the spicy-sweet scent of her hair and an odd, hungry feeling burrowed into his gut.

Damn. He ached to pull her into his arms. Something about this woman made him aware of how lonely he was. How hungry he was.

He wanted her. Hell's bells, any man would want her. But with Jeanne it was more than that. He liked her looks, her spirit. Liked her oddly inflected words. He liked talking to her. Jumping jennies, he just plain liked the woman.

He swallowed hard. "What did Montez want?"

One hand flew to her throat. "He…he wanted to kiss me."

Wash could sure understand that. Kissing her was something he himself had been thinking a lot about for the past two days. And nights.

A stifled groan floated up from the ground. Wash stepped off the porch and straddled the Spaniard. Dragging him upright by the back of his shirt, he planted a boot in his backside.

Damned randy snake.

"Get out of here, Montez. And don't come back. Pick up your pay from Rooney at the saloon."

Without looking at him, the Spaniard slouched unsteadily down the path and through the gate.

Wash couldn't look at Jeanne; he felt responsible. But she pinned him with an unflinching eye. "I do not like that those men come here."

Wash blew out a long breath. "Those men are my work crew for the railroad that's coming. A different crew will be here in a day or two to start clearing brush.

"Brush? What brush?"

Wash hesitated, gazing out into the darkness, envisioning Jeanne's lush fields of lavender glowing in the sun. God help him, he couldn't say it. Couldn't tell her the clearing crew was getting paid to chop down her precious crop.

"Brush," he echoed. "You know, tickle grass and small trees." He shot a look at her face. "Anything that's uh, in the way of laying track."

She turned to him, eyes narrowing. "I will not have such men at my farm."

"Jeanne, don't you understand?" Anger hardened his voice. "It isn't *your* farm. This land belongs to the railroad."

He kept a tight rein on his nerves and watched her mouth turn down, the light in her eyes dim. Maybe she'd cry or something. Her farm had to go. He expected her to crumple in the face of her impending loss. Instead she straightened her shoulders and bit her lower lip.

"Jeanne, don't you see? Many people will benefit from the railroad."

She began to crease tiny folds in her muslin apron. "No, I do not see," she blazed. "I and my Manette, we will not benefit! Do we not matter here in America?"

"Sure, you matter," Wash growled. "Every citizen matters. That's what this country is built on."

"But that is not true! If many people want one thing and two people do not want it, the many will win. Is that not so?"

Wash cleared his throat. "Well, uh, yeah. That's democracy. The majority rules."

Her chin came up. "But is that not unfair to the *not* majority people? To the two that wanted something else?"

He swallowed. Now that he thought about it, yeah, it did seem unfair.

Jeanne propped her hands at her waist. "So, I and my

daughter should be pushed out of our home because the people in town want a railroad, yes?"

She had a point, all right. What happened to the rights of a single individual under majority rule? Hell, he was a lawyer; he should have an answer. A war had just been fought between the North and the South over the right of a single state to secede from the union against the will of the government. So what gave Grant Sykes the right to decide that Jeanne Nicolet was not important and his Oregon Central line was?

Money, that's what. Ownership of the land. Sykes and the Oregon Central owned this land. The whole mess made his head ache.

"Well?" she demanded. Her eyes took on the most intriguing color he'd ever seen, kind of like green tree moss after a punishing rain. But they weren't soft like moss; they were hard as agate.

"All I know is that the railroad is coming through here. You have to get out of the way."

She gave him a long, steely look. "I will not move," she announced through tight lips. "Not until I harvest my lavender."

Good Lord, her precious lavender. This woman was the most single-minded female he'd ever encountered. His mother had been stubborn, but Jeanne…Jeanne was unmovable as a brick wall.

He reached out to touch her arm. "Jeanne, listen." Under his fingers the smooth gingham warmed with her body heat. A jolt of yearning skip-hopped into his vitals.

She was a singular woman, all right. She was the

starchiest female he'd ever encountered, all prickles and "but this's" and "but that's." Trying to reason with her reminded him of negotiating with an implacable Sioux chief. The Indians hadn't wanted to move, either, and the news that most of them had died of starvation on the winter trail to the reservation made him sick to his stomach. He couldn't stand to watch anything like that happen to Jeanne and her daughter.

But how was he going to convince her? What if he just hauled her into his arms and let her cry it out?

Because she wouldn't cry, that's what. Women with prickles didn't weep. Women with prickles poked back.

"Could we sit down and talk for a minute?"

She nodded, but he noticed her chin stayed tucked close to her chest. "*Oui*. I will make coffee." She called Manette in from the chicken house and opened the cabin door.

Grabbing off his hat, Wash crossed the entrance and followed her into the tiny kitchen. It smelled good, like fresh-baked bread. Four round loaves sat cooling on the wooden table.

It was quiet except for the whisper of trees in the soft wind. Good. Peace and quiet. Now he could make her see some sense.

"Jeanne…"

She kept her hands busy grinding the coffee mill and did not look up. "You like your coffee black, do you not?"

"I— Sure." Wash turned his hat around and around

in his fingers until the brim was sweat-damp. "Black is fine."

"*Bon.* I, too, like it black. And strong." She tipped the ground coffee into a waiting pot of cold water. Her hands shook so violently some of the coffee missed the pot and sifted over the counter.

Wash wiped one hand over the smooth wood, swept the spilled grounds into his hand, then looked around the tidy kitchen for some place to dump them. Finally, in desperation, he dropped them into the crown of his hat.

He stepped toward her. "Jeanne, we have to talk about—"

She moved to one side and with jerky motions began cracking eggs into an iron skillet. "In France I took my morning café with milk. *Maman* brought it to me in bed, and we would talk."

The thought of her in bed made his mouth go dry. "We're not in France," he growled. "We're here, in your kitchen."

"I was only twelve," she said quickly, running a fork through the eggs. "*Maman,* she was good to me. We had long talks about Papa and my little brother."

He moved toward her. "Jeanne, you're not twelve now."

She turned her back to him.

Dammit. He tramped out of the front door onto the porch, paced to the steps and back three times, then wheeled and strode back into the warm kitchen. He still cradled his Stetson with the coffee grains in the crown.

Jeanne was wrapping her apron around the handle of an iron skillet of scrambled eggs, which she then yanked off the stovetop. She headed straight for him. "*Très chaud*. Very hot."

"I like things hot." He spoke without thinking, then swallowed hard. He knew she'd heard him, because she clanked the skillet down hard onto the kitchen table.

"I learn from *Maman* how to cook. Our hens laid many—"

That was all he could take. "Would you just stand still for one damn minute and listen?" he shot. "One thing your mama didn't teach you was how to have a conversation!"

Jeanne sent him a look that would broil steak, and for a moment he thought he'd gotten past her defenses. But in the next second he saw he was mistaken.

"*Maman,*" she said in a determined tone, "had a special way with *une omelette*. She tip the pan just so..." Jeanne demonstrated, then pivoted away from the table and bent over the wooden sink, her back to him.

Dammit, he was trying to tell her something and she just plain wasn't going to listen. He stepped up behind her, close enough to smell her hair. "Stop talking about your *maman*."

Her head came up but her hands in the wooden sink fell idle. She'd heard him, all right. She just didn't want to admit it.

"Jeanne..."

She began to scrub hard at a china plate, then another, and another. Then a cup...

*To hell with it.* Wash groaned, spun on his heel and

stomped out the cabin door. Halfway across the porch he jammed his hat down on his head. It felt funny, kind of crumbly…

Hell, he'd forgotten about the coffee grounds in his hat.

Behind him he heard a ripple of her laughter. She stood in the doorway, one hand clapped over her mouth, her eyes shining with amusement.

With a curse he wheeled toward her. She backed up until she couldn't go any farther without scorching her skirt on the stove. He snatched off his Stetson, sailed it off into the dark and reached for her. He knew his actions were rough, but he'd had all he could take.

She shot him a look of surprise, her lips opening to protest, and without thinking he bent to find her mouth.

At the first touch of her lips, he knew he'd made a big, big mistake. Oh, God, she was sweet, and so soft. The pleasure of kissing her sent a skin-shriveling shudder up his backbone. Her lips were like 180-proof double-distilled brandy, and he drank until he was aching with want.

He kept kissing her until a strangled sound came out of his throat. He shouldn't be doing this, but he couldn't stop. She was the bone stuck in his craw, all right. The thing he couldn't swallow or cough up.

He felt like he'd died and gone to hell.

# Chapter Seven

*Mon Dieu!* What does this man think he is doing?

*Alors,* he was kissing her, that's what he was doing!

She lifted her hand to swat him across his tanned face, but as her arm rose, his lips moved suddenly deeper, more intensely on hers, and her resolve poofed away like so much dust. No man's kiss had ever been like this, not even Henri's on the night Manette was conceived.

She tipped her face to one side and still he did not stop moving his lips over hers. Surely God meant for a man and a woman to enjoy each other, but like this? With such abandon, such dark joy bubbling up inside her? About that, she did not know.

Her breasts were crushed against his chest and all at once she wanted to slip outside her skin and melt into his hot, hard body. Never in all her life had she had such a thought.

His demanding mouth asked and answered, and

asked again, while her most private parts swelled and ached. She should push him away, should... Ah, what she *should* do was of no importance.

He lifted his head and held her close, his chin resting against her temple. She closed her eyes, then snapped her lids open. "Would you perhaps want...?"

"Hell, yes," he said, his voice hoarse. His ragged breath ruffled the hair close to her ear.

*"... une omelette?"* she breathed.

Wash had no memory of his ride back to town. Rooney was at the saloon, as usual; he glanced up from the bar with a questioning look. "Hell, Wash, you look like you've been poleaxed."

Yeah. Something had smacked him over the head, all right. He felt happy like he'd never felt before. He sent Rooney what he knew was a sloppy smile but it was the best he could do with his brain still reeling from that kiss. He hunched his shoulders over the bar and tried to keep her name from hammering through his brain. *Jeanne. Jeanne.*

Rooney peered at him. "Got somethin' stuck in your throat?"

"Nah," he managed to croak. How was it Rooney always seemed to know what he was thinking?

"Mebbe heard some o' the talk around town about that French lady?"

Wash's head jerked up. "What talk?"

"Just...talk. You know, some of the townfolk are in a hurry to get the railroad through. Got money riding on it, you might say. Farmers want to ship their apples to the city. Ranchers are lookin' for markets they don't have to trail-up for. Even Miz Forester, the dressmaker, wants to bring customers from Gillette Springs. It's a two-day ride from Gillette Springs to Smoke River, but when the railroad—"

"What're you trying to tell me, Rooney?"

The older man gulped a swallow of the whiskey at his elbow. "Just that folks are in a sweat. Some of them are gettin' pretty het up."

"Yeah? Who?"

Rooney's black eyes slid away from his gaze. "There's some kinda meetin' at Whitey's barbershop. Mostly men—cowpokes and ranchers. Some shopkeepers. And that Spanish guy on your survey crew showed up."

"Montez."

"That's the one. Mean-lookin' son of a gun."

"I told Montez to pick up his pay and get out of town."

Rooney nodded. "He did pick up his pay."

Wash let out a breath of relief.

"But he didn't leave town."

His spine went rigid. "Where is he now?"

Rooney shrugged. "Dunno."

"The man's up to no good, I can smell it."

Rooney's salt-and-pepper eyebrows rose, but he said nothing.

The bartender slid a shot glass of whiskey in front of Wash and he downed it in one swallow. "That damned snake laid his hands on Miz Nicolet."

Rooney smoothed his beard with his little finger. "Did he, now? What's that to you?"

Wash dropped his head onto his clenched fists. He didn't know the answer to that one. He only knew that when he'd seen Montez manhandling Jeanne on her front porch something had come over him. Something hot and possessive.

Something he didn't want to think about.

"I'm going over to the boardinghouse," he muttered. "Change my shirt before supper. You coming?"

Rooney cast an appraising glance over the two empty poker tables in the center of the barroom. "Wouldn't wanna play a hand of five-card stud, wouldja?"

"Nope. Rather eat Mrs. Rose's fried chicken and gravy."

His stomach clenched at the memory of Jeanne offering him an omelet. He'd wanted to stay. *Forget the omelet—you wanted to kiss her again.*

Rooney was staying at the same boardinghouse, in the room just across the hall from Wash. Mrs. Rose had taken quite a shine to his half-Comanche friend. She always saved the biggest drumstick or the juiciest pork chop or the last dish of peach ice cream for Rooney, who accepted the gestures as if he'd spent his whole life being waited on. Wash knew different. His companion had lived a hardscrabble life. It surprised him how quickly his rough-and-ready friend had adjusted to being fawned over by pretty widows who ran boardinghouses.

Wash dragged himself off the bar stool and headed for the saloon entrance. He sure wished his mother hadn't sold the ranch. One of the things that had kept him going the two years he'd spent in that prison hellhole in Richmond was thinking about the ranch near Smoke

River. He'd dreamed about running fifty head of cattle and maybe some horses on the rolling seven hundred-acre Halliday Double H spread. There was something special about a place you called Home. Something worth fighting for.

Now, working for Sykes and the railroad kept him moving all over the Oregon and Washington territories. He never slept in the same bed more than twenty days at a time, but the money was good. And he was glad the railroad had sent him to Smoke River.

He could understand how Jeanne felt about being uprooted, forced out because a railroad line was coming through. She was caught between a slab of granite and a block of steel. His mother had sold out in a heartbeat after his father died; but Wash knew Jeanne would fight like a tiger to the end.

He pushed through the swinging doors and stepped out onto the board walkway. Just as he reached the barbershop where Whitey Kincaid offered haircuts and shaves and hot baths for fifty cents, a grumble of angry male voices spilled out of the open doorway. He strode on past but someone inside yelled the name "Nicolet." Instantly he doubled back.

And wished he hadn't. The small shop teemed with shouting men. They weren't getting shaves or haircuts or anything else, but they were getting plenty worked up over something. A premonition slowed his footsteps and he slipped inside to melt into the crowd.

"It ain't right!" someone yelled.

A clamor of voices rose in agreement and then Wash recognized the low, silky voice of Joe Montez.

The Spaniard was shouting something to a chorus of cheers. "She thinks she is too good for us!"

"We gotta do something," an older man roared.

A prickly sensation crawled up the back of Wash's neck. That damned Spanish rabble-rouser, what was he trying to do?

Montez was standing upright on one of Whitey's leather-upholstered barber chairs, addressing the unruly crowd. Wash stood up and made eye contact, and the man's face blanched.

Without thinking, Wash lunged for him, but Montez scrambled off the barber chair and vanished out the back door. By the time Wash reached the alley in pursuit, the only sign of his quarry was a swirl of dust stirred up by the man's boots and the fading thud of horse's hooves.

The raucous gathering at the barbershop set off a warning bell in his head. He didn't like the way his spine itched when he'd looked the men over, and he sure didn't like not knowing where Montez was headed.

He angled through a narrow vacant lot to the main street, noticing that the once lit-up barbershop interior was now black as the inside of a pistol barrel. He swore he could hear men's heavy breathing in the darkness.

Something was afoot. His instinct whispered that he wasn't going to like it.

The next morning Rooney stumbled into the empty boardinghouse dining room, squinting against the sunshine pouring through the yellow curtains. He was just in time for the last stack of Mrs. Rose's buckwheat pancakes, the same ones Wash was about to spear with his fork.

"Clearing crew's here," Wash announced. He shoved the maple syrup bottle toward Rooney's elbow.

"Yeah?"

"They're a day early. Got to delay them until…"

"Yeah," Rooney grunted again. "Guess Miz Nicolet's gotta move out of her cabin pronto."

"She's not going to budge until she harvests that lavender crop she's so proud of."

Rooney slopped syrup over the tower of pancakes on his plate. "Damned stubborn woman. Folks are itchin' to see some progress."

Wash gritted his teeth. "They'll have to wait."

Rooney's gray-and-black eyebrows did a little dance. "Don't the lady have a place to go?"

"No. Back to New Orleans, maybe. If I still had the ranch she could bunk out there."

"But you don't have the ranch. Yer momma saw to that. Guess she thought you were never comin' home."

Wash didn't answer right away. "The truth is I hadn't planned to come back to Smoke River. I figured everything I saw would remind me of Laura."

Rooney mopped syrup off his beard. "Well, the railroad sent you back here. Is it as bad as you thought?"

It was and it wasn't, he acknowledged. Memories of Laura and his sweet-sad time with her permeated every field and horse trail and flower-dotted meadow in the county. Even the bitterness was still there.

Rooney peered at him across the lace-covered dining table. "Still scared, are ya?"

"Hell, yes," Wash snapped. "A man gets his heart busted into little pieces only once. After that, he's damn gun-shy."

His mouth stuffed with pancakes, Rooney merely nodded. "So," he said after swallowing, "what're you gonna do?"

Wash pushed back his chair and stood up. "I'm going over to the bank, that's what I'm going to do."

He settled his hat and tramped down the short hallway and out the front door. His Stetson still smelled faintly of ground coffee beans.

## Chapter Eight

Rooney pushed his way through the bank lobby filled with ranchers and their wives, some in fancy dresses and big, showy hats. The chatter fell silent at the entrance of the large, craggy-looking man. He shouldered his way to the teller's cage.

"Wash!" he bellowed. "Wash Halliday, where are you?" His shout echoed off the wall and he pushed his way past the storekeeper's wife, Linda-Lou Ness.

"Well, I never!" she huffed. She turned away with a sniff loud enough to frighten a horse. Just one person met him with a smile, and that was Zinna Langfelder, the undertaker's spinster daughter.

"Good morning, Mr. Cloudman."

Rooney spared her a nod and pressed on through the grillwork gate. "Wash! We got trouble."

Wash was on his feet in a heartbeat, laying a hand

on his partner's muscled shoulder to slow him to a stop. "What's wrong?"

"Smoke! Don'tcha smell it? Comin' from the west, out near Green Valley."

Wash went cold all over. Jeanne's cabin!

Half an hour later he reined up on the cliff overlooking Jeanne's cabin and her lavender crop. From what he could see, the source of the gray-black smoke was either the chicken coop or the back side of the cabin. Or both.

"Must've been set on purpose," Rooney yelled. "Wind'll spread it to the trees, and the whole valley will go up."

Wash pounded down the steep trail, cursing under his breath. He didn't care whether it had been set or not; he cared only that the twelve-foot flames now licking one corner of Jeanne's cabin didn't swallow the small structure completely.

*But what does it matter?* The cabin was going to be torn down anyway when the clearing crew arrived. Sooner or later, Jeanne would have to get out.

But not this way!

A slim figure in a blue denim work skirt was clawing open the chicken coop door so the hens could scatter away from the fire. "Shoo!" she shouted. Waving her arms, she advanced on the clucking birds. "Shoo, I tell you!"

She straightened the instant she saw him at the gate. Wash dropped from his mount and started to run, Rooney close behind him. "Manette?" he yelled.

"Under the porch!"

He stooped, then went to his knees and scrabbled under the wood planking with one arm. His fingers brushed something soft, a girl's pinafore, maybe. He grabbed a handful and yanked.

Out tumbled Manette, dusty but grinning, a tiny green frog in her fist. Wash scooped her up and thrust the squirming girl into Rooney's arms. "Get her out of here."

Rooney carried the girl to his horse and headed up the steep canyon trail. The last thing Wash saw was Manette's rosy face turned up to the gruff horseman who held her securely in front of him. She was talking, lifting her frog so Rooney could admire it.

God help him, Wash thought with a little jerk in his heart. Rooney hated frogs.

He sensed Jeanne at his elbow and pivoted. "Get some blankets," he ordered. "Towels, anything."

She shoved her wool shawl into his hands and streaked through the open cabin door.

The fire was spreading. From the chicken coop to the side wall of the cabin, Wash could see nothing but greedy flames. He plunged toward the thickest smoke and attacked the fire with Jeanne's shawl.

No use. He beat at the flames, but the wool fiber began to smolder almost immediately, and the next thing he knew he was flailing away at the fire with a scrap of burning fabric. It smelled like scorched onions.

Then Jeanne was beside him, her arms so full of bedding and dishtowels she could scarcely see over the top. "Here." She dropped the load at his feet and grabbed the blanket on top. Wet, he noted. Smart girl. She had soaked everything under the kitchen spigot.

Without speaking, they whacked at the flames, beating the wet blankets against them in an uneven rhythm and stamping out rings of fire that ignited in the grass until they were soot-smeared and out of breath. Sparks had nibbled holes in all the blankets except for one bath towel that burst into flames in Jeanne's hands.

Smoke engulfed them. Wash could hear Jeanne coughing, and he dragged her upright and wrapped his bandanna over her nose and mouth. Then he ducked his own head under an embroidered tea towel and picked up his fire-singed blanket.

Foot by burning foot they beat down the flames, slapping wet towels against smoking boards, and stomping out bits of smoldering grass with their feet. Wash's bad leg ached, and the muscles in his arms stung. Jeanne showed no sign of slowing down, even though her slim arms must hurt like hell. Gasping to draw in clean air, they worked toward each other from the corners of the cabin.

At last the flames died, and the billows of acrid smoke began to dissipate. Trembling with exertion, they stumbled to a halt facing each other.

Jeanne's cheeks and forehead were streaked with soot and ash. Her denim skirt showed scorch marks where the hem had been singed. Lucky her petticoats hadn't caught fire! Her hair had come unpinned and now tumbled haphazardly about her shoulders. To Wash, she looked beautiful.

Dazed and red-eyed, they stared at each other. "Close

call," Wash grated. He gathered up the ruined blankets and towels and tossed them in a heap beside the porch. "Sorry about your sheets 'n things."

"I am not sorry," Jeanne announced, her voice raspy. "A few quilts—it is a small price to pay for my home."

"Rooney thinks someone started the fire on purpose. You see anyone around earlier this morning?"

She looked up, her face white. "*Non.* But I do see a horse, on the ridge."

"No rider?"

"*Non,* the horse only. Its color was strange…like the red glints in Manette's hair."

Montez. Had to be. By God he would pay for this.

Rooney clattered his horse down the hillside, a still-chattering Manette secure on his lap. He dismounted at the gate, lifted the girl down and sent her pelting down the path to her mother.

"You're all dirty, *Maman!*"

Jeanne knelt to clasp her tight. "*Oui, chou-chou,* I have been working hard."

Manette's blue eyes widened. "You need a bath. And Mr. Wash, too—he's even dirtier than you are!"

Rooney guffawed. "Observant little miss you got there, Miz Nicolet. Didja know she likes frogs?"

Jeanne stood up, Manette's arms still circling her waist.

"Thank you for keeping her safe, Mr.—?"

"Cloudman, ma'am."

"Mr. Cloud—"

"Rooney to my friends." He grinned at her, then

glanced at Wash. "Ya find out who set it? Wasn't a trace of anybody up on the ridge."

"Yeah, I know who it had to be. Tell the sheriff to put out a warrant for Joe Montez."

"Sure thing, Wash." His graying eyebrows waggled. "You stayin' here?"

Jeanne shot Wash a look, but he couldn't read it. He met her gaze and held it. "Thought I'd help clean up. Catch the mare and...maybe round up the chickens."

"Right." Rooney's tone betrayed his skepticism, but he saluted smartly and about-faced. "See ya tomorrow."

Jeanne jerked upright. "Tomorrow? You will stay here until tomorrow?"

"Thought I would, yes. I don't want you and Manette to be alone out here. I'll sleep out on the porch."

"That is...that is most kind."

Wash swallowed. That's not all it was, but he didn't want to think too hard about it now. He turned his back and strode off the porch. "I'll round up your mare, Jeanne. Probably didn't wander too far."

Her softly spoken *"Merci"* kicked his heartbeat up a notch. The woman had a voice like an angel. A seductive angel.

He found the mare in a narrow side canyon, munching quack grass. He slipped a rope over its head and led it back to the cabin where Jeanne kept the animal tied up. Wash rubbed it down with a handful of dry grass and hobbled her away from the scorched back wall of the cabin.

The chickens were another matter. Hens clucked from the field of lavender, but as soon as he drove one back to the coop he heard another that he couldn't see. He recalled there were six in all, but he tramped up and down among the fragrant bushes and couldn't find a single one.

After a frustrating hour, Jeanne appeared on the porch and motioned to him. "Here," she said as he mounted the step. She grasped his hand, turned it palm up and opened her fist. Dry corn kernels sprayed over his calluses.

Within twenty minutes, the five remaining hens had pecked their way along the trail of chicken-feed he'd dribbled out of his hand, right up to the coop. He slammed the wooden door after the last one.

Now what? Probably needed the wood box filled.

The wood box sat just outside the cabin door, next to a smaller box for kindling. Both containers were chock-full.

"Good Lord," he muttered. "This woman is damn self-sufficient. She sure doesn't need any help from me."

He plopped down on the porch and lowered his head into his hands. Laura had been helpless as a butterfly. He'd rescued her cats, helped her over fences, shaded her face with his hat when she started to sunburn. He'd felt needed. He'd liked the feeling it had given him—as if his presence had mattered.

Jeanne was about as helpless as a riled-up scorpion. She didn't need him. She didn't need anybody. What a woman!

Jeanne tiptoed out the door, took one look at Wash and quietly piled her arms full of small logs, then stuffed a handful of twigs and small broken limbs into her apron pocket. Wash didn't even raise his head.

*Alors,* he had been busy, and on her behalf, too. She had watched him rub down her mare and tie its foreleg to a wooden stake. She heard the chickens crooning contentedly, safe now in the coop.

The sun spilled warm light down on the man's dark head and wide shoulders; as she watched, his shadow on the porch floor lengthened. He was a handsome man, *un homme très beau,* with his tanned features and long legs that walked unevenly when he was tired. Oh, yes, she had noticed.

She liked the man, she admitted. She did not know why, she just felt a kinship between them. A mutual respect. She liked the way his gray eyes laughed at the world. The way his mouth curved into an occasional smile.

But, she reminded herself, she could not trust him. She would not ever again trust any man…and this man in particular. He worked for the railroad.

By suppertime, Wash had roused himself enough to appreciate the enticing smell of a bubbling pot of stew, and now a dilemma nagged at him. What about tonight?

He could roll up in his saddle blanket, but Jeanne had sacrificed her bedding to fight the fire. What would she and Manette do to keep warm? He asked the question over a brimming bowl of chicken stew and received a blank look.

"I have yet another quilt. Manette and I will be

perfectly comfortable." She piled two more biscuits onto his plate. "When I come from France to marry my husband, I bring my...how do you say...box of hope."

"Hope chest," Wash supplied while buttering his biscuit. "Young ladies fill them up with things for their marriage."

"Trousseau," she blurted. "I come with my trousseau. I have many quilts I make myself. And sheets with embroidery."

Wash leaned back in his chair. He didn't want to think about her embroidered sheets. "You burned some of them up today."

"*Oui,* I did. But I can make more. When I have money for my lavender, I will ask Monsieur Ness to order some muslin."

"Oh, no, your lavender," Wash groaned. "With the railroad coming you'll have to harvest early."

Her beautiful blue-green eyes turned to stone. "How early?"

"I'd say within a week. You'll have plenty of time, I promise."

A doubt niggled at his brain, but he squashed it down and ate another biscuit.


No night spent on the windswept plains of Kansas, or even in the prison barracks at Richmond, was as hard to get through as this one, wrapped in a blanket lying across Jeanne's cabin entrance. He rolled his lanky form over onto his other side. Porch sure was hard.

The air still smelled of smoke, both from the supper Jeanne had cooked on the woodstove in her kitchen and from the fire that had almost wiped out the whole cabin. Every little noise from inside brought him wide-awake. He heard Jeanne's soft, steady voice reading a bedtime story to Manette, in French. Heard the mumble of Manette's nighttime prayers. An owl *hoo-hooed* from a nearby fir tree, and then he heard the sigh of a corn-husk-stuffed mattress as a body lay down on it.

The bed Jeanne slept in was hidden behind a curtain that sectioned off part of the small cabin. Manette had her own bed, she had told him proudly. "*Maman* does not like my spider box under my pillow."

The cornhusks whispered again. And again. Was she sleepless, as well? Why?

She was frightened because of the fire and her smoky blankets and her mare and the chickens and…what? The more he thought about her, the more his hands burned to touch her skin.

His groin began to ache.

God help him, it was hot, urgent desire he felt, but Jeanne was not a woman he could tumble like a barroom dove. This woman was the kind a man courted, the kind who deserved a man's honorable intentions.

He didn't feel honorable. He was damn lonely and he was damn hungry. Still, the deepest need he felt was to just talk to her.

Talk! He couldn't remember if he and Laura had ever just talked. He rolled over once again and laid his forearm over his eyes.

# Chapter Nine

In the morning Jeanne dressed hurriedly and went to feed the chickens and her mare. She had to step over the man sleeping across her doorway; his breathing did not change so she knew she had not awakened him. She fed the mare some oats and flung handfuls of grain onto the ground for the chickens, then turned back toward the cabin.

Sunlight flashed off something metallic on the hillside and she caught her breath. At the head of the valley, five horsemen studied her lavender field. Dumbfounded, she stared at them.

One man gestured toward the ripening bushes and then pointed to her cabin.

Her neck hair began to itch. What did they want? One of the men untied a canvas-wrapped bundle from behind his saddle and dropped it onto the ground. The clank of metal brought her wide-awake. Tools. It was the railroad clearing crew Wash had mentioned.

They had come to clear her field!

Her home!

She whirled toward the cabin, raced up the porch steps making no effort to be quiet. Wash's inert body, still extended across her doorway, did not even twitch. Jeanne drew back her foot and buried the toe of her boot where she judged his midsection would be.

"You lied to me!" she screamed. "You promised I would have time to harvest—" She broke off to aim another blow.

A hand snaked out and caught her boot. "Good morning," a calm, sleep-fuzzy voice said. "Was there something you wanted?"

*"Oui,"* she shouted. *"Cochon!* I want you to suffer for what you did. I want—"

Wash sat up, still holding her foot. "Believe me, Jeanne, I am suffering."

"You mock me. I am so angry I could…" He released her foot and she drew it back to kick him again. Oh, she could not hurt him enough!

He raised both arms to protect his face. "For heaven's sake, what did I do?"

She faced him, planting her hands on her hips. "You know what you did. You lied to me. All men lie, but you—you are the worst! You promised!"

He struggled to his feet and they faced off. "What? What did I promise?"

"You promised I would have time to cut my lavender

before…before…" She could not bring herself to say it. "And now, this morning, they are here."

She pressed her lips together to keep them from trembling. She would *not* let him see her cry.

He took a step toward her. "Who is here?" He spoke with his jaw clenched, and she realized he was very, very angry. Even in his bare feet he towered over her. She straightened to her full height and lifted her chin.

"Five men from your railroad," she snapped. "They are here. Your clearing crew. And they have with them shovels and things to destroy my lavender. *Mon Dieu,* how could you lie to me about this?"

"Hell, I didn't lie to you."

"What do you call it, then? Those men are ready to cut—"

"They're here early, but I'll talk to them," he said, stuffing his feet into his boots. "Where are they now?"

Jeanne pointed beyond the chicken coop. "Up there, on the side of the hill."

Wash stalked off. He tried to reason with them, but the men said they were on Sykes's schedule, not his, and there was nothing he could do about it. When he returned she was still shaking with fury. "*Et alors?* Have those men not come to destroy my crop?"

He stepped up onto the porch and confronted her. "They won't cut your lavender today. They came to… uh…clear the buildings first."

"You mean my chicken house?" Her throat was so tight her voice cracked. "My cabin?"

"Yes."

"Today? You mean now?"

"Yes, today. Look, Jeanne, I'm as surprised as you are."

She bit her tongue to keep from screaming. "You are not surprised," she accused. "You knew this. You did not tell me the truth, you said I would have time—" She stopped to suck in an unsteady breath.

He stepped in closer to her, so close she could see the dark shadow of a beard on his chin, see his gray eyes burning with anger. And something else. Without thinking, she raised both arms and pounded her fists against his chest.

"I do not ever again trust you! I hate you!"

He wrapped his arms around her so tight she didn't have room between their bodies to keep pummeling him. Trapped, she dropped her head until her forehead rested on his shirtfront, blinking back the tears that stung into her eyes.

"Got it all out of your system?" he asked quietly.

"I will never get it 'out of my system,' as you say. Never."

"No doubt you're a woman of your word." He let out a breath that gusted warm against the crown of her head. She jerked, but did not look up.

"Of course," she muttered into his chest. "*I* do not ever lie!"

"Jeanne, believe me, I'm sorry about this."

"*Non,* you are not sorry. You want your railroad."

"Jeanne, just lis—"

"And I want my house. My lavender."

"Look, the house goes first. They're going to raze it

this afternoon, so you'll have to pack up your…" His voice clogged up and the unfinished sentence hung in the morning air.

"I will do no such thing! *Jamais!* Those men will have to chop me up with their shovels before I—"

Wash grabbed her shoulders and shook her, hard. "Hush up, will you? Just…be quiet." He looked at her oddly, hot light kindling in his eyes, and then his mouth was bruising hers. For an instant she forgot that she hated this man and gave herself up to the glorious sensation of his lips on hers. Her insides turned to warm molasses.

When at last he lifted his head, they were both breathing unevenly. He leaned his forehead against hers. "We'll get through this, Jeanne. Trust me— Oh, hell, never mind. I'll send one of the men into town for a wagon to haul your things."

In tight-lipped silence Jeanne made breakfast for Manette and Wash, scrambled eggs and the last of the bread for toast. Manette gobbled her plate clean; Wash pushed his eggs around and around with his fork and hoped Jeanne wouldn't notice.

No such luck. Jeanne noticed everything, even his uneaten piece of burnt toast.

"You are not hungry?" she inquired, her voice accusing.

Wash groaned inwardly. He *was* hungry, but not for scrambled eggs. He wanted another taste of her soft honey-sweet mouth.

A horse-drawn wagon rattled up outside. Wash

dropped his napkin beside his plate and bolted for the door.

The rest of the day he and Jeanne spent without speaking a word to each other while they packed up pots and skillets, china and tableware, and whatever bedding was undamaged after the fire. Wash even loaded Manette's prized spider box and her Mason jar full of grasshoppers, stuffing them between two quilts so Jeanne wouldn't be upset by the crawly things.

Two men from the clearing crew helped to jockey in the cast-iron woodstove and settle the chicken coop into the space remaining. Finally they tied Jeanne's gray mare to the back end with a lead rope.

She made a last inspection of the now-empty cabin, then marched out and climbed up onto the driver's bench next to Manette. Wash left General tied to a tree stump and drove the draft horse and the wagon up the winding trail to the ridge. At the top he reined to a halt.

"You might want to take one last look? Valley looks real pretty in this light."

She turned her face away but did not look down at the cabin. He picked up the reins. She kept her back rigid and her eyes fixed straight ahead for the three-mile trip to town. Not once did she glance back.

Rooney was waiting at the livery stable. Manette scrambled down from the wagon and threw her small arms about the older man's knees. Wash almost laughed at the look of consternation that crossed his friend's weathered face. Manette had apparently adopted him.

Rooney bent down to her level. "Hullo there, Little Miss. Got any new critters to show me?"

Wash arranged with the liveryman to store the loaded wagon until Jeanne had relocated. For tonight, she and Manette would sleep at the Smoke River Hotel.

All he wanted to do tonight was close his mind to the pained, set look on Jeanne's face. He could feel himself withdrawing from her; not letting himself feel anything had gotten him through his prison years. He figured it could get him through this.

"Care for a steak supper?" Rooney offered.

Jeanne shook her head. "I could not eat, Mr. Cloud— Rooney. I am not hungry."

"*I'm* hungry," Manette sang.

Rooney grinned. "Well, come along, then. I know a hungry miss when I see one. Wash, you joining us?"

Wash shook his head. He couldn't eat, either. "I'll get Jeanne settled at the hotel and then…"

He didn't know what then; he knew only that he couldn't stand to look at Jeanne's eyes any longer. In silence he walked her into the hotel foyer. The clerk scowled at Jeanne, but Wash ignored him and got her registered. Surreptitiously he even paid the bill. He knew her lavender crop would bring her some money, but it wasn't harvested yet. Right now, he'd bet she hadn't a penny to her name. He hoped she could harvest some of her lavender before…

Rooney and Manette walked into the hotel dining room, her small hand clasped in his big one. Jeanne watched them go, still with that stricken look on her face, then turned away to climb the stairs to her room.

He knew what being uprooted felt like. He didn't want

to think about Jeanne and her cabin. Mostly he didn't want to feel what she must be feeling.

He clumped down the hotel steps, marched three doors down to the Golden Partridge and ordered a double shot of Red Eye. After an hour Rooney sidled up beside him. "Finally got her all wised up, didja?"

"Don't make jokes, Rooney."

"Creepin' crickets, man. Wasn't a joke. She musta' finally heard what you been saying all along, and she caved in."

Wash raised his head enough to glare at his partner. "That woman never 'caves in.'"

Rooney busied himself pointing out to the bartender a bottle of scotch whiskey he fancied. "That bad, huh? Well, ya know what the Comanche say—'women and cats do as they please.'"

Wash didn't bother to answer. The less he thought about Jeanne Nicolet the sooner his railroad track would go down. Then he'd move on. One thing he liked about working for the Oregon Central—you never spent too much time in one town. There was always another site to scope out along Grant Sykes's planned route. Another clearing crew, another bunch of track layers.

Rooney signaled the bartender for another and propped his chin on his fists. "Right now you want out of this Smoke River mess, huh? Find a new town with no pretty widows growing lavender?"

"Right now," Wash said without looking up, "I don't know what I want."

"Got you comin' and goin', has she?" Rooney chuckled over his shot glass.

"Part of me wants her to be safe. Another part of me wants her to sweat in hell for making me—"

"And," Rooney added in an amused voice, "another part of you wants to clear out and leave it all behind, like a bad dream."

Wash groaned. "How'd an old coot like you ever get so damned smart?"

The older man laughed. "This old coot took to a woman once. Got more than I bargained for."

"She doesn't have her cabin anymore. The clearing crew is knocking it down."

"Right. I think it's prob'ly for the best, don't you?"

Wash felt his face flush hot. "You do, do you?"

"Yeah, I do. For one thing, Little Miss can go to school in town. And for another, with the new railroad line, Jeanne can ship her lavender sachets and smelly doodads all over the state." He shot Wash a sly smile. "Folks in Portland will smell as good as folks here in Smoke River."

Wash merely grunted. But he kept listening.

"New folks will settle here," Rooney went on. "Build ranch houses and schools, mebbe a church or two. Ranchers can ship their beef east without drivin' 'em two hundred miles to a railhead."

"Yeah."

Rooney punched his upper arm. "You told me you went to work for Sykes to do something constructive, to take the taste of killin' bluebellies and Indians off yer mind."

"Yeah, that's true."

"Well, son, now you've made the choice, you pay the price."

Wash lowered his head. "I've uprooted a woman and her child. She has nowhere to go. Sacrificed her crop. Even made a shambles out of trying to be a friend to her."

"Wise up, Wash. You ain't tryin' to be Jeanne's friend so much as—"

Wash drove his elbow into Rooney's ribs. The older man grabbed his side, coughed for a long minute, then choked out a sentence that turned Wash's belly upside-down.

"Ya damn fool! You're falling in love with her."

Rooney strolled off to join the poker game at the barroom table, leaving Wash with a lump in his belly as big as a cannonball.

# Chapter Ten

"No, Colonel Halliday," the pinch-faced clerk said. "She's not here at the hotel. Drove off before sunup with her daughter and an empty wagon."

Wash stared at the hotel desk clerk. "Wagon?"

"Yes, sir. Wobbly looking old—"

He was out the door of the hotel before the man had finished. He knew instinctively what Jeanne was up to; she would try desperately to harvest her lavender crop before the clearing crew could reach it. He should have planned this better, should have made the clearing crew listen to him yesterday.

At the livery stable, he borrowed Rooney's roan. The mare wasn't as fast as his own horse, but he'd left General tied up out in Green Valley where the chicken house had been. He walked the mare outside and squinted up at the sun. Just past noon. He climbed on, dug his spurs into the animal's flank and prayed to God he wouldn't be too late.

From the ridge he spotted the pile of boards that had been Jeanne's cabin and felt a knife rip into his gut. At the upper end of the valley the five-man clearing crew was felling pine trees and slashing their way through the surrounding brush, moving forward toward the spreading lavender field a square foot at a time.

When he spied Jeanne, the knife in his gut twisted. She was deep in the field, bent almost double, cutting the lavender stalks close to the ground with a hand scythe. When she had an armload, she trudged to the wagon parked where the cabin used to be and heaved it up over the side. Manette did a little stomping dance on top of it to tamp the load down. The wagon was one-third full; she'd harvested only about a quarter of her crop.

As he watched she leaned against the slat sides of the wagon and wiped her forehead with a corner of her apron. Manette offered her mother a glass jar of water, and Jeanne tipped her head back and gulped like a field hand. Then she patted her daughter's knee and turned back to pick up her scythe.

Wash spurred the horse forward to climb the hill to speak to the crew. "Cain't do it, Colonel. We gotta finish today. Gotta be at another site tomorrow, by order of Mr. Sykes. Can't afford to get behind, even by one day. You know how it is."

"I hate to ask this, boys, but could you work real slow? Give the lady time enough to gather in her crop."

Hell would be no worse than this, Jeanne thought. The merciless sun had beat down all morning, and now it was so hot even the sparrows were silent. She wiped her sweat-sticky face, glanced up to see how far the clearing crew had advanced, and sucked in her breath. The men were almost halfway down the hill to her field.

She swiveled toward the sound of horses' hooves.

She recognized Rooney's horse, but the rider... The rider turned out to be Wash. *"Mon Dieu,"* she muttered. "What next?"

He had not shaved, but his dark-shadowed face made her heart jump. Without a word he dismounted, took a hand scythe from his saddlebag and set to work beside her cutting lavender.

*Holy Mary, forgive me for kicking him in the stomach yesterday.* Truly she had never known a man such as this.

A few minutes later the tall man in faded jeans tramped past her on his way to the wagon with a load of lavender balanced in his arms. "Smells good," was all he said.

She straightened. "Is Spanish lavender," she said in a purposely matter-of-fact tone.

They spoke no other words from that moment on, just cut and gathered, cut and gathered as fast as they could wield their scythes. By midafternoon the wagon bed was only half-full and Jeanne began to wonder how she could keep going. The intense heat was so suffocating she could scarcely breathe. Clouds of tiny gnats swarmed around her face and her hair felt itchy, as if something were crawling on her scalp.

Three rows over, Wash worked on, in spite of the stifling air, the gnats, even the bees. He must be as miserable as she was. He'd brought two canteens of water; every so often he dribbled some out and sloshed it over his face. Once he poured some on his shirttail, strode over to where she was working and wiped the cool, wet fabric over her face.

Wash shot a glance at Jeanne. Her face was gray with exhaustion but she gave him a wobbly smile and his heart floated free in his chest. It would be a real horse race to finish the field before the clearing crew reached it, but he knew he had to try.

Twilight fell. The clearing crew had reached the bottom of the hill and were moving relentlessly toward the lavender field. They labored on, heedless of the fading light and buzzing insects until Jeanne gave a yelp. She'd swiped at a section of lavender and hit her foot instead. Good thing she was wearing boots.

By dusk, the field was almost completely mowed, and the clearing crew was bearing down on them. All that remained were a few square yards of growth near what had been the cabin. Wash knew she'd want every last frond of the stuff; he stood up and signaled the clearing crew to take a break.

They worked until they couldn't see clearly in the growing darkness, and Wash lit a kerosene lamp and walked the valley perimeter. Every last stalk of lavender had been cut. It made him feel so good he laughed out loud.

Jeanne staggered toward him, her scythe dragging from her hand. "What is funny?" she demanded.

"We're finished," he said.

"The entire crop?" Her voice turned hoarse. "I cannot believe it is true."

Wash nodded. "Every last bush." He pointed to the wagon, where a tower of lavender stalks rose from the bed and spilled over the sides. *"C'est t-très beau,"* he stammered.

She stared at him, then laughed. *"Votre francais c'est très mal."*

"Shouldn't have switched to Latin, I guess. More use for a lawyer than French." Wash spread his saddle blanket over the loaded wagon and roped it down tight. Then he climbed onto the bench and shoved over to his left to make room for Jeanne and Manette. He drove the creaking wagon up to the ridge. At the top, the clearing crew waited with General, Rooney's horse, and Jeanne's gray mare. They tied the horses to the tailgate.

The crew rode on ahead, and the wagon rattled and groaned its way into town. Every few minutes Jeanne reached one hand behind her and stroked the fronds of lavender.

Watching her made his throat tight.

He drove the wagon straight into the livery stable, nodded to the liveryman and jockeyed it into place next to the smaller wagon they had filled yesterday with Jeanne's belongings. Manette lay sound asleep with her head in Jeanne's lap. She smoothed her daughter's red-gold hair and for a moment the three of them sat in silence. The warm air smelled of horses and fresh straw. And lavender.

Never in her life had she been this tired, not even walking day after day alongside the wagons that had brought her to Oregon. Her arms ached, her legs were wobbly with fatigue. And her face, her hair—she must look like a sunburned scarecrow.

But she'd harvested all her lavender! She would have meat and milk for Manette, and at this moment that was all she cared about.

Wash half turned to her. "You all right?"

She nodded, and he climbed down and began to unhook the rig. He kept his head down but she thought a smile touched his mouth. He was pleased, then, with their day's work? Or was he pleased that his precious railroad could now roll its iron tracks over her farm?

Men liked nothing better than to win. Henri had bragged that he was the best swordsman in New Orleans; it would have been better had he spent his time practicing marksmanship with his rifle. And this man, Wash Halliday…well, she could not say what she thought of him.

She was so weary her thinking was confused, but she was not so weary she could not feel the inexplicable pull toward the man who was now lifting her sleeping daughter into his arms. She stumbled down from the wagon seat to walk close beside him, up the stairs to the hotel's second floor. He paused at the door to her room while she unlocked it. Light spilled in from the doorway, illuminating the room she and Manette slept in.

He entered as if expecting to be ambushed, then gently deposited Manette on the big double bed. When he straightened Jeanne laid her hand on his muscled forearm. He flinched the tiniest bit, and somehow she guessed he was weighing his reticence about her against his masculine need. That pleased her.

"You have been very kind," she said. "You are a good man, Monsieur Wash. I am sorry that I kick you, and I thank you for today."

The oddest expression crossed his face, and in his gray eyes she suddenly saw both wariness and raw desire.

"Are you hungry?" he whispered.

"It does not matter. I cannot leave Manette."

Then he did a strange thing. He reached out and laid his hand against her cheek. For a moment she did not move and then an irrational yearning tugged at her. She wanted to turn her mouth into his palm.

She leaned toward him. Oh, if he would only hold her in his strong arms and make her fears go away. She hadn't known a woman could be so desperately lonely at times; perhaps he would talk with her? God knew she had no one else to talk to—no friends. No family.

But he dropped his arm and stepped away. Something in him held back. *Alors,* she should not have kicked him in the stomach yesterday.

*Mon Dieu,* would she never learn not to strike out first and questions later?

## Chapter Eleven

Wash moved through the open hotel-room door and closed it decisively behind him. No use prolonging it; he'd accomplished what he set out to do, even though it had cost this woman everything she had. Now his mind was rolling up all his doubts in a ball and bouncing it off his heart.

Was it worth it? No one was paying a higher price for this damn rail line than Jeanne, not even Grant Sykes, who was shelling out hundred-dollar bills like Christmas candy canes. Just thinking about Jeanne's cabin and the look in her eyes when she'd seen the pile of boards at the site made him feel rotten.

He hadn't felt like this since the War. Sykes would probably give him another raise for being an efficient instrument of destruction. And on top of everything, Rooney was right: he was falling in love with Jeanne Nicolet.

What was he going to do?

He decided to pay a visit to the sheriff and ask about Joe Montez. The answer unsettled him.

"Sure, I ran into Montez couple of days back. Said he was leaving town, but my deputy spied him setting up camp in the woods somewhere near River Fork Road.

Wash felt his belly turn to ice. He had to find Montez; he had a feeling the Spaniard meant bad business.

In the hotel dining room, he caught Rita's eye and ordered a picnic basket with a jar of chicken soup, half a loaf of bread and three hard-boiled eggs. Then he tramped back up the stairs and left the basket outside Jeanne's door, tapped softly and fled. He could break a horse in half an hour, but right now he hadn't enough grit to face Jeanne again.

The next morning, Wash found the burned remains of Montez's campsite but no sign of the man. Maybe he'd been spooked by the deputy who'd seen him, but had the Spaniard hightailed it out of the county?

Wash didn't think so. The man seemed to have a grudge of some kind against Jeanne.

He rode out to Green Valley to supervise the clearing crew in cutting timber and laying the split logs onto the four-foot-wide cleared track the men had leveled in preparation for the iron rail sections. The rolling bunkhouse for the workers had already reached the town of Colville, twenty miles to the west; another week of laying the three miles of track a day credited to the Chinese laborers Sykes hired and they'd be at the rim of Green Valley.

On the site, it was turning into another scorching day.

By noon, Wash and the five-man clearing crew were tired and sweaty and thirsty. By quitting time they were hot and cranky. When they straggled back to town, he bought the men cold beers at the Golden Partridge, had himself a bath and a shave at the barbershop and decided to visit the hotel to check on Jeanne and her daughter.

He was not prepared for the shock he got when he spoke to the desk clerk.

"Sorry, Colonel Halliday, Miz Nicolet checked out this morning."

"Checked out! Where'd she go?"

"Over to the livery stable, I think. Said something about finding a place to live. That's the last I saw of her."

A place to live? What kind of place can she find with not one red cent to her name? He'd sure as hell find out in a hurry. He headed for the livery stable.

One of the wagons—the one loaded with Jeanne's household items—was gone. The liveryman shrugged and raised his hands, palms up. "How should I know where some stubborn female spends her time?"

Wash started asking questions. Someone at the barbershop had seen her drive off to the south, but it wasn't until Wash cornered storekeeper Carl Ness in the narrow aisle between men's boots and seed corn that he learned the truth.

"The MacAllister ranch out on Swine Creek!" Wash thundered. "That old place was run-down six years ago when I left. Unless they've discovered gold in the creek, it can't be worth a hill of beans now."

"Ain't worth a hill of beans, Colonel," Ness replied.

"Thad MacAllister's growin' barley. Yessir, he's had four or five years of good crops. In fact, his threshing crew left just last Sunday."

Wash remounted his horse and headed south, toward Swine Creek. What did Jeanne want with an old used-up barley field? He kicked General into a gallop.

Jeanne saw the man riding toward her across the shorn barley field and her stomach knotted. What would he think about her decision?

*Alors,* it did not matter what the tall man who bossed the railroad crews thought. What mattered was what *she* thought. Mr. MacAllister had been surprisingly nice; she and Manette were safe here in his empty bunkhouse, sheltered under a weathered but sturdy roof. She could draw water from the nearby creek and she could cook supper over the potbellied stove. At this point she asked for nothing more.

She watched Wash circle her new abode, a scowl on his face. He dismounted with jerky motions and came striding up to the open door.

"Jeanne!" he yelled.

"I am here," she said quietly. "Inside."

He stomped into the tiny building and stopped short in front of her. "What the hell do you think you're doing out here in MacAllister's bunkhouse? Where is Manette?"

She met his angry look with a calm voice. At least she hoped it was calm; inside she was most definitely not calm.

"Do not shout, please. Manette is asleep."

"Where?" he shouted.

She gestured to the upper bunk bed behind her. "She is tired from yesterday. I, too, am tired." She looked pointedly at the lower bunk where she had just finished laying out sheets and quilts on the thin cornhusk mattress.

Wash glanced at the small stove that sat at one end of the room. She had not quite finished starting the fire; a thin spiral of smoke escaped from the iron firebox into the room.

"Jeanne, you can't stay here. This is a bunkhouse, for farm crews, not a hotel. Not even a cabin."

"I know very well what it is," she shot back. "Monsieur MacAllister offered it and I—I took it." She did not add that it was only a temporary lodging until she earned some money from her lavender crop. Or that she had swept and scrubbed all morning to get rid of the dirt. Or that she was frightened about the future and uneasy about camping out here alone. Instead she pointed out the gingham curtains she had tacked over the single window and the work skirts and aprons hanging on wooden pegs along one wall.

But she could see by his expression that he was not impressed. From the deepening frown on his tanned face, he was far from approving of what she had done. Well, so be it.

"Jeanne you can't live out here."

"I can. And I will."

"Alone? It's not safe."

In answer she lifted the rifle leaning beside the door

and aimed it out the door. He shifted quickly away from her line of sight.

"Look, MacAllister isn't going to keep an eye on you. He lives in the ranch house a mile up the road. He can't even see the bunkhouse from his place."

"But I do not want his eye on me."

"Jeanne, dammit, listen to me. You're a woman—"

"That does not mean I am helpless."

He barked out a laugh. "No one would ever think of you as helpless! Misguided, maybe. Hardheaded as a Sioux brave on the warpath. But not helpless." He sighed and shook his head.

"Not—"

She held up one hand to stop his speech. "I will make it all right. I *must* make it all right. Do you not see that, Monsieur Railroad Man? It is necessary for me and my Manette to survive. When I sell my lavender, when I have money, then I will find another place."

Wash clumped twice around the little stove, then halted and propped his hands on his hips. He looked so angry she took a step backward.

"I can't look after you. During the day I'll be out in Green Valley supervising the crews."

"There is no need to—"

"Oh, yes, there is! I will be here at night."

"You need not be here!" It came out a bit harsher than she had intended, but she knew she was right. She did not need Wash Halliday to protect her.

"I'll be here," he growled. "Just don't shoot me when you hear my horse."

"I will not feed you," she warned. "I have enough only for Manette and myself."

He took a step toward her. "I'll eat in town."

She raised her chin. "You will not wake Manette."

"Not unless you shoot me. She'll wake up when she hears the shot."

"I will not shoot."

He looked up at the ceiling, his fists opening and closing. "You are more trouble than any woman I've ever known."

"*Oui,* that must be true. Otherwise, you would not make such a noise."

Wash gave up. He pivoted away from her and stomped outside to his horse. How in Heaven's name had he been brought to his knees by this slip of a woman in a blue gingham dress?

He found Rooney lingering over his coffee at the Rose Cottage boardinghouse; Wash poured himself a cup of the brew and explained the situation.

"I can't rest easy while she's out there alone."

"Yer even less easy when she's *not* alone. 'Specially when you're the one who's with her."

"Rooney, how 'bout you keep a watch over Miz Nicolet and Manette during the day? I'll take over at night."

Rooney sent him a wry look. "You mean days I get to bust my knees huntin' for bugs with Little Miss and nights you get to sleep on her doorstep?"

"Damn right."

"Deal," Rooney shot.

Wash reached the railroad site in time to start the

crew hacking the roadbed down the hillside into the canyon. All that day he couldn't erase the picture of Jeanne, so mad at him she looked like a fluffed up banty chicken, her green-blue eyes studying him with that wary look he'd come to know. Who was it she didn't trust? Him?

Or herself?

At supper in the boardinghouse that night Wash was the last one to sit down at the table. He took an empty chair across from Rooney and dug into the fried chicken and mashed potatoes Mrs. Rose had saved for him while his partner pared his fingernails and then cleaned them with his pocketknife. Rooney was wearing a new shirt.

"What's up?" he inquired, his mouth half-full of mashed potatoes.

"Hell, man, it's Saturday night."

"So?" Wash gulped down a mouthful of coffee.

Rooney tapped his folded blade against Wash's chest. "You dead or alive in there? Big barn dance out at the Jensen place tonight. Sarah—Miz Rose, that is—invited me to go with her.

Wash stared at him, a drumstick halfway to his mouth. "'Sarah,' huh? If I live to be two hundred I'll never understand your appeal to women."

Rooney chuckled. "I'm halfway handsome and all the way smart, that's why."

Wash chewed in silence.

"Now you, on t'other hand, are all-the-way handsome but only half smart! If you was *all* smart you'd see what's starin' you in the face."

"And what's that?"

"Jeanne Nicolet, that's what."

Wash shoveled in potatoes and said nothing.

Rooney waggled his salt-and-pepper eyebrows. "She 'n Little Miss will be goin' to the dance tonight. Jeanne's figurin' to make friends with some of the townfolk and try to sell some of her lavender sacks."

"Sachets," Wash corrected.

"French, huh? Figures."

"Yeah? Well, my friend, I won't be going to the dance tonight."

"Wouldn't count on it, son." Rooney straightened the collar on his new shirt, smoothed down the cuffs, and headed for the kitchen.

"Sarah? You 'bout ready?"

## Chapter Twelve

Wash took his time riding out to MacAllister's, trying to sort out his feelings about Jeanne Nicolet. She was annoying as hell and prickly as a cactus. But he liked her. In addition she was so good to look at he hadn't stopped wanting her since he'd laid eyes on her.

He gazed up at the beginning of a colorful sunset. The shorn barley fields glowed with a rich, golden light and purple-tinged clouds hung over the mountains in the distance. He'd always thought this part of the country was beautiful. Hadn't realized how much he'd missed it in the years he'd been away.

He let General pick his way slowly toward the bunkhouse where a spiral of smoke curled from the stovepipe on the roof. The empty wagon sat next to the structure and…dammit, there was another clothesline draped with lacy undergarments flapping in the breeze. Wash groaned aloud. This woman would try a man's patience until it snapped.

Before he could dismount the door swung open and Manette sprang out, dressed in a crisp white pinafore. She tipped her face up, watching him slip out of the saddle. He bent his knees and hunched down to her level, ignoring the stab of pain in his wounded hip.

"I wanna look for grasshoppers, but *Maman* says I can't cuz we're going to a dance."

"You ever been to a dance before?"

"No. And I don't want to."

Wash had to laugh. At what point in a young girl's life did she get interested in dances?

"I see," he said. "You'd rather hunt for grass—"

Jeanne appeared in the doorway and he broke off. She wore a yellow dress made of some kind of soft-looking stuff. She'd let her hair down and it brushed her shoulders in dark waves. He'd like to run his fingers through it. In the gauzy almost-evening light she looked like an angel. Over her arm she carried a basket of lavender sachets.

*"Bon soir,"* she called.

Very slowly he rose to his feet and snaked off his wide-brimmed hat, his mouth suddenly dry as tumbleweed. He had to clear his throat twice before he could utter a word.

"Manette says you're going—"

*"Oui,* to the dance at Peter and Roberta Jensen's barn. They were very kind to invite me."

"How're you going to get there, walk?"

"But of course! It is only one half of a mile. Ten minutes!"

His mouth opened and before he could close it, words he hadn't expected came tumbling out. "I could drive you in the wagon."

*What was he saying?* He didn't want to go anywhere near that barn dance. He especially did not want to be anywhere near Jeanne in that yellow dress. Every time he looked at her, his britches felt too tight.

She gazed at him, considering his impulsive offer, probably weighing all the reasons she would prefer to walk. Apparently she didn't want his help. Well, let her walk if she was so independent. He hoped she'd get cockleburs in her stockings.

He looked skyward where the moon floated above them like a fat orange pumpkin sailing close to the earth. He guessed she was still mad enough about the railroad to spit nails. She wouldn't want to be within a mile of him, much less sitting next to him on the wagon bench.

*"Bon,"* she said abruptly. She gestured toward the slat-wood vehicle pulled up next to the bunkhouse. "Would you hitch up my horse?"

Wash stood motionless, wondering if he'd heard right. Hitch up...? Yeah, he'd heard right.

His hands shook when he nudged the bridle over her gray mare's head. By the time he'd linked the traces to the wagon axle, he was so nervous the horse sidled away from him.

What the devil was wrong with him? He'd be sitting next to Jeanne for maybe five minutes while he drove the wagon to the Jensen place. Five minutes, that was all. And he would position Manette between them.

He lifted the girl up onto the wagon bench, then offered a helping hand to Jeanne. She ignored it, stepped up on the axle and settled herself into place beside her daughter. Wash tramped around to the other side, climbed up and flapped the lines. The mare started forward.

Jeanne smoothed out her soft yellow dress and sat in rigid silence while Manette clapped her hands and began to hum a tuneless song. Jeanne leaned sideways to put her arm around her daughter and he caught a whiff of that indefinable scent that rose from her hair. Like lilac blooms, with a dash of…cloves? Whatever it was, it made him ache with an old, old hunger he thought he'd never feel again.

The Jensens' barn, actually their threshing barn, was lit up like a Kansas City carnival. Candlelit lanterns lined the path; music poured out the double doors which stood wide open as townsfolk crowded to get inside.

The interior was warm, smelling of pine planks and coffee and tobacco smoke and ladies' scented powder. At one end of the room a long table was laden with cakes and pies, glass bowls of lemonade punch, two speckle-ware coffeepots, and even a few bottles of whiskey for the men. Jeanne set her basket of sachets next to the lemonade.

In the opposite corner Thad MacAllister and Whitey Kincaid sawed away on their fiddles, and Seth Rubens jauntily plucked a washtub bass. Upturned wooden boxes served as chairs along one wall, and an area behind the refreshment table had been set aside for makeshift beds for young children and a few cradles for infants.

Wash felt suddenly out of place in the overwarm, noisy atmosphere. For some reason the friendly spirit of the gathering grated on his nerves. He knew almost everyone. Some folks he'd known since he was in knee pants on his dad's ranch, but he still felt he didn't belong.

Jeanne was whirled away into a square dance set and Rooney strode across the polished floor and bowed before Manette. "Now, then, Little Miss, I'm gonna teach you how to dance."

Wash found himself standing against the far wall, trying not to watch Jeanne lifting her arm to make a Ladies' Star in the center of her square. She was clearly working hard to mend some bridges with the townsfolk. Instead he concentrated on Rooney and Manette. The girl placed her feet on top of Rooney's big boots, so that when he stepped, she stepped. Together they moved about the floor in a dance of sorts, Manette grinning up at Rooney, her eyes shining. Rooney, the big galoot, was one big smile.

Wash blew out a pent-up breath. He was surrounded by a bustling crowd of people yet he felt lonelier than he could ever remember. He edged toward the whiskey on the refreshment table. He downed one hefty slug, and then another, and began to feel more alive.

The music changed to a polka. He searched the dancing couples for Jeanne, found her with Carl Ness, the mercantile owner. Looked like Carl had warmed toward her; he was teaching her the steps. She looked distracted and kept stumbling over her partner's feet. He guessed they didn't polka in New Orleans.

A tall young cowboy cut in on Carl, and then another fellow with a handsome blond mustache cut in on the cowboy. The mustache held her too close, and Wash clenched his jaw. *Don't manhandle her, you big oaf. This one is a Lady with a capital* L.

He watched as long as he could stand it, then shouldered his way onto the waxed floor. When her partner swung her close enough, Wash reached out, snagged his arm around her waist, and spun her out of Mustache's arms and into his own.

*"Merci!"* she whispered. "I thought he was going to eat me!"

"I thought so, too."

She said nothing, and their conversation died. Wash tried to concentrate on moving his feet. The fiddles moved into a slow waltz, which made it easier in one way—he knew the steps—but harder in another: he was holding her in his arms. Her hair smelled of flowers and under the billowy yellow dress she was warm and soft. He held her slightly apart from him, afraid he would crush her.

Which was exactly what he wanted to do. After a slight hesitation he pulled her closer, so close her tumbled hair brushed his bare hand splayed against her back.

"What do you think about when you are dancing?" she murmured.

"About the railroad, I guess." *No, you don't. You think about Jeanne.*

She swallowed. "I never stop thinking about it. It has changed everything. I feel...lost. Everything I have worked so hard for is gone. It makes me feel—how you say?—helpless. Marooned, like a ship with no place to go."

Wash nodded, grazing her forehead with his chin. "Partly I'm sorry about it. But partly I'm glad, too."

"Are you glad for this? For the dancing?"

"Some," he answered honestly.

"It is not comfortable for you, then? Why is that?"

At that moment he forgot everything except the feel of her pliant body in his arms. He forgot why he was here in Jensens' barn. He forgot to move his feet.

She tipped her head back to look at him. "Why?" she repeated.

He stopped dancing. She didn't seem to notice, but stood still, closed in the circle of his arms. "Because," he said at last, "I can't be near you and not want you."

His words hung in the air between them, as if a bell were summoning them. For a long time neither of them moved, but then she dropped her head to rest her cheek against his shoulder. When she reached her hand up and curved her fingers across the back of his neck, Wash gritted his teeth. He was finding it hard to breathe. Hard to think. He wanted to hold her close enough to feel her breasts against his chest. Oh, he wanted to taste her nipples.

He wanted to— Oh, hell. Her hand was clasped in his in proper waltz position; he drew it to his breastbone and folded his fingers over hers.

What in hell was wrong with him? He began to move

slower, and he forgot to think about the steps. They moved at the periphery of the other dancing couples, past the refreshment table, past the musicians in the corner.

Jeanne closed her eyes. She drew in an uneven breath and let herself drift between the sob of the violin and the thrum of his heartbeat. She liked his smell, of leather and sweat and…ah, it did not matter what else; it was just good. All of him was good. *Très beau.*

She needed some lemonade.

*Non,* she needed some whiskey.

*Mon Dieu,* she needed…him.

The music stopped, but they kept moving together, their bodies almost touching. His mouth grazed her forehead; the yellow ruffles on her bodice brushed against his shirtfront.

The violin struck up a reel. Jeanne heard the faster tempo but she did not want to stop their slow journey together. It was almost like making love, his body asking, hers answering. At the thought she sucked in a gulp of air and felt tears sting into her eyes. It was such pleasure being close to him! It made her nerves sing in a way they had not since she was a girl in France.

*Mon Dieu!* Was she falling in—?

A rough hand grasped her forearm and yanked her out of Wash's arms. She stumbled, then found herself dragged against another man's body.

"Aye, *señora,*" a silky voice said. "Now I will have that kiss, no?"

The Spaniard! The one Wash had chased away that

night. She opened her mouth to shout, but another voice, low and menacing, interrupted.

"Take your hands off her, Montez."

For a second nothing happened. The Spaniard tightened his hold, and then Wash slipped one arm about her waist and simultaneously rammed his other elbow into the man's windpipe.

The man doubled over, gasping for air.

Wash propelled her to the sidelines. "Let's get out of here."

He spun at a woman's cry from across the room. Montez had halfway straightened and now he was pulling a knife from inside his boot. Wash thrust Jeanne behind him and stepped forward. Out of the corner of his eye he saw Rooney lift Manette onto a chair protected behind the refreshment table. Rooney could smell a fight a mile away.

Jeanne gave a stifled cry. Damn, he didn't want her mixed up in this; he'd have to keep himself between her and Montez until she could leave the barn.

Montez crouched, the blade in his right hand sweeping in an arc as he advanced. The man's steps were slow and deliberate, his eyes glittering, his breathing raspy. Wash had had plenty of practice during the Sioux skirmishes, but at least he'd had a knife of his own. Now, he had nothing. *It wouldn't be fun, but he'd done it before.*

He lifted both arms and began circling to the left, drawing Montez's attention away from Jeanne. If he could get in close enough, under the Spaniard's blade…

He crouched and kept moving to the left, drawing closer bit by bit. He couldn't take his eyes off the shiny knife Montez brandished—some kind of silvery blade with a carved black handle. The Spaniard would have to raise his arm to stab downward at Wash. Or he could strike up from waist level and catch him in the rib cage.

He moved in. "Come on, Montez. Come and get me."

The Spaniard's lips drew back in a feral grin. "I will kill you, Boss Man."

"I don't think so." Wash feinted with his left hand, and when Montez followed with his knife, Wash lunged inside the blade's arc, close enough to the man's body to hamper his thrust. Before Montez could rip the blade into Wash's side, Wash shot his right fist into the man's shoulder and with his left arm knocked Montez's elbow up.

Montez yelped, and the knife clattered onto the barn floor.

Wash dived for it, but the sheriff stomped out of nowhere and pinned it under his boot. Then he lifted his coat back to reveal his holstered sidearm.

"Come along, Montez. Got a nice cool jail cell waitin' for ya."

Wash was breathing hard, but inside his gut the knot of anger and fear was dissolving in a rush of masculine triumph. He watched the sheriff march the Spaniard out the side door. Outside, he found Jeanne leaning against the side of the barn, her eyes huge, her fingers clasped over her mouth. Rooney appeared with Manette clinging to his hand.

"Thought I'd have to patch you up, Wash."

Wash barked out a half laugh. "Maybe next time."

"Huh! Guess I'd better stock up on bandages. And whiskey," he added with a grin.

Wash chuckled. All at once he realized how tired he felt, as if his legs had turned to lead. His hip hurt like hell.

"I'm getting too old for this," he muttered.

"Get some sleep," Rooney advised. "You got a carload of Chinese track layers comin' tomorrow."

Wash groaned and turned away to see Jeanne and Manette starting for the wagon. He'd just see them safely back to MacAllister's bunkhouse and then…

He couldn't think clearly beyond that. Maybe he didn't want to.

## Chapter Thirteen

**W**ash guided the mare away from Jensen's barn and used the moon's light to pick out the path between the bare fields. Seated next to him on the wagon bench, Jeanne twisted to the side and leaned over Manette, who had wrapped herself in a soft quilt and curled up in the wagon bed. "Are you comfortable, *chou-chou?*"

"*Oui, Maman.* But I am sleepy. I have danced a long time with Monsieur Rooney."

Beside her on the bench Wash chuckled. He lifted the reins but he was watching Jeanne and he dropped one leather line. "Damn," he said under his breath. "Guess I'm a little shaky. Sorry the evening had to end in a fight."

Jeanne reached a still-trembling hand to pull the quilt up over Manette's shoulders. "D-damn," she repeated with a soft laugh. "I, too, am shaky."

Wash shot her a quick look as he urged the horse and

wagon forward. Her face was white as flour, but she held her head high and looked straight ahead. She sure didn't show her feelings.

He could understand that. He rarely showed his own feelings, especially about a woman. Just one small shove would push him back into the safe cave he'd built. Feelings were scary things. And dangerous.

Jeanne settled her hands in her lap. "I do not like the West very much," she announced.

Wash nodded. "Life out here can be hard. There's not many who can stick it out."

"But I have nowhere else to go."

"Would you want to go back to France?"

There was a long silence. "I do not know. My *maman* is now dead. Even the cottage where I grew up is gone."

"Do you want to leave Smoke River?"

"I want a small piece of land to farm," she said. "I will find one here."

He heard the determination in her words but her voice said something else. She was scared. Not of Montez, but of being vulnerable. With looks like hers, he guessed she'd rebuffed a number of overamorous men. He'd fought Montez to protect her, but maybe she didn't need protecting. This woman seemed more concerned about finding farmland than avoiding the unwanted attention of a randy Spaniard.

Suddenly she pointed at something beside the path. "Look!"

An old abandoned plow sat in the stubbled field. Moonlight bathed the metal in silvery light, and Wash slowed the horse to admire the picture it made against the dark earth.

"Pretty," he remarked.

"Useful," she said instantly. "I will come back for it tomorrow."

"You want that old rusty thing?"

"*Oui,* I do want it."

He flapped the reins to speed up. "Well, I'll be… What the he— What for?"

Her laugh rang out. "To plow with, of course!"

"Jeanne, is that all you think about, farming? Growing your lavender?"

"Ah, no," she said slowly. "But it is of importance, you see, because of Manette." She glanced over her shoulder at her sleeping child. *"Compris?"*

No, he didn't *"compris."* But maybe it didn't matter. Maybe he would never understand this woman beside him, but he knew one thing: the brush of her skirt against his thigh, the hint of her warm body underneath all those yards of calico, was enough to make his mouth dry and his palms sweaty.

He turned his face away and gulped in air that didn't smell of lilacs and something spicy. He wanted her. How he wanted her. He was so hard he ached. If he wasn't careful he'd forget all about his safe little cave.

He circled the mare around the bunkhouse and parked the wagon next to the wall. It was a relief to climb down and ease the turgid pressure from inside his jeans. He loosened the mare's cinch but left the horse hitched up to the wagon for Jeanne.

She rose with a swish of her skirt and waited. He

didn't dare lift her down from the bench; he knew he'd be unable to lay his hands on her waist and stop there. She'd be in his arms in a heartbeat and he doubted he could bring himself to release her. She'd feel the bulge in his jeans and she'd know everything.

And, dammit, if he kissed her, as he ached to do, he'd be a goner.

Instead he reached into the wagon bed and lifted the sleeping Manette into his arms, snugging the quilt close around her small form. Jeanne climbed down, unlocked the bunkhouse door and swung it wide for him. He heard a match rake across something—the stove top, he guessed—and then the glow of a kerosene lantern washed the small room in soft light. She held the lamp up high so he could see.

Wash angled his burden inside, feet first, then sent Jeanne a questioning look. She murmured something in French and pointed to the top bunk. He heaved the sleeping child up onto the waiting sheets and tucked the quilt around her.

Jeanne dipped water from a bucket into her speckled blue coffeepot, then turned toward Wash. In the flickering light his face looked set and stubborn. And his eyes, which were usually gray with flecks of dusty blue, were now almost black.

"*Café?*" she asked quietly.

His mouth tightened. "No."

"I make it anyway, for myself, so is no trouble."

"No." He turned away from her. "Thanks anyway," he added, and moved toward the door.

Such a man. So strong and yet so gentle with Manette.

Why was he not that way with her? He had kissed her, she reflected. Twice, in fact. But both times he had been angry. She could not remember the circumstances, only the taste of his firm mouth on hers, the scent of his skin, smoky and sweet at the same time. She also remembered the look in his gaze when the kiss had ended—as if he'd been shot between the eyes.

*Mon Dieu,* he was looking at her now in that same way. *Alors, do you not want him to look at you?* See all of her, see past the fear that she would not be able to feed her daughter, the pain of being uprooted from her home. And the determination that she knew thinned her lips into an unsmiling line.

They had danced close to each other tonight, so close that she could not read his expression without tipping her head back and breaking the spell. What was he thinking? What did he want?

She swallowed. What did *she* want?

He had reached the door now. *What did she want?* She wanted to matter to someone. To *him*.

She stepped toward him and laid her hand on his arm. When he turned to face her, she uttered a single word.

"Stay."

Wash groaned softly. "You're sure you want me to?"

"*Oui,* I am sure."

"Jeanne…Jeanne, you know I want you. Don't ask me to stay unless—"

"I am sure," she repeated. "I have been sure for three days."

He unfolded his fists and closed his fingers about her

shoulders, pulled her close and kissed her. He took his time, let his lips do all the talking that was needed—or maybe not needed. When he broke the kiss she felt a quiver of disappointment. *More. She wanted more.*

She raised her face to his. He bent to blow out the lantern, then gathered her tight in his arms. "Where do you sleep?" he whispered.

"Below Manette. There." She tipped her head toward the bottom of the bunk.

"We'll wake her."

Jeanne shook her head. "We will not wake her."

He lifted her into his arms, took a single step toward the bunk and then set her on her feet again. The next thing she knew he was cupping her breasts, then pressing her hips into his groin.

"Buttons?" he murmured.

She could not stop smiling into the dark. *"Oui."*

He gave a half groan, half chuckle. "Not *if*, Jeanne. I mean *where?*"

Without speaking she guided his hand to her throat, where the top button was hidden beneath a ruffle.

Wash let his fingers trail down the front of her dress. Twenty buttons. Twenty damned buttons. How many buttons did a woman need to close up a dress? And these were little tiny ones.

His fingers shook, but he began to slip the buttons free. When he was halfway to her waist, she lifted her hands to start on his muslin shirt. Under his knuckles he could feel her body's heat, feel her heart beating steadily as he worked his way down. His thumbs brushed across her breasts, and she moaned softly.

Her nipples hardened, and the instant he could open the bodice of her dress he slid his hands inside to touch her. She wore only a camisole underneath, tied with a ribbon bow. He jerked it free and smoothed his hands over her breasts, then moved around to her back to feel the small, lumpy bones of her spine, then back to cup the firm globes against his palms.

He bent to take one nipple in his mouth. She tasted sweet, like ripe cherries, like a ripe pomegranate he'd tasted once in Mexico. He closed his lips over the erect bud and heard her breath hiss inward.

Good. Maybe she was as starved for this as he was.

"Take my shirt off," he whispered.

She undid the rest of the buttons quickly, pushed the fabric off his shoulders, and then her hands dropped to fumble with his belt buckle.

He gritted his teeth. He'd never last until he got her undressed; the drive to take her, to be inside her, was too hot and insistent. He lifted his head and forced his hands back to the little pearl disks that held her dress together all the way to her belly. When he had freed them all, her dress dropped to her feet. The loosened camisole followed.

He caught her hands, busy with the metal closings of his jeans, and lifted them against his bare chest. Quickly he shrugged his shirt off one shoulder, then tore the garment free.

She made a small sound and moved to the bed wearing only her lacy drawers. Wash shucked off his own drawers and reached for the tie at her waist. It came away in his hand. He splayed his fingers over the subtle swell of her stomach, then over the curve of her buttocks.

For a moment he couldn't draw breath. She turned to face him and his throat closed up. She took one step forward and lifted her arms around his neck.

He could feel her naked body from his thighs to his chest. He caught her mouth under his and edged them to the bed.

Not much room in the bottom bunk. He wrapped his arms around her, pushed her down on the mattress, and rolled on top of her. He bit his lip. The mattress—her cornhusk mattress, he realized—made a scratchy rustle, and she choked off a laugh.

"Not funny," he murmured. "Can't move around much."

She blew out a long sigh. "Then don't."

She arched upward and he forgot to breathe. He was poised right at her entrance. If she moved again he'd…

Then he was inside her, enveloped in velvety heat and softness, her hands urging him to thrust. He forgot all about the crackly mattress and did what she invited.

It was brief but intense. At his climax he kept himself from shouting aloud by biting down hard on his lower lip, but when her body began to spasm with her own release, she cried out and he covered her mouth with his.

Later, when their breathing returned to normal, they made love again, face-to-face, and slowly.

For hours afterward, Wash lay holding Jeanne in his arms, her warm body pressed against his, her head nestled between his neck and his shoulder. He hadn't had a woman in four years, and yeah, he was more than a bit in need. But nothing—*nothing!*—had ever been like this. He felt different. Alive.

And scared like he'd never been before.

When the faint light through the gingham-curtained window shaded from gray to peach, he carefully edged away from her sleeping form, pulled on his jeans and shirt and carefully stepped out of the door carrying his boots in his hand.

# *Chapter Fourteen*

**J**eanne woke to find herself alone. She scrambled out of bed and flung open the door of the bunkhouse, but Wash's horse was no longer tied up beside the wagon. In its place was the old rusty plow she'd seen last night. He must have ridden back to find it and dragged it over to the bunkhouse after...after they had made love last night.

She studied the worn-out farm implement and smiled. That man was remarkable. *Formidable.* Wash Halliday paid attention to her with more than his body. A shiver of remembered pleasure danced into her belly. Most of all she remembered the small things: his hands in her hair, his low voice murmuring her name, his tongue stroking her intimate places. Never had she experienced such a night!

All at once she wanted to weep. She gazed up into the dazzling blue morning sky, wondering about the man who had moved her so much. How did a man know when to thrust hard and when to take the time to draw things out?

*Mon Dieu,* she wanted it all over again!

She gazed down at the plow resting against the bunkhouse wall. And how did he know this was exactly what she wanted to find on this glorious morning?

She pivoted and reentered the bunkhouse. "Manette? Wake up, *chou-chou.* After breakfast we must ride into town."

Carl Ness, the mercantile owner, gave Jeanne a friendly smile. She had feared the townspeople at first, even Monsieur Ness. She struggled to speak their language, and they thought her prickly and unfriendly. She was not unfriendly; she was so frightened she could scarcely swallow. But that she could never admit.

Now Carl shook his graying head. "No, Miz Nicolet, haven't seen Colonel Halliday this morning. Might be he's still sleepin' over at Mrs. Rose's boardinghouse where he stays. I heard there was some kinda fracas out at Jensens' barn last night."

"Ah, no, he cannot be sleep—" She bit her tongue just in time. Could he have left her bed and crawled into his own to get some real rest? Her cheeks grew warm.

"About your lavender wreaths, Miz Nicolet?"

"Ah, yes. I will bring my wreaths this afternoon."

"And some more of them sachets?" he said eagerly. "My women customers keep askin' about them, and about the Lavender Lady, too. Seems they can't get enough of your pretty little bags of good-smelling herbs, especially in this heat."

Jeanne spun toward the front door. "I will bring some," she called over her shoulder.

Outside on the walkway in front of the mercantile Manette was perched in a bent rocking chair, watching a ladybug crawl over her palm. "I saw Monsieur Rooney," she said without moving her uplifted arm. "He went inside that place over there." She pointed to the Golden Partridge saloon.

"*Bon.* But we shall not bother him. Come, I have work to do."

In the livery stable Jeanne gathered up an armload of lavender fronds from the towering wagon load they had brought in two days ago and carefully laid them in an empty chickenfeed sack Carl Ness had given her. She calculated quickly in her head. There would be enough for five or six wreaths plus six or eight small sachet bags.

"And now," she announced to Manette, "we need some ribbon and…"

But Manette was down on her hands and knees scrabbling through the straw looking for crawling things. Jeanne shivered at the thought of her daughter's precious Spider Box. She watched her daughter's diligent search and realized that she must keep herself busy today, as well. So busy she would have no time to think about last night.

She sucked in a long breath. His scent still clung to her skin, and in her belly a flock of birds soared up into flight.

She studied Manette's busy fingers among the weeds. Very busy. She must make at least seven wreaths. Perhaps even eight.

They paid a quick visit to Verena Forester, the dressmaker, where Jeanne bargained for lengths of ribbon, a warm coat for Manette and enough brushed sateen for the sachet bags. At last she hoisted the sack of lavender up behind her mare and set off leading the animal with Manette's hand clasped in hers. Her daughter's other hand was closed tight over some six-legged treasure. Jeanne let out a long sigh.

Soon…very soon, she and Manette would once more be safe and snug in a house of their own. She straightened her shoulders, adjusted her drooping straw sunhat and marched forward. To accomplish that she would have to work very hard.

*C'est la vie.* She had worked hard before.

Wash reined his horse to a halt at his first glimpse of the huge black steam engine puffing along on the last three hundred yards of newly laid iron track. Not bad, he thought. From Colville to Smoke River in five days; that meant laying four miles of track a day. Better than the last set of shovel-monkeys Sykes had sent—twenty-five burly Irish farmers fresh off the boat.

A whistle screeched and a low rumbling began in the three-deck rolling bunkhouse pushed by the train engine. At least fifty men with long black pigtails and odd dishpan-shaped hats swarmed out of the structure. Most of them looked like they weighed around one hundred pounds with their floppy blue trousers soaking wet.

These were his graders? His track-laying crew? He groaned in disbelief.

The head man sped forward on skinny legs, keeping well clear of General's hooves. Wash nodded at the man. "Sykes sent you Celestials after all, I see."

Snapping black eyes peered up at him. "Good yes, boss. Sykes very smart man. Chinese man work good, you will see." He stuck out a thin arm. "My name Sam."

Wash grunted, then reached down to clasp the man's small hand. He sure as hell would see. Sykes spoke highly of the Chinese work gangs that were beginning to grade the Central Pacific roadbed out of Sacramento. These were the best pick-and-shovel men, so Sykes had insisted. Talk was cheap. The work would tell the story. And if Sykes was wrong, he'd send his Chinese back so fast their pigtails would stand on end.

More diminutive men poured out of the three-tier bunkhouse, forming up in groups behind a single pajama-clad leader. Wash was mildly surprised at the level of organization.

"Have these men had breakfast?"

Sam nodded and grinned. "Oh, yes, boss. Eat very early, before sunup."

"Where's your dining car?"

"No need. Cook work at stove inside." Sam tipped his head toward the bunkhouse. "All eat, all finished. We work now." He grinned up at Wash, his dark, intelligent eyes shining.

Maybe Sykes knew a thing or two after all. He dismounted and handed the reins to a young Chinese boy who darted forward.

"Lin will take good care of horse," Sam assured him. "Now, we go to work?"

"Yeah, now we go to work. I need a roadbed cleared into that valley ahead. The far end has a fair grade, but this end's pretty level, mostly brush, some trees." He paused to gauge the Chinese man's reaction.

Sam's head hadn't stopped nodding since Wash opened his mouth. "All understood, boss. We clear land."

He barked an order in Chinese to the assembled workers and they raced for the flat railcar behind the bunkhouse and returned with shovels and picks, mauls and axes. Again they formed themselves into ranks.

Sam was beaming. "Ready, boss?"

Wash had to smile. If they were half as efficient at clearing a six-foot-wide swath through Green Valley as they were lining up, they'd be worth their weight in gold.

"Let's go, then."

The Chinese followed him at a respectful distance until he reached the valley edge, where he stopped and pointed. "Start right here."

Sam shouted something at the men behind him and they split into teams of four and fell on the brush like locusts.

Sam saluted smartly. "Reach flat part of valley by supper, boss."

Like hell, Wash thought. But as the morning wore

on, the teams of men cut and hacked with more energy than he'd ever seen in a grading crew. They looked like blue-trousered ants chewing their way down the gentle slope.

Only one gentle grade would be needed on this end of the valley, he judged. The route out at the other end of the valley would be much tougher. He'd figure out the gradients tonight after supper at the boardinghouse. Tonight he'd get Rooney to stay out at MacAllister's place and watch over Jeanne.

*You coward,* a voice whispered. Right. He didn't trust himself anywhere near her.

He jerked his attention to a tall pine being cut up into short log lengths. Firewood for the cook, he figured.

Wash helped stack the logs, then watched in disbelief as the small wiry men wielding axes split them in half, then in half again so four chunks of firewood fell away from the axe like an opening flower.

He offered to help stack the logs, but Sam waved him off as a small wooden hand cart appeared, pulled by two Chinese. They trundled the cart right up to the canyon edge and before Wash could blink it was loaded up to the rim with wood and rolling back toward the bunkhouse.

Wash wondered if Sykes knew how little direction his Celestials needed once they understood the task at hand. Of course he knew; that's why he owned a railroad that was already making money.

At noon, the Chinese cook rang the bunkhouse dinner gong. Wash had no taste for the strange vegetables the crew ate, so he retrieved his horse from the boy, Lin, rode back into town and headed for the hotel dining room. Mrs. Rose served breakfast and supper at the boardinghouse, but no midday meal.

Rita at the hotel dining room greeted him with a broad smile. "Haven't seen you in a while, Colonel."

"Been busy, Rita."

"Mmm-hmm, I heard. Got the Lavender Lady out of Green Valley, didja?"

"Yep, I did." Out of the frying pan and straight into the fire. He took a table next to the window and fidgeted until the white-aproned waitress brought some coffee.

Rita poured his cup full and plopped down a sugar bowl. "I hear the Lavender Lady's got no place to live now. Is that true?"

Wash bent his head over the steaming cup. "Pretty much, yeah. She's camping out at MacAllister's bunk-house right now. I feel pretty rotten about—"

"Wouldn't worry too much, Colonel. Look there." Rita tipped her gray curls toward the paned glass at his elbow. Across the street Jeanne was leading her gray mare toward the edge of town; the animal was so loaded with a bag of something it looked more like a camel than a horse.

Rita waited. "What'll you have, Colonel?"

"A large helping of crow," he grumbled.

"How about a steak 'n some fries instead?"

"Sure." He hadn't heard a word the waitress had uttered, but he figured it didn't matter. He wasn't the least bit hungry.

Rita propped her hands on her hips and followed the

direction of Wash's gaze. "I wouldn't worry too much about her," she said in a matter-of-fact tone.

"Yeah? Why not?"

"That's one smart, hardworkin' woman. She did just fine before you and the railroad got here. She'll do just fine when you leave."

Wash worked on believing that, watching Jeanne march along, her head held high, her steps determined. She paused at the dressmaker's and grasped her daughter's hand. Just as she turned toward the shop door, sunlight washed the face beneath the floppy hat. His pulse sped up. Whatever it was she was so intent on this morning, she couldn't look more beautiful.

He picked up his fork, then put it down. He couldn't watch. The devil of it was he couldn't *not* watch.

With Rita and the platter of steak and potatoes came a dark-faced Rooney. The older man turned a chair backward, settled himself across from Wash and inhaled dramatically.

"Smells good." He waggled his finger at Rita to order the same. "Izzat breakfast or lunch?"

"Both."

"Thought so. You never turned up for Miz Rose's biscuits 'n gravy this mornin'."

"Grading crew arrived," Wash offered in explanation. There was more—lots more—but he wasn't inclined to talk about it.

Rooney nodded slowly. "Oh. Sure."

Wash swallowed a lump of fried potatoes. "Sykes sent some Chinese. Work like tigers."

"They take much overseein'?" Rooney's black-and-gray eyebrows went up and down twice while waiting for an answer.

"Not much. They're good men. Why?"

"Just wonderin'."

Wash closed his lips over a bite of steak. No way did his partner "just wonder" about something. He surveyed his friend's craggy face while he chewed.

"What do you want to know, Rooney?"

"I wanna know who's gonna keep watch over Jeanne and Little Miss at night?"

Wash stopped eating. "You are. Go on out to MacAllister's after supper, when it gets dark."

"You know Montez is still in jail, don'tcha?"

"Yeah, I know. I checked with the sheriff."

Rooney frowned. "You don't want to watch over her yourself, huh? Kinda strange for a man who's got his britches in—"

"I've got some paperwork to do. Canyon's pretty steep at the far end, and I've got to figure—"

Rooney snorted. "Don't bother lyin' to me, son. She scared ya last night, right?"

Wash clanked his fork onto the china plate and sat without moving for a full minute. Then he sent a long, hard look straight into the older man's twinkling onyx eyes.

"Yeah, you're right, Rooney. Worse than any Sioux ambush we ever lived through." In some ways Rooney was still scouting for him, even though the older man was now his paymaster and second-in-command of his crews.

# Chapter Fifteen

Jeanne dangled her work boots over the sparse grass and weeds beyond the single wooden step she perched on, meticulously weaving the dried strands of lavender into generous wreaths that she tied at the top with a wide purple ribbon.

She paused to rub the muscles of her shoulders. Four completed wreaths hung from nails she had driven into the bunkhouse wall; she knew she would need at least twice that many, but her neck was growing stiff from looking down at the fronds of lavender in her lap.

Idly she watched Manette gather a fistful of the yellow dandelions dotting the stubbly hay field. Her daughter was fascinated by the sizes and shapes of growing things—even weeds. How she wished the girl would collect flower blossoms or pretty leaves in her secret box instead of spiders!

But she had to laugh. When she herself was a girl,

growing up in France, she had collected cocoons—hundreds of them. *Maman* must have worried over her the same way Jeanne fretted over Manette.

Manette could now attend the Smoke River school instead of doing her lessons at home. The school had been too far away for someone who lived miles out of town, in Green Valley. But, besides her warm winter coat she would need shoes. And, Jeanne thought with a stab of anxiety, a proper home and nourishing food.

She puffed her breath upward to chase a loose tendril of hair off her forehead and flexed her shoulders, resuming her work on the wreaths. It took money to buy food and warm clothing; her only source of income was the lavender sachets and wreaths she made and sold at the mercantile. She bit her lip. Would they earn enough?

"Look, *Maman,* I am making a daisy chain!"

"Those are dandelions, *chou-chou,* not daisies. But they will be very pretty." And thank You, God, for a respite from the crawly insects Manette gathered wherever she went.

She bent over the wreath once again and seamlessly wove in the last strands, all the while thinking about Wash Halliday. When she was with him, she felt valued. And…beautiful.

A shard of doubt poked into her thoughts and she gazed toward the distant hills. They had exchanged no words since last night; how would it be between them when they met again?

It would be dark soon; she must think about supper, not the man who smelled of leather and smoke and had spent all night with his arms wrapped around her.

The setting sun bathed the bunkhouse and the wagon parked beside it in gold light, and a blush of crimson washed over the mountains to the east. Would he come tonight?

The low thud of horse's hooves brought her head up. Yes! He was here! Her heart skittered under her apron top. Heavens, what should she say to him?

Manette's squeal of joy cut through her uncertainty. "Look, *Maman,* it is Monsieur Rooney!"

Jeanne clenched her teeth. It was Rooney and not Wash who rode up in a froth of dust. She swallowed back a surprisingly sharp prick of disappointment.

Manette dashed toward the gray-haired man. "Look what I made!" She held up the chain of yellow dandelions. Rooney dismounted and squatted on his haunches at her level, and the girl draped the necklace about his throat.

"It's for you," she said with a happy laugh.

Rooney said nothing for a moment, and then Jeanne saw that his eyes were shiny.

"Well, thank you, Little Miss. Nicest necklace I've ever had." The older man rose and tramped toward Jeanne.

"Evenin', Jeanne. All quiet and peaceful out here?"

"*Oui,* all is quiet. Except for Manette reciting stories to the dandelions. Her favorite stories," she added with a laugh. "In French."

Rooney chuckled. "Now that's somethin' I didn't know about dandelions. Understand French, do they?"

"I was about to prepare supper. Would you join us?"

"Oh, no, ma'am. I ate already at the boarding-house."

"Perhaps some *café,* then?"

Manette flung her arms about Rooney's knees. "Oh, yes, you want some coffee, don't you? Say yes, Rooney. Please say yes."

"Well… Listen, Jeanne, I hope you won't mind, but Wash sent me out to watch over you tonight."

"Oh?" Even to herself she sounded puzzled. "Wash is not coming?"

"Yeah, well, no. He's got some figurin' to do for his railroad crew tonight and— To be frank, Jeanne, I'd like to roll out my pallet and stay the night, kinda keep an eye on things."

"Ah. Of course." With trembling hands she gathered up the wreath makings, rolled up the leftover lavender fronds in an old blanket and set it just inside the doorway.

Rooney cleared his throat. "I thought maybe we could do some talking. Maybe there's some things I might explain about my partner."

Jeanne stopped short at the bunkhouse door. "What things?"

Rooney wiped one hand over his sweaty forehead. "Uh, maybe we could have us a conversation later, over coffee? After Little Miss goes to bed."

"I am not going to bed!" Manette announced.

Rooney hunched down to where she stood gazing up at him. "Why not? You afeared of ghosts?"

The girl giggled. "No, I'm not."

Rooney's voice dropped. "Or maybe spirits or demons that go bump in the dark?"

"N-no. I'm not going to bed because you're here!"

Rooney straightened. "Well, now, Little Miss, I'm gonna be here for a while." He shot Jeanne a look.

Jeanne nodded. She wanted Rooney to stay. She was not afraid of being alone at night, but she wanted to talk about Wash.

"Come inside, both of you. I will make supper. And some *café*."

Rooney stepped over the threshold into the bunkhouse and snatched off his gray hat. Jeanne pointed to a hook beside the door and waited. She knew the instant he spotted her shotgun, mounted over the door; his head bent slowly and his eyes fastened on her hands.

"Yes," she said in answer to his unspoken question. "I can shoot it.

Rooney scratched his salt-and-pepper beard. "Oh, I don't doubt that, Jeanne."

"What surprises you, then?"

"Just that…well, I didn't figure you was as self-sufficient as you're turnin' out to be. You know, bein' a French lady from a big city like New Orleans."

Jeanne turned to stir up the fire in the potbellied stove.

"I am not in New Orleans, now."

Rooney grunted and plopped onto a weathered straightback chair, then shot up, turned it around and straddled it, folding his hands on the back. Manette clambered onto the adjacent chair and pinned him with a blue-eyed stare. "I want my chair backward, too."

Rooney laughed, then reversed the chair for her and continued his speculative perusal of Jeanne. She could tell he was studying her. She lifted the skillet onto the stove, and tried to calm the flutters in her stomach. Did he know Wash had been with her last night?

*Did he know something about Wash she should know?*

She fixed thin, delicate pancakes in the skillet, each one rolled around slivers of hard cheese. *Fromagettes* she called them. Manette gobbled down seven—seven! *Mon Dieu,* in six months, her daughter would grow out of any clothes Jeanne could purchase for school.

She poured Rooney's coffee and made a diluted cup for Manette—mostly milk from Monsieur MacAllister's cow. Little by little her head drooped onto the table, her eyelids closing.

Jeanne unbuttoned the weed-stained pinafore, wrestled a muslin nightgown over Manette's head and tucked her under the quilt on the top bunk.

Rooney was washing their plates in the basin of water heating on the stove; the skillet he wiped spotless with a clean scrap of cloth and hung it up on the wall. Then he refilled both cups with the last of the coffee in the speckleware pot and waited for Jeanne to reseat herself at the inverted wooden fruit crate she used as a dining table.

"Manette was most active today," she remarked. "She will sleep soundly."

"Meanin' we can talk now?" Rooney asked from the stove.

Jeanne sighed. "*Oui.* She will not hear us."

"Just as well, Jeanne. This is grown-up talk."

She ignored her coffee and fisted her hands in her lap.

"About Wash?"

"Yup. I've known Wash a long time. Scouted for him in the army out of Fort Kearney, and when he decided to come back to Oregon to work for the railroad, I came with him. He grew up here, ya know."

Jeanne studied the man's sun-lined face. "Where was your home, Rooney?"

"Comanche country. Up around Kansas. Now my home is wherever we travel. See, Wash risked his life to save mine once in a skirmish with the Sioux, and I swore then I'd protect him, no matter where he went."

"And now he has come back to Smoke River?" Jeanne questioned.

Rooney resumed his place on the reversed chair at the table. "Well, not right away. He had some bad feelings 'bout the place, but by the time he'd hired on with Sykes and the Oregon-Central, he'd pretty much got over it."

Jeanne felt her entire body go still. "What was 'it'?"

Now she would find out about the strange reticence she had sensed in Wash from the beginning? About whatever burden he carried inside that colored his sometimes harsh attitude toward her.

"Well, first he was wounded in the War. He spent some awful years in a Confederate prison, and it takes a man some time to feel normal after somethin' like that. For a long while he was mighty withdrawn, like he'd crawled into a shell."

Rooney shot her a look. "You understand what I'm talkin' about? He was all busted up inside."

"I do understand, yes." She unknotted her hands and sipped her cooling coffee. "It must have been terrible for him."

Rooney chuckled, but when she met his gaze, his eyes were dark with pain. "Naw, it got 'terrible' lots earlier, before he left Smoke River and joined the army. There was this girl, see. Laura Gannon. She jilted him, ran off with another man right before their weddin', just before he left for the War. Broke him up somethin' awful... things pretty much went downhill from there."

Jeanne wasn't sure she wanted to hear any more, especially about Laura Gannon. Something close to jealousy pinched her heart.

But Rooney went right on talking. "Wash wasn't himself for years after that. After he got out of that Yankee prison, he drank a lot and crawled right back into that shell he'd been buildin'. To make a long story short, Jeanne, when the railroad sent him to Smoke River, Wash carried a girl-shaped hole in his heart and a chip on his shoulder the size of a railroad tie."

Jeanne frowned. "What means 'chip on his shoulder'?"

Rooney smoothed his hand over his beard. "Means he's kinda mad at the world and everybody in it. 'Specially women. Attractive women. Like you."

She sat without speaking for a long time. What could she say? Wash was scarred inside. Likely he did not want involvement with her; he was still too vulnerable.

"I see," she breathed. "I understand what you are

trying to tell me, Rooney. I would guard my heart against this man, but it is too late."

Rooney just grinned. "Kinda figured that out, Jeanne. Just wanted you to know the why of his behavior. It's got nothin' to do with you personal-like."

"*Au contraire*. It has everything to do with me. I think Wash has taken a step toward life again, and I think he didn't expect to. Perhaps he did not even *want* to. He is a brave man when it comes to being a man—managing his railroad crews, fighting a bad man like Monsieur Montez to protect me."

"Yeah, you got that right."

Jeanne swallowed and went on. "But he is perhaps not so brave when it comes to a woman? Is it… I mean, do you think that may come with time?"

"Dunno. It gets complicated when it's a woman like you, a woman who's right pretty, sure, but one he really likes underneath." He swirled the coffee dregs in his cup around and around. "I just plain don't know."

"Oh." She blinked hard to keep the hot tears from spilling over.

"Now, I've always been a bettin' man," Rooney said. "Can't hardly walk past a card game or a horse race… I'd ride a hundred miles for a good horse race."

Afraid her voice would crack, Jeanne just looked at him.

Unexpectedly he reached across the table and clumsily patted her hand. "I'll tell you this, though—this looks to me like a pretty good race shapin' up right now. And I'm bettin' you're gonna win."

A shaky laugh escaped her. "A horse race, is it? You

mean Wash will run for his shell and I must head him off before he buries himself?"

"Somethin' like that, yeah. If you choose to."

She closed her eyes. "Oh, Rooney, I am not skilled at this kind of game. I do not think—"

"That's exactly right," he interrupted. "You just hold that there, and *don't* think."

Rooney unrolled his pallet in the niche between the wooden wagon and the bunkhouse, stretched out and ran his hand over his eyes. By jingo, he hadn't done this much talking since his years scaring around the plains with Wash, and then he'd mostly listened. Something about Jeanne just made a man open up.

He rolled over, pulling the wool army blanket up around his chin. That woman made a man feel…bigger than his usual self. And that's exactly what Wash Halliday needed, something—someone—to grow toward.

He lay perfectly still and gazed up at the bright stars dotting the night sky. "Life gives life," he murmured, remembering an old Indian chant. *God keep you both, and may your days together be good and long upon the earth.*

The next thing he knew a shaft of hot sunlight was blinding him. He shrugged out of his bedroll just in time to see Jeanne set off for the stream lugging a bucket. He hoped that meant coffee sometime in the next half hour. Thinking about Wash and the widow Nicolet last night sure hadn't left time for much shut-eye.

He stayed for coffee with Jeanne, then, because she

was short of food, he rode into town for bacon and scrambled eggs at the boardinghouse. After he'd teased Mrs. Rose about her undercooked bacon, he rode out to the rail spur at the Green Valley site.

Wash and his team of Celestials had carved out and graded a gentle slope down the hillside to the valley floor. Amazing what these small, tough men could accomplish working together as a team.

He wished things between a man and a woman could be resolved as efficiently. Maybe Wash should ask his Chinese crew for advice in the courtship department!

Or maybe not, noting how haggard his partner looked this morning. Jaw tight. Eyes like gray thunderheads.

"Mornin'," Rooney called to him as he emerged from the canyon.

Wash just grunted.

Rooney dismounted and peered over the edge toward the east end. "You figure out your gradients for the steep end of the valley yonder?"

"Nope."

Rooney smothered a grin. "Distracted, were ya?"

Wash's stony gaze met his. "Mind your own business."

"Aw, come on, son. What's got a burr up your britches on a morning this beautiful?"

"Didn't sleep much," Wash snapped. Inside, Rooney exulted. Outside he tried to look sympathetic.

"Had me a fine time with Jeanne and Little Miss last night," he offered. He lifted the wilted remains of the dandelion chain which still hung around his neck. "Little Miss made me a necklace."

Wash took a step toward him. "How is Jeanne? Any trouble?"

"Not trouble, exactly. Just a bit of unrest. Jeanne's anxious to sell her lavender things to the mercantile. She needs the money."

Wash gave a curt nod of acknowledgment. Rooney waited as long as he could stand it, then said, "Jeanne's comin' out to Green Valley around noon today. Bringin' you…um—" he scrambled to come up with a believable lie "—uh…bringin' you some lunch."

"What for?"

"Jes' bein' friendly like, you know—"

"I plan to eat in town," Wash said with a scowl.

"Well, ya damn fool, *un*-plan it! Won't hurt you none to be nice to the lady whose valley you're tearing up for your railroad."

Wash's face changed. He stared at Rooney and finally gave a low grunt and another short nod.

Rooney blew out his breath. Well, by damn! He'd better hustle on back to town and catch Jeanne at the mercantile, let her know about the picnic lunch she'd "promised" to bring.

He signed to Wash, mounted and turned the roan toward town. Funny, he didn't feel a bit of guilt for the falsehood he'd fabricated.

Wash saw his partner touch spurs to his mount and disappear in a cloud of dust. So, Jeanne was coming out and bringing his lunch. Nice gesture, he guessed. At the thought of seeing her again his stomach floated up just under his rib cage and flipped over.

Part of him didn't want to lay eyes on her. Another larger part wanted to smell her hair and put his hands on her skin. But what the hell would he say to her after their night together?

Judas and Joseph! Sooner or later he'd have to own up to being damn scared.

He snorted and began to tramp back down the valley slope. Scared? That was like describing a thunderstorm as a spring shower. The worst part...

Aw, hell, he couldn't even say it. The worst part was that he was beginning to recognize that he cared about her; and, not only that, he still wanted her. He wasn't sure he would ever stop wanting her.

## Chapter Sixteen

All that morning Wash thought about seeing Jeanne again. What would he say to her? It felt as if he was watching himself from outside his skin, and what he saw was a man in turmoil. A longing ate at his gut and nibbled away at his spirit, but his fear chewed him up like that rusty plow Jeanne wanted, dragged over a barren field.

He climbed up to the valley rim and scanned the road that stretched toward town. "Never thought of myself as a coward," he muttered. "Learn something new every day."

A puff of dust caught his eye, about a mile away; he watched it move toward him. Oh, Lord, it was Jeanne's gray mare. He couldn't wait to see her again, hear her voice. He hadn't stopped thinking about her for the last twenty-four hours.

On the other hand, he wanted to drive her from his thoughts. Hell's bells, she'd tied him up in knots.

The gray mare halted a good ten yards from where he stood. He studied his boots for a long moment, afraid to look at her. His heartbeat tripled, slamming against his rib cage like the hooves of a wild horse. Not even a Sioux war party evoked a fear like this.

She gave him a half smile. "Hello, Wash." That was all it took for the war party to attack.

"Jeanne," he acknowledged. He looked up at her, then wished he hadn't. A glow of hot sunlight spilled around her shoulders where she sat her horse; her straw hat was tipped down to shade her face, but then she lifted her head and her eyes met his.

The bottom fell out of his belly.

She held up a wicker hamper. "I brought you some lunch. And some coffee."

His legs started toward her of their own accord. She handed the basket down to him and slipped off the mare into his arms. She smelled good, like soap. He wanted to kiss her so much his chest ached.

"It's…good to see you," he managed. The truth was he was stunned at how happy the sight of Jeanne Nicolet made him.

She stepped away from him. "It is awkward, too, is it not?"

She didn't wait for an answer, but moved past him and pointed across to the opposite side of the valley.

"Over there is my thinking spot. It would be nice for a picnic, no?"

*No.* The thought of sitting close to her in some shady

bower made his hands curl into fists. "Sure," he found himself answering.

She started off, walking purposefully along the horse trail that skirted the valley rim. He could see she was used to walking; he had to lengthen his stride to keep up with her. He concentrated on the sway of her blue checked skirt and tried to keep his mind off her backside.

"Where is Manette?" he wondered aloud. It was the only thing he could think of to say.

"At the hotel dining room. Rooney is filling her up with strawberry ice cream."

"Rooney is a good man."

"*Oui.* He is a good friend, as well. Manette likes him."

She didn't explain, but she didn't have to. Wash knew his partner must have told Jeanne all about Laura Gannon. He felt completely exposed.

Within ten minutes they had circled the valley rim and all at once Jeanne stepped off the path and led him to a spot where a vine maple had woven itself between two elders to form a sun-dappled trellis.

"Here," she announced. She reached for the hamper he carried and flipped open the hinged wicker top. Then she bent her head and rummaged in the basket.

Wash tried not to let his eyes linger on her bare neck. He held his breath until spots danced in his vision to avoid inhaling the scent of her hair.

She spread a blue gingham tablecloth over a grassy spot and settled herself on one corner, her legs folded under her skirt. She sure liked blue gingham. Her dress was blue gingham, and he remembered the blue gingham curtains she'd hung over the bunkhouse window. She must have brought an entire bolt from New Orleans when she'd come West.

Wash plopped the hamper in the center of the table-cloth and took the opposite corner, stretching his long legs out until the tips of his boots almost brushed the white petticoat poking from under the flounces of her dress.

"Are you hungry?"

Her question sent a red-hot knife up his spine. "Sure," he groaned. Damn, but he was hungry.

"I am, too. Very hungry. I have been working hard this morning."

"Yeah?" With relief, Wash grabbed on to the conversational thread. "Working on what?" He accepted something wrapped up in a napkin—blue gingham, again—and watched her pour coffee from a Mason jar wrapped in a thick towel.

"On my lavender, of course. Surely you do not think my work ends with cutting a wagonload of lavender? My work is just beginning."

Wash unfolded the napkin and bit into a still-warm pancake of some sort, rolled-up and filled with something. Melted cheese. His belly was going to heaven.

"This morning," she went on, "I sold ten wreaths to Monsieur Ness at the mercantile for ten cents each, and seventeen small sachets for five cents apiece." She flashed him a proud smile.

"I have now almost two whole dollars!"

Wash couldn't help grinning at the note of triumph

in her voice. He took another, larger bite of the pancake. "What will you do with your earnings?"

Her eyes—those green-blue eyes that had pulled at him the first time he'd met her—blinked and widened until they looked like two lumps of turquoise. "Why, I will rent a house, of course. For Manette and me!"

"With two dollars? Jeanne, that's not enough to—"

"But it *will* be. I am making more wreaths and…" Her voice trailed off. "You do not think I can rent a house?"

Wash reached for another napkin-wrapped pancake. "I started to say no, but I've watched you for the last seven days and I'd guess you can do pretty much anything you set your mind to."

The oddest look came over her face, half questioning, half challenging. Instantly her expression altered. He'd give two dollars just to know what she was thinking.

*"Alors,"* she said thoughtfully. "I am glad you think so."

"What do you call these pancake-things?" he asked quickly. "Sure taste good."

"They are called *fromagettes*. Little cheeses. You make a thin pancake and roll—" She bit off the words. He was staring at her mouth with a strange expression, as if he wanted to—

Jeanne's throat closed. He wanted to kiss her! *Oh, yes, please yes.* She wanted him to. She rested her eating hand in her lap and leaned toward him.

"Jeanne," he said, his voice low.

*"Oui?"* She held her breath, waiting.

"All I've thought about the past two days is you. Making love to you. And I don't think—"

She released a sigh. "Rooney said something very wise last night. He said, 'Don't think.'"

Wash stood up suddenly and turned his back. "Tell Rooney to mind his own business."

She thought for a long minute. In the quiet she could hear the cry of a hawk soaring overhead, mingled with the murmur of wind in the treetops. Finally she rose and moved toward him, so close his ragged breathing was audible.

She raised her hand, rested her palm against his back. "Perhaps we should not talk. Perhaps between us silence is enough."

He turned and she stepped into his arms. He kissed her until she grew dizzy, until the rasp of his breath against her temple made her weak with wanting. And then he set her away from him.

"I have to get back to work," he said, his voice rough. He began to gather up the picnic remains and the tablecloth and stuff them into the hamper.

*"Mon Dieu,"* she said to fill the awkward silence. "For a large man you have a very small appetite."

For the rest of the day Wash drove himself and his Chinese crew, without mercy. The tough, wiry Celestials easily weathered the grinding hours spent hacking the brush and trees away from the planned rail bed. They smoothed it level, or as level as it could get considering the required angle of descent into the valley.

Wash himself took down the three remaining fir trees

on the sloping hillside. He didn't have to help out, he just needed to work off the steam he'd built up trying to keep his hands off Jeanne.

He leaned on his ax handle and watched the last evergreen tilt, then crack and smash onto the ground with a *whump* that made the earth tremble. Before he could shoulder his ax, the little figures in floppy blue pajamas were crawling over the felled tree, limbing it up like energetic ants. They cut it into six-foot lengths, split them and laid them crosswise on the cleared road-bed, flat side up. Wash counted the number of ties as he worked his way down the incline, figuring out how many iron rails would be needed to lay track the next day.

The Chinese worked without stopping. Amazing men. He understood now why Sykes had hired them; when this line was completed, Sam and his boys would be sent to the Sierras as graders and powder-monkeys to blast tunnels into the rock.

Late in the day he watched the crew lay track right up to the valley rim, and it was a sight to see. A flat car behind the rolling bunkhouse carried rails to within a hundred yards of the site, then the rails were loaded onto an iron-wheeled cart which was pushed to the end of the tracks. It took eight of the wiry men to hoist one length of iron clear of the cart and drop it in place, right side up. A second team swarmed over it, pounding spikes which fastened the rail to the split-wood tie underneath.

At that point another crew took over and in a matter of seconds, more rails were carted up and dropped into place. Wash calculated three rails went down about every minute, a feat of unbelievable coordination and teamwork.

At six o'clock the Chinese scampered up the incline to the bunkhouse car where the cook had supper waiting. Wash was tired; the old war injury to his hip was throbbing, but he didn't want to go back to town just yet. He'd wait until he was sure Jeanne and her daughter had gone back to MacAllister's bunkhouse; then he'd ride into town and eat supper. Mrs. Rose served up dinner around sundown.

He spent the hour walking the length of the valley, double-checking the spiked joint bars that held the individual rails together, recalculating the gradient and figuring what would be required to lay track over curves less than twenty-four degrees as the railroad climbed out of the opposite end of the valley.

He felt good about the railroad. Thirty-five dollars a month per man was a small price to pay for schools and churches, a telegraph office, maybe even a hospital. It would improve life for the whole county. Trained schoolteachers could come from Portland; homesteaders could haul their belongings to a farm five times faster on a train than in a wagon. Oranges could be shipped in to Smoke River before they got moldy! The railroad meant civilization in this rough, raw land and Wash liked being a part of it. It was, he had reflected often enough, lots better than killing men and blowing up bridges.

But, in spite of his feelings of pride and accomplishment, this stretch of railroad didn't bring the euphoria he usually felt at seeing a line take shape. Something was missing.

Maybe it was coming back to Smoke River and facing all those memories of Laura. Maybe it was because of what he'd been through in the War. He rolled around in his mind all the possible sources of his vague dissatisfaction, but he took care to put Jeanne in a separate niche. She had nothing to do with his work. "Nothing," he snorted. She had something to do with a man's physical need for a woman, with his hunger for connection.

But that was all.

# Chapter Seventeen

Jeanne stripped the hard green peas out of their pods with short, jerky motions. "That man," she grumbled to Rooney, who sat across from her with a kettle full of the shelled vegetables. "I wish I did not like him so much!"

Manette, crouched in a corner of the bunkhouse, poked her head up. "Who? *Maman?*"

"Monsieur Halliday." She aimed a handful of peas into the kettle cradled between Rooney's knees. "He is forward, and then backward, and then…" She pressed her lips into a tight line.

"I think he is a nice man, *Maman.*" Her daughter bent once more to peek under the bunkhouse. "I like him."

Rooney chuckled from his perch on an old log he'd rolled up to use as a chair and tossed his own handful of peas into the kettle.

"He *is* a nice man, *chou-chou.*"

Too nice. She ached for him to be bolder. More forward. With Wash she approached the edge of impropriety and she had never felt that way before—not even with Henri. But it appeared Wash did not feel the same.

"Little Miss is right," Rooney offered. "Wash is a good man." He eyed her with a sly smile. "You don't agree on that, Jeanne?"

Absently Jeanne nibbled the end of her empty pea pod. "*Oui,* he is…good." She wrinkled her nose at the sour taste and sailed it onto the battered cookie sheet near Rooney's boots where the garbage was collecting.

Rooney's eyebrows rose. "Well, now, there's 'good' and then there's 'good.'" *Good* as in steady and responsible, and *good* as in too danged polite sometimes.

A short laugh burst out of her mouth. "This afternoon on our picnic, he was so well-behaved it made me angry!"

"Glad to hear it," Rooney quipped.

She pinned him with a hard look. "Which are you glad to hear—that he behaved or that I was angry?"

Rooney slid the cookie sheet to one side, leaned over, and patted her arm. "Like I said, Jeanne, he's got some knots inside he has to work out."

"Ah, I understand, of course. But could he not…I mean, he might…"

"No, ma'am, he's not gonna. Not till he's ready. Wash never does anything without thinkin' it through two or three times. And, Jeanne, I gotta tell ya, when it comes to you, he's probably already thought it over a dozen times."

"He is afraid of me, no?"

"Not 'xactly."

Jeanne gathered up another handful of pea pods. "Well, what, exact—"

A sharp cry sliced through the late afternoon air. Jeanne sprang to her feet, scattering shelled peas onto the ground.

"Manette? *Manette!*"

Rooney was already on his knees reaching one arm under the corner of the bunkhouse where Manette had been. He grasped one ankle and dragged the girl out on her belly; Jeanne flew to lift her upright.

Manette began to scream. Two small puncture wounds showed on the girl's forearm, and Rooney groaned. He got to his feet and whistled for his roan.

"Are you hurt?" Jeanne cried. "What is it, *chou-chou?*"

Rooney plucked the girl up and set her on his horse. "Snakebite," he said as he mounted behind her. "Get yer horse, Jeanne. I'm takin' her to the doctor in town. Gotta move fast."

Jeanne stood frozen with disbelief. One minute she was shelling peas on a peaceful afternoon, and the next her daughter was in danger.

"Jeanne!" Rooney shouted at her. "Move!"

He tore the blue bandanna from around his neck, fashioned a tourniquet on Manette's upper arm and twisted it tight using a short twig. "Lie quiet, Little Miss. You'll be better off if you don't move around much." He leaned sideways and peered down at the girl's white face. "You hear me?"

"Yes," she whimpered, her voice choked with tears. "I hear you. My arm hurts!"

"It's gonna hurt for a little while, Missy. You just sit quiet and hold on to the pommel here." He positioned both her small hands on the hard leather knob, wrapped his left arm around her waist and spurred the horse toward town.

Jeanne ran for her gray mare, stood on the stump to clamber up onto the horse's back and dug her heels into its flanks. The horse bolted forward into a cloud of Rooney's dust. She put her head down alongside the mare's neck and began to pray.

She caught up with Rooney at the edge of town and followed him to the boardinghouse where he was staying. Jeanne reined to a stop right behind him.

"Doc Graham lives here, too," Rooney panted.

She slid off the mare and lifted her arms for Manette. Rooney handed her down, dismounted and pounded up the porch stairs.

"Sarah!" he yelled.

A woman's figure appeared behind the screen door and took one look. "In here," she cried. She swung the door open. "I'll get the doctor."

Rooney lifted Manette from Jeanne's arms into his own. "Gotta climb the stairs," he explained. "Too heavy for you."

Manette's eyes drooped shut, opened, then closed again and her head lolled against Rooney's chest. Her daughter's face was flushed scarlet, her breathing too fast. Jeanne covered her mouth with both hands

The woman called Sarah stood next to an open

doorway on the second floor. "In here." With Jeanne at his heels, Rooney charged into the room where a tall silver-haired man pointed to the single bed.

"Rattlesnake," Rooney barked as he laid Manette on the quilted coverlet.

"How long ago?" the doctor asked.

"Maybe twenty minutes."

The tall man swore under his breath, loosened the tourniquet and retightened it. "Gonna be close." He bent forward with his shiny metal stethoscope.

"Doc, this here's the girl's mama, Jeanne Nicolet."

The doctor glanced up. "The Lavender Lady? Heard a good deal about you, ma'am, but don't have time to be sociable just now."

Jeanne's vision started to dim. She bent at the waist, sucked in air and began to sob.

Rooney laid his arm across her shoulders. "Try not to waste yer strength cryin', Jeanne. Doc Graham's the best doctor in the county."

She nodded, swiping the tears off her cheeks with shaking fingers.

Sarah, the landlady, beckoned. "Come on, Miz Nicolet. You sit down here and I'll be right back with some coffee."

Rooney steered Jeanne to a wing chair near the curtained window. She couldn't think. Couldn't talk. And she must not cry. It always upset Manette to hear her cry. Suddenly she wanted Wash, wanted his arms around her.

Rooney seemed to read her thoughts. He tiptoed forward, peeked at Manette's still form on the bed, then tramped over to Jeanne.

"I'll ride out to Green Valley and get Wash."

She gazed up at his sun-weathered face and the long-ish graying hair. Without a word she rose and pressed her lips to his cheek. In the next moment she heard his heavy boots clomp down the stairs.

Wash heard the oncoming horse and instinctively reined up. Whoever it was sure had a burr under his saddle. When he recognized Rooney's roan gelding, a boulder thunked into his belly. Something was wrong. Through all the years Rooney had scouted for him, he'd rarely driven a horse that hard.

The roan made a wide circle around Wash and his mount, then pulled up short. "Got trouble," the older man yelled over the panting of his horse. "Little Miss got bit by a rattler."

Wash frowned. "Where is she?"

"Boardinghouse. Doc Graham's tendin' her."

Wash sent silent thanks for the hardy physicians who practiced their profession on the frontier.

He lifted his reins. "Jeanne?"

"With Manette, at the boardinghouse."

Wash spurred General so hard the gelding jumped sideways. He waited a split second for Rooney to catch up, then the two men set off for town at a full gallop.

Rattlesnake! How the hell—? But he knew the answer. Probably tried to catch the damn thing. He gulped back a snort. Lord almighty, Jeanne must be frantic.

He could not think beyond getting to her. He sucked

in a determined breath and concentrated on guiding his horse's pounding hooves around rocks and prairie-dog holes. Rooney rode at his shoulder.

At the boardinghouse a young boy—Sarah's grandson, Rooney explained—led their mounts off down the street to the stable. Wash paused to brush the trail dust off his trousers and shirtfront while Rooney mounted the porch steps and burst through the screen door. Wash was on his heels.

Sarah hurried to meet them, pointed up the staircase and signaled for quiet. "She's sleeping now. Doc says she'll probably be all right, but of course poor Miz Nicolet can't believe him."

Wash removed his hat. "Can we go up?" He found himself convulsively mashing the brim until Rooney reached over and lifted it out of his hands.

Wash turned toward the staircase. All he could think of was reaching Jeanne, shielding her from the anguish she must be feeling.

Sarah laid a hand on Rooney's arm. "Doc Graham's back is bothering him. Could one of you carry the girl?"

"Sure," both men replied in unison.

Upstairs, Rooney tapped once on the doctor's door and quietly pushed it open. Manette lay asleep on the single bed, her breathing labored. The doctor held her wrist, counting her pulse. Jeanne stood by the window, watching the wind in the maple trees outside. Her arms were wrapped tight across her midriff.

"Jeanne." She turned at his voice and Wash strode across the room. She gave a small cry and stumbled into his arms, laying her swollen face on his shoulder. He held her until her body stopped trembling.

"Doc says she'll probably be okay," he whispered. Jeanne nodded but did not raise her head.

Rooney zigzagged around the doctor and bent over Manette. At Doc Graham's nod, he lifted the girl and started for the hallway.

Wash slipped his arm around Jeanne's shoulders and pivoted her toward the door. "Come on. Mrs. Rose has made sleeping arrangements for you. There's an extra bed in Rooney's room for you and Manette. Rooney can bunk in with me."

Dr. Graham held the door open. "Keep sponging her off, Mrs. Nicolet. It will help to keep the fever down."

"Yes, I will do that," Jeanne murmured.

Outside in the hallway, Wash spoke aloud. "Have you eaten?"

"No," she croaked. "I…could not." She stumbled against him, then righted herself and let him help her into Rooney's room. The older man gently laid Manette's still form on the bed and covered her with the quilt he kept folded up at the bottom.

Wash steered a wobbly Jeanne toward the other small bed.

"Hold on a minute," Rooney said. "Let's you 'n me move the beds close together so Jeanne can watch over Little Miss without gettin' up and down."

The men butted the beds together. Wash led Jeanne over to the unoccupied one, sat her down on the edge, and knelt so he could look into her face. "Jeanne, you have to keep up your strength. You have to eat."

She moved her head up and down in agreement, but she didn't take her eyes off her daughter.

Rooney signaled to Wash and the two men tiptoed out into the hallway. "Breaks yer heart, don't it?" the older man said on a sigh.

Wash's throat was so tight he couldn't answer.

"How 'bout some supper? Sarah saved us some chicken and potato salad."

In answer Wash gripped Rooney's thick shoulder and squeezed hard.

He and Rooney finished off the leftover fried chicken and most of the potato salad. Wash drew the line at the strawberry shortcake, poured himself another cup of coffee and stepped into the kitchen, where Mrs. Rose was washing the last of the supper dishes.

The landlady glanced up in surprise.

"I just wanted to thank you, ma'am. Jeanne and her daughter are…well, you know, they're both important to me. And Rooney," he added quickly.

# *Chapter Eighteen*

At the knock on her door, Jeanne looked up to see Wash step quietly into the room and move toward her with a china bowl of something in one hand and a spoon in the other. He glanced at Manette. "Any change?"

She shook her head. He settled himself beside her on the extra bed and presented the bowl. "I want you to eat this."

She sniffed the contents. It looked lumpy, but it smelled good. "What is it?"

"Bread and milk. My mother used to make it when I was sick with the measles."

She dipped in the spoon and put a tiny bite in her mouth. The milk was warm and comforting and the bread fragrant with butter and something sweet. "Sugar?"

"A bit. I like sugar."

"Good," she pronounced.

Wash grinned. "If you like this, wait till you try my rolled-up sugar sandwich."

*Rolled-up sugar...* What a kind, thoughtful thing to do, bringing her something to eat. Suddenly she wanted to throw her arms around his neck and kiss him. But the bowl rested on her lap. She would kiss him later. If he would let her. She was beginning to see that her need for support warred with his need to stay uninvolved.

While she finished the last spoonful, Wash moved to the kerosene lamp on the bureau and turned the flame down. Jeanne had to smile. He must have noticed how tired she was.

She ran her gaze over Manette. The cool washcloth she'd been sponging her daughter's face and neck with was drying out. She plunged it into the basin of cool water at the foot of the bed, wrung it out and rearranged it over her daughter's mottled face.

Wash watched her every move. "I've got a clean shirt Manette could sleep in, if you'd like."

"A shirt?"

"You know, use it as a nightgown. I'll bring one for you, too."

"Yes, thank you. That would be nice."

He picked up the ceramic bowl, left the room and returned a few minutes later with not one but two plain blue muslin shirts.

He laid them at the foot of the bed.

Jeanne looked at him long and hard. He was not asking anything of her; he was simply taking care of her needs the best way he knew how. She had not felt taken care of since she'd left France; Henri had been too young, too irresponsible and there had never been anyone else.

But this man… He was doing something instinctively that would probably frighten him to death if he took a moment to think about it.

Wash's face was drawn with fatigue. He smelled of sweat and leather. And the slight hitch in his gait was growing more pronounced with every step he took. Yet here he was, bringing her supper, bringing his shirt for a nightgown. He was a split man, was that how one said it? One part of him divided against the other part.

Her eyes stung. *Vraiment,* Rooney was indeed right: Wash Halliday was a good man. *Un homme de bien,* her mother would say.

He touched her shoulder, moved toward the door, then stopped abruptly with his hand on the knob. "I'm going out to the wash house to get cleaned up, check on my horse. I'll be back in half an hour."

Yes, a good man. She didn't care one *sou* what he smelled like.


Rooney rolled over on the pallet he'd laid out on the floor beside Wash's bed, spied his partner, and blinked at the third clean shirt he drew out of the bureau. "You already took two, how many shirts you need?"

Wash studied the man and gestured toward the unoccupied bed. "Use my bed, Rooney. I might not be back for a while."

His partner sat bolt upright. "Huh?" He scratched his beard, and then a grin spread over his lined face. "Oh. I see."

"No," Wash said, his voice quiet. "You don't see. I figured Jeanne might…might need me for something." He shooed Rooney off the pallet and began to roll it up.

"She sure as hell does!" Rooney crawled under the covers on Wash's empty bed.

"Yeah?" He was only half listening to his partner.

"Well, son, she does need you. Her daughter might be dyin' and Jeanne needs a strong arm to lean on and maybe some comfort talk."

Wash stood up and shoved the pallet under one arm. "I'm no good at that, Rooney. I won't know what to say."

Rooney barked out a *huh*. Then, "She sure don't need a strong, silent man in a spiffed-up shirt."

Wash hesitated. He hadn't really thought about exactly what he was doing; he was driven by something inside him, something that whispered that he had to be there with her. Maybe he didn't know what to say, or do, but he knew he couldn't be away from her right now.

"'Night, Rooney." He opened the door and stepped out into the hallway.

"'Night, Wash. See you at breakfast."

Wash paced up and down the hall outside Jeanne's door for a good ten minutes before he worked up the courage to lay his hand on the knob.

He guessed it didn't much matter how helpless he felt; right now all he wanted was for Manette to be okay and for Jeanne to hold steady.

He bowed his head. Was this too much to ask from a man who hadn't prayed in years?

He rapped against the wood and didn't wait.

Soft golden lantern light bathed the room. Jeanne was curled up in a ball, asleep at the head of the bed, one hand extended to rest on her daughter's arm. She had slipped one of his shirts over Manette's head; the sleeves were rolled up to her elbows. Her left arm looked red and puffy, but her breathing had quieted some.

He draped his clean shirt over the back of a chair and slid onto the bed beside Jeanne. She didn't move. He touched her shoulder, and she jolted awake.

"Oh, it is you," she said in a sleep-fuzzed voice. "I am glad it is you."

A curious warmth burrowed into his chest and he couldn't get enough air.

"Take off your dress, Jeanne. By morning it'll be a mess of wrinkles." He began to unbutton her gingham shirtwaist. She wasn't really awake, he realized. Probably wouldn't remember a thing come morning. He worked the dress down off her shoulders.

The instant her hand was free, she reached out to touch Manette, then, without opening her eyes, let her head droop down onto her extended arm.

Wash slid his fingers along the waistband of her skirt, found the button closure at the back and gently slipped it free. He tugged it over her hips, unknotted her petticoat tie and pulled it off, as well.

Her work boots sat on the floor beside the bed. Wash looked at them a long time, then shucked his own and set them next to hers. His blue muslin shirt settled easily over her head and shoulders; he half wished it had buttons down the front instead of the neck placket. Then he could…

Oh, no, he couldn't! He stood up quickly, draped her garments over the chair and blew out the lamp. The sky outside the single window was black as coal dust. When his eyes had adjusted to the dark, he carefully eased onto the bed next to where Jeanne lay, gently lifted her hand away from Manette's swollen arm and straightened Jeanne's pantalette-covered legs. Then he rolled her body toward him so her back snugged up against his chest. With one hand he searched for the wire pins holding her hair in its bun at the back of her neck, drew them out and stuffed them into his trouser pocket. Her dark, silk-soft waves spilled over his hands and he clenched his teeth.

He pressed his lips against the crown of her head and breathed in the spicy-sweet scent he knew he would never forget. Her soft, even breathing told him she was asleep, but his heart began to hammer so hard he was afraid she might feel it against her spine.

For a long, long time Wash stared up at the ceiling, wondering what the hell he thought he was doing, and at the same time knowing deep in his gut that, whatever it was, it was the right thing.

Long past midnight, Jeanne woke with a small jerk and immediately reached out to touch Manette in the adjoining bed. Her skin was still hot, but the snake-bitten arm Jeanne felt under her palm seemed less swollen.

She rose up partway to dip the cloth in the basin of cool water and smoothed it over Manette's hot face and neck. It was then that her sleep-fogged brain began to register that she was not alone in the bed.

Most definitely she was not alone! Wash lay next to her, asleep, his bare chest rhythmically rising and falling, one arm flung out across the quilt toward her. Had she lain next to him all these hours? She emitted a tiny gasp. *Incroyable.* And how had she come to be wearing his shirt? She did not remember.

Or did she? She recalled his voice speaking low in her ear, but *Mon Dieu!* Her skirt and petticoat were gone. Underneath Wash's blue shirt she wore nothing but a lacy wisp of a camisole and her ruffled drawers.

Her face heated. He had undressed her? Surely not. But it was clear that he had done exactly that. With trembling fingers she lifted the cooling cloth from Manette's forehead and ran it over her own burning cheeks.

And then she had to smile. This man was unlike any she had known before. He was skittish about a relationship with her, yet when there was need, he was here beside her, caring for her the best way he knew.

She remembered that night after the Jensens' dance, those wondrous hours in his arms. And she understood.

Or thought she did. He wanted her, but he was not sure how far he dared to step into her life.

She leaned over the side of the bed, dipped the cloth in the cool water and wrung it out before replacing it on Manette's sweat-sticky forehead.

Releasing an unsteady breath, she gazed down at the man who slept beside her. Now what? She knew things about Wash, things that Rooney had confided and more that she had deduced on her own. Wash Halliday had been badly burned by a woman, and he would not willingly wade into that fire again. On top of that, he had been injured in the War.

What, she wondered for the thousandth time in the past two days, did he really want? Yes, he desired her. But would he want more outside of satisfying a perfectly understandable male hunger?

And what did *she* want? She swallowed a soft laugh. At this moment she knew exactly what *she* wanted. And tomorrow?

Tomorrow she would see. Tomorrow she would want Manette to be well. Tomorrow she would want to somehow make a new home for her daughter.

And tomorrow she would want…him, still. *Oh, Lord, help me, my body is at war with my mind.*

She gave Manette a final look and slid her body down close to Wash. He did not move, did not even twitch an eyelid. Sound asleep. She smiled to herself. She would wake him up in a way he would not forget.

She pulled the makeshift nightgown over her head and untied the ribbon at the neck of her camisole. When it crumpled off her shoulders, she lifted Wash's hand and laid it over her breast. The warmth of his fingers stirred her flesh; her nipples hardened and a flood of delicious heat flowed from her cheeks all the way down to her toes.

Careful not to wake him—at least not completely— she wriggled out of the long-legged ruffled drawers and worked the pantalettes down over her hips. With abandon she tossed away both garments.

Naked, she stretched out beside him, close enough to feel his hard, warm body against hers. He still wore his denims, but for now it did not matter.

Wash murmured in his sleep. She brushed her lips across his cheek, blew gently in his ear and repositioned his hand on her breast. He gave a low moan, but his eyelids remained closed.

She let her hand drift to his crotch and laid it slowly and deliberately over the swelling. Still he did not awaken. Even when she began drawing her fingers along the length of his manhood.

Then with no warning a hand of steel clamped around her wrist. "Jeanne," he murmured. "Careful."

Her eyelids flew open. "You are awake?" she whispered.

"Very much awake." The laughter in his voice made her entire body flush with heat.

"Oh, but I thought—"

"Don't think," he breathed near her ear. "And for Heaven's sake, don't stop."

An irrational, blinding sense of joy swept through her. Her skin felt as if it were brushed with melted chocolate, and the place between her legs began to ache. It was glorious to be near him, to feel such exquisite sensations, so sweet and hot. Tears stung into her eyes.

Wash released her wrist and ran his hand up her bare arm. She reached again for his crotch, but he rolled away from her and then she heard the pop of buttons being released. He shucked off his jeans and underdrawers in one motion, then lay down next to her and pulled her close.

"Wash…" she murmured.

"Manette asleep?" he asked, his voice hoarse.

"Yes."

"Thank Heavens."

"She seems better. Cooler."

He did not answer. Instead he covered her mouth with his and she tried to stifle a cry of delight. His lips explored and aroused, told her of his hunger and asked for what he wanted.

"Oh, yes," she whispered against his mouth. "Yes."

While his lips moved over hers he began to touch her all over, slowly moving his hands on her skin as if dawn were hours and hours away and these precious stolen moments would last forever. Up her belly, across her breasts, into the shell of her ear. Her breathing grew heavy and uneven.

He lifted his mouth from hers and nibbled his way with quick, hot kisses down to her breast. "Jeanne," he whispered, his voice unsteady. *"Jeanne."*

She stretched luxuriously, lifting her arms over her head and raising one knee. Slowly Wash pressed her leg down flat on the bed and reached one hand to cup her buttocks. Then he rose over her and positioned himself at her entrance.

"Wash…"

"Shhhh. We have to do this quietly."

He entered her with one slow, deep thrust and she could not help smiling. "Next time," she murmured, "I wish to make all the noise I want." She arched her back, taking him even deeper, and when he sucked in his breath she pressed her fingers against his lips.

He made it slow and languorous, and he made it last and last until Jeanne thought she could not stifle the cries that rose within her. When she started to come to her release Wash caught her mouth under his and rode with her until her spasms subsided and his own release began.

# Chapter Nineteen

Wash glanced sideways at Rooney when he entered the dining room, gestured at the coffeepot on the cherrywood sideboard, and then sat in the empty seat beside his friend. Rooney filled a coffee cup for him, then refilled his own. Wash inhaled the fragrant steam. Hot and black, just the way he liked it.

He sniffed the air appreciatively. Bacon…and scrambled eggs! He felt like he hadn't eaten in a week. He spooned a double helping of eggs from the china platter onto his plate and lifted his fork.

Rooney eyed the mound of food on his plate. "Get a good night's sleep, didja?"

Wash chuckled. "You sly old fox, you want me to lie to you?"

"Okay by me, as long as it's imaginative."

Wash chuckled. "Shut up and let me eat my breakfast."

"Sure thing, Wash." Rooney ducked his head over his coffee cup. "Musta' been some night," he muttered.

Wash munched up a crisp slice of bacon and swallowed it. "Why do you say that?" he asked as blandly as he could manage.

"Cuz you just poured maple syrup all over yer eggs."

Wash stared at the gooey mess he'd made. "Tastes great, Rooney. Ought to try it sometime."

Rooney choked on a mouthful of coffee and spent the next ten minutes in silence, watching Wash eat. "Sure are hungry," he said when his partner loaded up his plate again. He waited expectantly for a reply.

"Thought you'd never notice," Wash quipped. He liked sparring with Rooney; it kept him on his toes.

"Huh! Thought you'd never get yer appetite back. Jeanne told me about yer picnic yesterday. Said you ate two itty-bitty cheese pancakes and went right back to work."

Wash downed the last forkful of scrambled eggs. "Rooney?"

"Yeah, Wash?"

"Mind your own business." He tossed his napkin onto the table and strode out onto the front porch.

"Well, hell," Rooney said under his breath. "You *are* my business. You and Jeanne. And Manette." He heard the screen door slam and knew Wash was off to the stable.

"I'll be out at the site all day," Wash called over his shoulder. "Take care of Jeanne."

On the ride out to Green Valley Wash let his gaze

roam. The cloudless, robin's-egg-blue sky overhead hinted at another scorching day. Finches twittered among the maple trees, which were just beginning to turn gold. Lord, he loved this country!

He'd left Jeanne at the first flush of peach light through the bedroom window, but he was still going to be late. By the time he got to the site, Sam would have most of the valley covered in railroad ties. He half wished the quick, industrious little men would slow down a little; the minute they got the track up the incline at the far end of the valley…

He couldn't finish the thought. He couldn't let himself think about that now; there was too much to be accomplished, and then…

Then it would be time to move on.

Couldn't think about that, either. He dismounted, turned General over to the eager Chinese boy who scampered out of the bunkhouse and clenched his jaw. Rooney said he was burying himself in his work for the Oregon Central, and might be that was true. Sometimes he wondered if he was letting this railroad job eat up his life.

What life? He had no life outside of the railroad; he'd wanted it that way for years.

Jeanne woke to sunshine streaming in the window. Wash was gone—the side of the bed where he had lain was cold. He must have left her hours ago.

Tentatively she stretched her legs, then raised her knees and winced at the tenderness between her thighs.

Did men get sore from…? Probably not. Most men had more of such athletic practice than women.

On the other hand, Wash was not like "most men." Wash was Wash. He had loved her thoroughly last night and then absented himself before she woke. She would not complain about it. She would not even question him about their on-again, off-again relationship.

Except for the occasional delicious night of sensuous indulgence, chances were she would never know how things really stood between them. Wash was afraid of commitment.

*Would you want him to change?* She thought that over while she dragged her body off the bed and drew on her clothes. No, she did not want him to change. She wanted him as he was. He was like a wounded animal who needed to run free until he realized he didn't need to run any longer.

Jeanne bent over Manette, still asleep on the other bed, and noticed the blue shirt she wore as a nightgown was soaking wet. Her fever had broken during the night! She laid her palm on her daughter's forehead. Cool, but a bit sticky. She would sponge her off with fresh water when she woke up.

A tap on the door and then Dr. Graham's voice announced, "Let me examine your daughter, Mrs. Nicolet. You go on down to breakfast."

"But I—"

"Mrs. Nicolet, you need to eat." Gently but firmly the tall, silver-haired physician ushered her out into the hallway.

The dining table was empty except for Rooney, who sat hunched over a cup of coffee.

"May I join you?"

"Oh, sure, Jeanne. Sure. Not much left after Wash finished, though."

"*Bon*. I have not much appetite."

Rooney sent her a quick, sly look. "Any partic'lar reason?"

"No."

His grin faded. "Oh."

Jeanne concentrated on the coffee Rooney poured into her china cup. "Yes," she amended. "There is a reason."

"Are you all right, Jeanne? You don't seem too sure this mornin'."

She bent her head. "Oh, Rooney, I don't know." She drew in a slow, shaky breath. "I don't know if I am happy or sad."

Rooney nodded. "How's Little Miss?"

"Better, I think. Her fever broke last night. Dr. Graham is with her now."

"She wake up yet?"

Jeanne shook her head. "Not yet. And her arm—"

"Bruised black 'n blue, I'd guess."

"And yellow and purple! It looks terrible."

"That'll pass. Point this mornin' is to keep Big Miss goin'. So eat up, now."

Sarah bustled in from the kitchen with a plate piled high with toast. "Shall I scramble a couple of eggs for you, dearie?"

Jeanne looked up at the older woman and tried to

smile. Tears stung into her eyes. "You are very kind, but—"

Sarah shot a look at Rooney, who was just reaching for a slice of toast. "Maybe that's because a certain older gentleman is mighty fond of your daughter."

Rooney paused with his hand over the jam jar. "Now, Sarah…"

"Might also be a younger gentleman who's fond of—"

"Sarah!" Rooney interrupted. "Could you bring us some more, um, toast?"

The landlady looked pointedly at the existing stack of toast and pursed her lips. Rooney met her gaze. "Please?" he added. Mrs. Rose retreated to her kitchen and Rooney cocked his head at Jeanne.

"Wanna talk some?"

Jeanne sighed. "About Wash?" She felt her cheeks grow warm. "I do not know what to think, or do, about that man."

"Well, cheer up, Jeanne, honey. Wash don't know what to do about you, either."

She couldn't help laughing. She slathered strawberry jam on a thick slice of buttered toast and bit an almost perfect circle off one corner.

Rooney's black eyes twinkled. "It's good to hear you laugh. Been pretty grim around here since that rattler lunched on Little Miss's arm. You think I could visit her for a bit this mornin'?"

"Most certainly," a deep male voice answered. Dr. Graham stepped through the double glass doors, plopped his black leather bag on an empty chair and touched

Jeanne's shoulder. "Your daughter is going to be good as new in a few days, Mrs. Nicolet."

Jeanne clasped the older man's hand in both of hers but she could not speak.

He patted her arm. "I'll check on your daughter again this evening."

"Oh, thank you! Thank you so much."

She felt so relieved she devoured the entire stack of toast, then absentmindedly gobbled down the scrambled eggs Mrs. Rose set in front of her. The landlady exchanged a secret smile with Rooney and again disappeared into the kitchen.

The minute Jeanne and Rooney entered the upstairs bedroom, Manette's eyes popped open. "*Maman?* I'm hungry!"

"Are you, *chou-chou?*" She worked to keep her voice from cracking. "*Bon!* I will bring some breakfast for you, and after you have eaten, we will have a bath."

Manette grimaced. "Do I have to?"

"Yes, you do."

"But I don't want a bath."

"Well," Rooney interjected, "you know what? You hafta hurry up and get well so I can show you some secrets about rattlesnakes."

Jeanne flinched.

"What kind of secrets?" Manette queried.

Rooney caught Jeanne's eye and winked. "Oh, things like how to see 'em before they see you. How to listen for their rattles." He sent another wink to Jeanne. "And how they taste when you fry 'em up in bacon grease."

*"Ewwww,"* Jeanne and Manette said in unison. Rooney just chuckled.

"I'll make you a bet, Little Miss. I'll bet that you can't tell the difference between a bite of chicken and a bite of rattlesnake."

Manette's blue eyes snapped with interest. "What'll you bet, Rooney?"

Jeanne rolled her eyes to the ceiling and headed to the kitchen to boil an egg for her daughter. And heat some water for a sponge bath. The last thing she heard before the door closed behind her was the low murmur of Rooney's voice and her daughter's high, clear laughter.

The sound brought tears to her eyes.

Wash reined in at the valley's edge and sat his horse watching the Chinese crew heave and drop the heavy rails and drive the iron spikes in place. The metal track glinted in the sun like two silver ribbons.

Gradually the crew pushed their way along the length of the valley floor, and as the day grew hotter, the Chinese crew seemed to work even faster. By tomorrow they'd be ready to blast through the steep canyon wall at the far end with dynamite and a measure of caution.

Wash had always disliked setting charges, disliked the anxious, pregnant wait until the explosion rumbled and the lookout man shouted "All clear."

He still had a hard time with sudden loud noises; blasting the Green Valley Cut would make his nerves so jumpy he wouldn't sleep nights. But there would be no blasting for a while since the route through Green

Valley and on to Gillette Springs would run across flat ground.

He studied the thousands of acres of fertile land that stretched to the distant mountains and wondered suddenly if Jeanne could file a homesteader's claim on some of that land. Oregon didn't allow Indians to gain land this way, but what about a woman? He laughed out loud. If there was a way to do it, Jeanne would find it. He'd never known a woman quite like her.

He'd petitioned Sykes two weeks ago about the $400 Jeanne had been swindled out of. He wanted her to have the money to help her make a new start. With $400 she could buy any building in town! But without a doubt she'd want a house. A home for herself and her daughter.

His head jerked up at a chuffing noise at the valley rim. A steam engine was puffing its way along the newly laid track, black smoke billowing from the smokestack. The locomotive slowed to a crawl and the engineer leaned out of his window, waving a mail pouch.

The train stopped just behind the flatbed car full of iron track sections and sat steaming in place until Wash spurred General and rode over to the hissing engine.

"You George Washington Halliday?" the engineer yelled.

Wash nodded.

"Letter for you." The man leaned out and tossed down the mail pouch. "Must be important, cuz now I've gotta get this baby all the way back to Portland goin' backward!"

Wash snagged the hurtling pouch and waved his

thanks. What could be so important that Sykes would send a train instead of a rider?

Inside he found two envelopes, both from Grant Sykes. The first contained a check for $400, made out to Jeanne Nicolet. Wash looked up at the clear blue sky overhead and felt his heart lift. His efforts on her behalf had not been in vain.

Hallelujah! He could hardly wait to see the look on her face. He would add his own salary for the month… then she could buy anything she wanted.

The second envelope contained a letter from Sykes. Wash unfolded it, read it over, then read it again. It wasn't unexpected, but he hadn't thought it would come this soon.

*"Move on to Gillette Springs. Survey the area between the river and P. Henderson's cattle ranch. Calculate the angle of the curves and…"*

He refolded the letter and stuffed it and Jeanne's check into his shirt pocket. The sky, the trees, even the shimmers of hot summer air along the railroad tracks, dimmed to gray, as if a cloud had swallowed up the sun.

What was wrong? He'd surveyed dozens of river-to-ranch routes, calculated hundreds of arcs and grades. He'd always found the best boardinghouse for himself and Rooney, gotten to know the sheriff and the bartender at the saloon. This job wouldn't be any different.

But right now, just thinking about it, it sure felt different, like something was stuck in his craw. There was one thing he'd never faced before, and now it was staring him in the face like a big black locomotive. When they finished laying track through the Green Valley Cut, he'd thought the hard part would be over.

Wash swore aloud. No, dammit, the hard part wouldn't be over.

The hard part would be saying goodbye to Jeanne.

# Chapter Twenty

$W$ash stayed at the site long after the aroma of chicken and exotic spices drifted on the still air and the Chinese cook summoned the crew to supper. Twice he walked the entire length of the tracks up to the proposed cut, calculating where to set blasting caps the next morning and how much dynamite he had to work with. By the time he had tramped back up to the rim, his hip was aching.

Still, he put off returning to town, finding small cleanup tasks to keep himself occupied. Finally his grumbling stomach demanded that he eat. Maybe he'd take supper in the hotel dining room instead of at Mrs. Rose's crowded table; food wouldn't be as good, but it would be quieter. He needed time to think. He mounted General and headed back to town.

He had always moved on to his next assignment as the Oregon Central Railroad connected Portland with smaller cities and towns; he'd never experienced such a wrench at the prospect.

As he rode he tried to sort out his mixed feelings. In an odd way part of him was relieved; his absence could answer the nagging questions about his feelings for Jeanne. Another part of him was so full of regret at leaving her he couldn't think straight.

Usually he felt deep-down satisfaction at a job well done.

But instead of feeling satisfied about this job in Green Valley, he felt dead inside. He didn't feel like celebrating as he and Rooney usually did over a shot of Red Eye at the saloon.

The closer he got to town, the more uneasy he felt. Lights flickered along the main street when he rode in and tied up at the hotel. Maybe he'd feel better with some of Rita's steak and potatoes filling his belly.

*No, he didn't want to see Jeanne.* Not yet. Not until he'd decided what he would say to her. But an hour later, even though his stomach was full of dinner plus apple pie and a half gallon of black coffee, the empty feeling was still there. A weight like a blacksmith's anvil pressed on his chest, crushing down harder with every breath.

He wanted to see Jeanne.

He paid his supper bill and drifted next door to the Golden Partridge. Need for Jeanne made his whole body ache. But dammit, he didn't feel right making love to her now, knowing he would be leaving so soon. That knowledge in itself made his heart constrict. He hadn't seen this coming. If he'd thought it through that night after the Jensens' dance, maybe he'd never...

But he knew better. He hadn't thought, he'd just let himself feel something he hadn't allowed himself to feel since Laura.

Rooney strode through the saloon's swinging doors, sized up the table of cowboys and ranchers engaged in a poker game, then settled himself beside Wash at the bar.

"Been here long?" He signaled the bartender.

"Nope."

Rooney ordered a beer. "Missed you at supper."

"Stayed late at the site."

"Missed one of Sarah's fine meat loaves."

Wash downed the last of his whiskey and signaled for a fill-up. "Guess I did."

"Missed the sheriff's visit, too. Seems Montez is on the loose."

Wash's head came up, but all he did was grunt.

Rooney eyed him sideways. "Missed seein' Little Miss an' me playin' checkers."

"Yeah? Did she win?"

Rooney chose not to answer that. "Missed seein' Jeanne, too."

Wash said nothing.

"You gonna sleep at the boardinghouse tonight?"

That thought carved a gut full of red-hot desire in Wash's belly. He said nothing.

Rooney leaned closer. "Heard from Sykes, didja? He movin' you on to Gillette Springs?"

"How'd you know that?" Wash grumbled.

Rooney tapped his head with one long forefinger. "Comanche smarts, I guess. Haven't seen you with such a long face since Laur—"

"Shut up, Rooney."

But his partner just grinned and clapped him on the shoulder. "Don't worry, son. You'll live." Then he ambled off to join the poker game.

Jeanne waved at Tom Roper, the liveryman, and walked on past him into the interior of the stable. Tom had been friendlier since the railroad had made such progress, and since he'd seen her wagonload of lavender; in fact, he had nodded his head in admiration.

It was dark inside the stable, and it smelled of straw and horses. She left the broad hinged door open so she could see her way to the wagon loaded with her harvested lavender. Even from here, she could smell the fragrant lavender fronds.

She sucked in a deep breath and closed her eyes. *I thank you, God, for the life of my child and for the bounty of my field.*

Abruptly the door swung shut with a thump and Jeanne's eyelids snapped open. She could see nothing but thick, velvety blackness.

"Monsieur Roper?"

Silence.

"Tom?"

And then a low, oily voice spoke close to her ear. *"Buenas noches, señora."*

Wash finally dragged himself up the boardinghouse porch steps, hoping to see Jeanne, but she was not there.

"No, Colonel," Mrs. Rose explained. "She worked all afternoon makin' those pretty wreaths of hers. Just now she's gone over to the livery stable to get some more lavender."

"How long ago?"

The landlady pursed her thin lips. "About half an hour, I'd say. I've been watching over Manette until she gets back. Should be any minute now."

A sense of unease settled in his chest. *Montez is loose.* All at once he needed to see Jeanne, wanted to make sure she was all right.

He wheeled toward the staircase, took the steps two at a time and burst into his room. From the top shelf of the carved wooden armoire in the corner he withdrew his gun belt, slid six cartridges into his revolver and strapped the weapon around his hip. He couldn't really say why, just following an instinct.

The main street was dimly lit. The mercantile was closed and the only light shone from the saloon and the front windows of the hotel. Wash moved quietly toward the edge of town and the livery stable, staying in the shadows and working to keep his breathing steady. On cat feet he drew near the barnlike structure that held horses and the wagon loaded with Jeanne's lavender crop.

The wide door was shut, but the owner, Tom Roper, was in the adjacent yard working on a pinto quarter horse by lantern light. Wash signaled his intention to enter the stable. Tom waved him on and Wash automatically slowed his steps.

No sound came from inside. No lamplight showed

under the broad door. He approached the closed entrance at an angle, and when he was close enough to touch the wall, he unholstered his gun and flipped the safety off. Very deliberately he laid his left hand on the one-by-four board that served as a door handle and yanked it back, hard. The door shuddered open.

Wash stepped into the gloomy interior. "Jeanne?"

Silence. The hair on the back of his neck began to bristle.

"Jeanne? Where are you?"

A rustle of straw drew his attention, and in the next instant he heard a familiar voice.

"The lady, she ees not here, *señor*."

"Montez! What are you doing here?"

"I sneaked in to visit…with my horse. We are good *amigos,* me and my horse."

Wash turned toward the voice. It came from his left and he squinted, waiting for his eyes to adjust to the darkness. "Where is Mrs. Nicolet?"

"She don' like me because my skin is darker than her preetty milky-white skin. I do not know where she is, *señor.*"

The Spaniard was lying. "I don't believe you." Gradually he could make out the shadowy outline of the man's frame.

"I cannot help that." Montez made a slight movement with one arm. Wash studied the outline of the Spaniard's body and noticed something that made his blood run cold. Why would the man's shape look wider than it had a moment before?

*Because he was hiding Jeanne behind him.*

Sweat dampened the neckband of his shirt. He couldn't shoot for fear of catching Jeanne with the bullet. At least he could tell she was standing up, and that meant she was conscious. And maybe—*maybe*—Montez hadn't hurt her.

Over the sound of Montez's raspy breathing Wash could hear the whistled signals Tom was using to train the pinto out in the yard. If he could get Jeanne to run for the stable door...

Maybe if he spoke in French, Montez would not understand, but Jeanne would. He racked his brain for the right words.

*"Je compris,"* he managed. That told her he knew she was there, hidden behind the Spaniard.

What next? Run for the door. *"Vas au fenestre."* He pronounced each word with elaborate care.

"Speak American," Montez snapped.

Wash ignored him. *"Vas quand je dis* trois." Go when I say *three*.

Suddenly Montez had a knife in his hand.

*"Un,"* Wash said. He waited two interminable breaths.

*"Deux."*

The Spaniard hunched his body and came at him, the knife glinting silver.

*"Trois!"* Wash yelled. The blade sliced his shoulder, but the sound of small boots and the stable door crashing open told him Jeanne had escaped.

Montez launched himself again, leading with his blade. Wash clenched his teeth so hard his jaw cracked. In half a second he'd be a dead man.

He slammed his elbow into the Spaniard's chin just as a searing pain pierced his shoulder. He swore aloud. Without thinking, Wash brought his revolver up and fired.

Montez crumpled to the stable floor.

Wash heard a woman's cry and then Tom Roper's shout. He shook his head to clear it and walked toward the liveryman.

"Better get the sheriff, Tom. There's a dead man lying on your floor."

# Chapter Twenty-One

From the moment Montez sprawled on the floor, everything seemed to happen at once. Jeanne flew back into the stable and walked straight into Wash's arms, in spite of the blood seeping through his shirt from the knife slice.

"The gunshot," she said in a strangled voice. "I thought it was you."

Wash just tightened his arms about her shaking body.

Tom Roper bent over the Spaniard's inert form, his hands propped at his waist. "What's he wanted for?"

"Breaking out of jail, for one thing," Sheriff Dan Rubens said from the doorway. He was followed by his new young deputy, Curt Tempelhaus, who took one look and turned ashen.

"And maybe assault," Wash added. He bent and put

his mouth against Jeanne's temple. She was trembling so hard the lace cuffs at her wrists fluttered.

"Did he hurt you?" he asked quietly.

She shook her head. "*N-non*. But he touch me, here." She laid one hand on her breast and a shudder racked her frame. The top four buttons on her shirtwaist had been ripped free of the buttonholes; Jeanne clutched it together at her throat.

Wash had to bite his tongue to keep his voice calm. "Anywhere else?"

She buried her face against his shoulder. "My neck." Her voice was muffled but not tearful. Gently he tipped her chin up and perused her skin from throat to hairline. An angry red band encircled her neck. Finger marks. Wash felt his control wobble.

The sheriff straightened. "Anybody else here at the time?"

Tom Roper cleared his throat. "Far as I knew, Miz Nicolet was the only one in the stable, Sheriff. Until Colonel Halliday came, just a few minutes ago."

The short, graying sheriff turned to Wash. "You know the dead man, Colonel?"

Wash nodded. "Yeah. He worked on my survey crew. I fired him a while back."

The sheriff nodded and a frown pulled his gray eyebrows together. "Will you be around a while longer, Colonel? Might have an inquest."

"Long enough," Wash answered. "Maybe another week."

Jeanne's body went absolutely still.

Oh, hell! He had not told her about leaving. This was

a cowardly, backhanded way of letting her know, but he hadn't had a chance to explain about Sykes or the letter or what his work for the railroad entailed. He prayed it would help that he had a $400 check for her in his pocket.

The sheriff glanced once in Wash's direction and stalked out. Liveryman Tom coiled and recoiled a length of rope and finally exited to see to the horse he'd been training.

In the next minute the undertaker and his wagon rattled in and took the body away.

For a long time Jeanne said nothing, just stood there in the circle of his arms. When she stepped back to look up at him, there was fire in her green eyes.

"You are leaving." Her voice sounded tight as new barbed wire.

"Jeanne, let me explain. The letter came just this after—"

She snapped her head up. "You have known this all along? That you would be leaving?"

He began to perspire. "Yes. I didn't exactly know how to tell you."

Her face was white as paste, her eyes bruised looking. Wash swallowed hard. "I'd give anything if you hadn't found out this way."

Her voice hardened. "It does not matter how I found out. I should have guessed long ago."

"Jeanne…" He reached for her but she jerked away.

"Do not touch me!"

"At least let me explain."

Her lips formed a thin line. "You do not need to explain. I understand well enough."

He closed his hand around her upper arm. "Listen to me, dammit!"

Her eyes went wide, then instantly narrowed. "*Alors,* I am listening."

Wash gritted his teeth. "I wanted to tell you, I just didn't know how. When I got to the boardinghouse Mrs. Rose said you weren't there, that you'd gone to the livery stable to get more lavender."

"And so?" She spit the words at him.

"Rooney told me Montez was loose. I didn't want you to be alone here."

Jeanne moved away from him and was silent for a long moment. "For that I am grateful," she said, trying to keep her voice steady. "I am angry because..."

"Because I'm leaving? Or because I didn't tell you before?"

She dropped her head to hide her face, then raised it immediately. "Why did you want to tell me at all? Is it because we are...close?"

He caught her wrist and pulled her toward him. "We're more than 'close,' Jeanne, and you know it."

Jeanne let out a shaky sigh. "*Oui,* I do."

He had a strange expression on his suntanned face, as if something in his mouth had turned sour. For a moment a twinge of sympathy tempered her fury, but she brushed it aside. It felt much more satisfying to be angry.

"I've known I'd be leaving all along," he said quietly. "I just didn't know when."

"Perhaps it does not matter?" She hated the way she sounded, like a quarrelsome fishwife.

"It matters," he said. "I just don't know what to do about it."

Jeanne straightened her spine. "I could perhaps go with you?" She had to ask; she could not simply wipe him out of her heart.

"You and Manette, you mean?" Wash shook his head. "I'd only be there a month at the most, then Sykes will move me on to another town."

"No. That I cannot do. Manette must remain in one place to go to school."

Wash groaned. "This afternoon I thought hard about the Oregon Central. About resigning my position. Sykes could replace me and I could stay here. Work at something else."

"You must not do that," she said. "I know what your work means to you." His job with the railroad was his way of healing his past wounds. He'd said it was his salvation. She could not ask him to forego that.

He looked up at the ceiling, his lips tense. "Gillette Springs is only forty miles east. Maybe I could—"

She stopped his lips with her fingers. "*Non,* you could not. You would exhaust yourself riding back and forth for only a few hours together."

He caught her hand, turned it over and pressed a kiss into the center of her palm. "Jeanne, if we're not careful, we're going to talk ourselves out of something we—"

"Something we both want?" she blazed. "Is it not clear that we want two different things?" She turned away and started for the stable door. "You want your railroad, and I want a home for Manette and a place to grow my lavender."

Wash walked beside her without speaking. At the boardinghouse, Mrs. Rose took one look at Wash's haggard face, bandaged the knife slice on his shoulder and poured him a cup of double-strength coffee.

"I heard about the fracas over at the livery stable. You both look like you've been through one of those new-fangled clothes wringers." The landlady brewed a cup of peppermint tea for Jeanne and shooed her upstairs with a glass of warm milk for Manette.

In tense silence Wash and Jeanne climbed the stairs to Manette's room. Rooney was perched on the edge of the neatly made bed, reading aloud from an open book on his lap while Manette sprawled on her belly, her chin propped in her hands. Rooney marked his place with a finger and looked up.

"Heard about Montez," he said. "Too bad."

Wash and Jeanne glanced at each other. Rooney cleared his throat and continued the tale of *The Orphan Princess.* "'Then the cruel king ordered the guards to lock his daughter in the dungeon.'"

"But that's not fair!" Manette objected. "It wasn't her fault his glass horse broke."

Rooney wet his lips. "That's just the way it is, Little Miss. Life ain't fair sometimes."

Behind him, Jeanne sucked in an audible breath. Rooney shot a glance at Wash.

Manette cocked her head at him. "Why isn't it always fair?"

"Well…" Rooney scratched his beard. "Uh…if things

was always the same, always fair and always just, it'd be like having sunshine every single day. Wouldn't it get kinda boring?"

"No!" the girl shouted.

*"Non."* Jeanne murmured.

"Not on your life," Wash growled.

Jeanne set the milk on the nightstand. "Finish your story, *chou-chou.* Then you must go to sleep."

Wash caught Jeanne's eye and tipped his chin toward the hallway.

She shook her head.

He grasped her elbow and propelled her into the hall and down the stairs. "There's a lawn swing out on the front porch. We need to talk."

She hesitated. "It will do no good, Wash. We are headed down two different paths."

"Please, Jeanne. There's more I want to say."

His eyes looked smoky, like the blued steel of his revolver, and in their depths was an expression she could not read. Desperation?

She said nothing and let him guide her through the screen door to the wide front porch. The late summer night was quiet except for the rhythmic scrape of crickets and an occasional burst of song from an evening sparrow in the pepper tree overhanging the porch. Honeysuckle twined along the front fence, wafting a flowery scent on the warm air.

Jeanne drew in a shuddery breath. "The night is beautiful, is it not?"

Wash settled his long form onto the porch swing,

pulled Jeanne down beside him and pushed off with his foot.

"Jeanne…"

"I have always liked summer," she said quickly. "I came to Oregon in the summer, across the desert in a schooner wagon."

"Alone?"

"Ah, no. I joined a wagon train. It is dangerous for a woman and a child to travel alone across the country."

"Must have been hard traveling," he said in a low voice.

"We came by rail to El Paso. That part was not difficult."

"Jeanne…"

"Manette liked the train," she added without a pause. "And—"

Wash groaned. "You know what?"

She blinked. "No, what?"

"You're not letting me talk again. Won't let me say something I've been wanting to say."

She dropped her head until her chin brushed the lace at her throat. "It is because I am frightened."

"Frightened of what? Of me?"

"Oh, no. Not of you. Well, yes, in a way."

He twisted to face her. "'Yes' in what way?"

She raised her head and looked straight into his eyes. "I do not want to be unhappy."

"I don't want you to be unhappy. I'm trying to figure—"

"Wash." She laid her hand on his forearm. "It is not possible. When you are gone, I will miss you." She lifted her hand away and laid it in her lap. "But I will manage."

"I imagine you will," he said drily.

"*Oui,* I must. A woman should not depend on a man for happiness. I have to make the best of *my* life."

Wash's throat began to ache. "I have something for you. The railroad's paying you for the land you got cheated out of, so…" He dug in his shirt pocket. "Here's a check for your $400."

"*Vraiment?* But I thought—"

"Don't think, Jeanne. You've got enough money now to do anything you want, buy a house. Buy another farm."

He slipped his own monthly pay into her hand. "My room and board is paid up for six months. I want you and Manette to stay here in town, at the boardinghouse."

"But I cannot repay you!"

"I don't ask for repayment. I need to know you'll be safe and warm, come winter."

"This will matter to you? Even though you will be gone?"

"Damn right, it matters to me."

Her eyes shone with tears. "You are a good man, Wash."

Wash tried to smile. "Well, hell, this 'good man' is not feeling very good about things right now."

But something inside him eased, now that he'd told her everything. Everything he could afford to tell her, that is. He couldn't tell her that he loved her; he wasn't really sure what that would be like. He wanted her, for damn sure, but that wasn't the same thing, and he'd be lying if he said it was.

In all the years since Laura, this was the first time he'd really cared about a woman. But his mind felt hazy and unfocused, and some kind of knot in his gut wouldn't let him think it through.

## Chapter Twenty-Two

W ash had no appetite for breakfast the next morning, but he did need coffee. All night he'd wrestled with nightmares: the first time he'd killed a Johnny Reb, the first time he'd kissed Laura Gannon behind the schoolhouse. The last time he'd seen her before the War, driving her own rig out of Smoke River on the day she was to marry him.

Maybe if he could sort all those blasted memories out, he'd be able to think straight.

The long table gradually filled up with boarders chattering about yesterday's shooting at the livery stable and whether it would rain on Sunday's Church Ladies' social. And... Where was Mrs. Nicolet and her charming daughter this morning?

Rooney tramped in and without a word settled into the chair next to him.

"Is little Manette better this morning?" the school-teacher who boarded with Mrs. Rose asked.

Rooney just grunted, and the woman turned her attention to the platter of pancakes in the center of the table. Half an hour later Jeanne entered, a silent Manette clinging to her hand. Jeanne nodded a Good Morning but said nothing and she did not look at Wash but seated herself and her daughter across the table from him. Rooney rose to fill her cup with hot coffee. Manette's cup he filled to the top with mostly milk and Jeanne added a splash of coffee.

Her gaze moved from the pancakes to the china cream pitcher on the sideboard, but she clearly avoided looking at Wash. Her mouth didn't look pinched like it had yesterday, but she wasn't smiling, either. She wasn't even close.

Wash lingered over a third cup of coffee, hoping she'd say something, but she remained as talkative as a fence post. Finally he couldn't stand it any longer. He pushed away from the table and stood up.

She didn't even glance at him.

But Rooney did. The older man met Wash's gaze and shrugged his shoulders. Wash could read the man's thoughts as if they were smoke signals. *Hell, I don't know what's goin' on with you two!*

Wash wished he did. Last night Jeanne had been angry; today he didn't know what she was. Resigned, maybe. A lump of iron dropped into his stomach. Whatever she was feeling he'd better keep his mind off it; today he and his crew would be blasting through rock to carve out the Green Valley Cut.

He signed to Rooney and strode outside, purposely keeping his eyes away from the porch swing. He could still feel Jeanne's warmth next to him, still smell the fresh scent of her hair.

Out at the site, he unlocked the kegs of black powder and carefully parceled out bags of the stuff to Sam and the grinning team members lined up behind him. The Chinese sure loved things that exploded; each time a charge sent off, they stood rapt as if expecting colored streamers and shooting stars to pop out.

The workers reached the sheer granite face at the valley's end and progress along the Cut slowed to mere inches. All day the men pounded holes in the rock with iron hand drills and stuffed them with black powder. When the fuses were lit, each blast brought a shower of rocky shrapnel.

It was hot, sweaty labor. When a fuse didn't ignite, it was Wash who shimmied up the rock to inspect the failed charge and either relight the half-burned corded string or tamp in more explosive powder.

Made him sweat some. The headman, Sam, tried to wave him off. "Much danger, boss. Blow off hand."

"Yeah, well someone has to do it." Wash refused to imperil any of the crew under his supervision. He'd never sent a man into battle or to do a job that he himself wouldn't undertake, and he wasn't about to start now. Maybe he was a damn fool, but he felt responsible for his men.

Little by little the path blasted through the granite grew wide enough to allow the six-foot railroad ties and the steel rails that would be spaced four feet, eight inches apart. By midday, both Wash and the crew were gray with sifted dust from the exploding rock. Even his face felt sandy with the acrid-smelling stuff.

About noon, Rooney rode in, took one look at the advancing Cut and then at Wash's dust-coated face and loosed a tirade of curses. "Ya crazy idiot, ya wanna get yerself blown to smithereens? Jeanne will never forgive you."

"Then don't tell her!" Wash snapped. "A man does what he has to." Besides, Jeanne wouldn't forgive him for much more than just handling the explosive powder.

Rooney leaned sideways on his strawberry roan and spit so close to Wash's boots he had to jump out of the way. "Huh! I s'pose right about now you find this easier than dealing with Jeanne."

"Yeah? What would you know about Jeanne and me?"

"Enough. You might be riskin' your skin out here, but dyin' is a coward's way out."

"Talk straight, Rooney. You know I'm no coward. What are you trying to say?"

Rooney rolled his eyes at the blue sky overhead. "Gettin' blowed up is one thing. Gettin' flayed down to your vitals by a riled-up woman is another. I figure you're just plain scared."

"She's riled up, is she?"

Rooney spit at Wash's feet again. "Dunno. She's all closed up like a morning glory before the sun rises. She hasn't popped yet, but she sure will if you get yerself killed."

"She still at the boardinghouse?"

"Nah. She took Little Miss and rode out to MacAllister's bunkhouse. Said she had some work to do."

Wash wheeled away from his friend's piercing gaze and wished the roaring in his head would ease up. Might be he was still flinchy around loud noises, like he'd been after the War. Or maybe he was too close to the charges when they went off.

Or, dammit, maybe it was the constant imagined conversation with Jeanne that was getting his brain all mixed up. Anyway, his head was starting to hurt like hell.

He grabbed the bridle of Rooney's horse. "Either get down and help me finish this job or clear out and leave me be."

Rooney snorted. "Seein' as how you're in a worse mood than Jeanne, I guess I'll clear out." He tried to rein away, but Wash held onto the bridle. He softened his tone. "I'll see you at supper."

Wash released his hold on the horse and Rooney sidled away from him. "And don't ask me to ride out an' keep an eye on Jeanne!"

"Why not?"

"Why not?" Rooney aimed another glob of spit close to Wash's dusty boots. "Because Jeanne is *your* responsibility, not mine. You're the one that got her all fussed up in the first place."

"You're right, you old buzzard."

Rooney cocked his ear toward him. "Well, that's more like it!"

"Now clear out." Wash slapped Rooney's mount on the rump and watched with satisfaction as the horse jolted into a canter. Anything to get rid of the man's incessant nattering. "Damned nosy, interfering, know-it-all Comanche," he muttered.

Wash reached for the black powder tin looped to his belt and stopped short. He did want to protect Jeanne, keep her safe. He'd never looked at it that way before, but yes, he did feel responsible for her.

His chest tightened as if a huge fist were squeezing from the inside. He didn't want to feel responsible. Didn't want to feel a tie between Jeanne and himself. He let out a heavy groan. Didn't matter what he wanted, the tie was already there.

Taking in an uneven breath, he yelled for Sam. "Let's get back to blasting."

Within ten minutes, the sound of rock ripping away from its bed of earth cut through the otherwise tranquil morning, and all through the long, powder-dusted afternoon, Wash thought about responsibility. Each time he crept up a slab of rock to fix a fuse that failed to ignite or fill the hole with more of the grainy black explosive, he rolled questions around in his brain. Questions about his past. About his life now.

About the years to come.

Dying would be easy; it was *living* that was hard. He thought that over while he reached into a drilled-out hole to make sure the fuse cord touched the charge. Being alive meant you felt things: a father's untimely death; a prison guard's brutality; a lover's betrayal. Being alive meant you got attached to things.

And people. The headache pounding in his temples kicked up a notch. He tamped down the powder and resecured the fuse, then found his mind wandering again. It didn't take a genius to know he was attached to Jeanne. Not hog-tied and squealing, but…well… attached. He liked her more than he'd liked any woman, even Laura. But…

But.

Using the flint and steel he carried in his back pocket, he created a spark and bent to fan it with his breath. When the flame sizzled along the fuse cord, he shinnied down the rock face.

Just in time—the charge went off sooner than he expected. All he could do was turn away and hunch his shoulders against the rain of granite bits. Hell, it was like a thunderstorm of rocks.

When the dust cleared, Sam grabbed his arm and dragged him away through the smoke. "Not good you get hurt." The Chinese man shook his forefinger in Wash's face. "Should not take chance."

"Wait a minute, Sam. Who's the boss around here?"

In answer, Sam jabbed the same forefinger into Wash's chest. "Stupid. Dumb. Make no sense." He kept jabbing.

Wash opened his mouth to protest, but his throat was so clogged he could make only a wheezing sound.

"Boss see now," Sam crowed in triumph. "Voice gone."

Wash shook his head, then gulped water from the canteen he carried at his hip. "I'm okay, Sam. Just parched."

"And stupid," the Chinese muttered. He loped back the ten yards to the advancing tracks.

Maybe so, Wash acknowledged. Maybe Rooney was right, he'd rather risk dying than living with more pain of the female variety.

A stab of agony shot across the top of his head and settled behind his eyes. When he turned to follow Sam back up to the rim he found he was unsteady on his feet. And dizzy, he noted after he'd gone two steps.

The six o'clock dinner gong reverberated into the canyon. Like well-organized ants, the crew lined up four abreast and double-timed it up to the rim and their waiting supper. Sam flashed him a grin as he jogged past.

Wash tried to smile back but the effort made his teeth ache.

What was the matter with him?

*Nothing that an hour's rest and some whiskey wouldn't cure.*

The young Chinese boy, Lin, led his horse over and Wash heaved his weight into the saddle, fighting off waves of nausea. Nothing serious, he told himself. Just the "too's" again: Too much coffee. Too much work. Too much thinking.

Too much remembering.

He kicked General into a canter but immediately slowed him to a gentle walk. Maybe he'd hit his head on something. He chuckled, then bit his lip against the surge of pain.

He'd hit his heart on something, too.

By the time he reached town, it was dusk, and

whenever he moved his head the throbbing in his temples and behind his eyes felt like a cannonball exploding in his brain. If he didn't look down at the ground his head didn't spin so bad, so he stared across the plain at the pink and orange sunset against the mountains on the far horizon. He carefully walked his mount to the boardinghouse and dismounted at the front gate. Mrs. Rose was clipping back her honeysuckle. Wash asked if her grandson could take his horse on over to the livery stable.

The landlady looked puzzled for a moment, then peered up at his face. "Land sakes, you look awful," she blurted.

"Mostly rock dust," he told her. "And maybe a bit of a headache."

She shoved her hand-shears into her apron pocket and studied him more closely, looking especially hard at his eyes. "Go right on up to your room, Colonel, and I'll bring some tea."

"Coffee?" he said hopefully.

"Tea," she insisted. "Made from willow bark. Best remedy for a headache."

He watched her young grandson lead General off down the street, then dragged himself up the stairs, shucked his boots and his hat, and stretched out on his bed. The quilt underneath him smelled of soap and sunshine.

His eyelids drifted shut. He lay without moving until he heard the thump of footsteps on the stairs and the swish of his door opening. Someone—Mrs. Rose—laid a cool washcloth across his face and settled a mug of odd-smelling liquid onto his chest. She lifted one of his hands and positioned it around the mug to hold it in place.

"Sip it," the woman ordered. She wiped the grit off his face with the cloth, wrung it out in a basin of water and laid it over his closed eyes. "Doc Graham said something about a 'vascular spasm.'"

"Never heard of it," Wash muttered. "Don't tell Jeanne."

"Don't need to. But it appears you've got one, and I aim to fix it."

Mrs. Rose, he thought hazily, was a singular woman.

"Thanks," he murmured. The last thing he remembered was gulping down the bitter tea.

Hours later he woke up when a gentle hand drew the cloth from his eyes, freshened it in cool water and replaced it.

"Supper over?"

"Mmm-hmm."

"Your grandson see to my horse?"

"Mmm-hmm."

Wash drew in a long breath of dust-free air and realized his head no longer ached. His mind felt fuzzy and slow, as if he'd downed too many shots of whiskey in too short a time. But what the hell? He'd felt unfocused like this before, like that night with Jeanne after the Jensens' dance.

Thinking about that made him feel good inside and then sent a needle of agony through his eyeballs.

Thinking about leaving town in a few days made his gut hurt.

A hand again set a mug on his chest and steadied it against his curved palm. He breathed in the smell of coffee and couldn't help smiling.

"Thanks, Mrs. Rose. You sure know what a man needs when he's down." It *was* Mrs. Rose, wasn't it?

He heard a sniff and then the click of the door as it closed.

Didn't matter what she thought; he'd been ambushed by a temporary weakness and he was grateful for her attention. A cup of coffee was a small thing, maybe, but at the right time it sure meant a lot. By Jupiter, he sure admired a woman's intuition.

# *Chapter Twenty-Three*

Wash woke with a start when Rooney tramped into his room.

"Heard you was feelin' kinda puny."

Wash didn't bother to open his eyes. "Better now. Mrs. Rose made me some tea."

"That's some woman," Rooney said softly. "One in a million."

"Make that two in a million. Jeanne's mighty unusual, too."

Rooney was quiet for a long minute. "Wash, when you figure on movin' on to Gillette Springs?"

"Two or three days. I want to get the rails laid all the way through the Cut we're blasting."

"You mind if I lay out my pallet in here tonight? Jeanne and Little Miss are—"

"Sure." His chest felt warm all at once, as if filled with light knowing she was just across the hall and not out at the bunkhouse tonight. Maybe he'd see her at breakfast.

Rooney lit the kerosene lamp and Wash rolled over, away from the light. He heard the older man flap open his rolled-up pallet and mutter to himself as he straightened the blanket edges. Wash drifted toward sleep thinking about Rooney, how much he owed the older man, how much he valued his friendship. He wondered if he'd ever told him that.

His last thoughts before sleep were about Jeanne, how beautiful her voice was when she read to her daughter in French. And what a maddeningly independent, stubborn woman she was.

He woke the next morning still thinking about her. Rooney had already rolled up his bedroll and leaned it in the corner. Wash guessed he'd already be at breakfast in the dining room downstairs.

And so would Jeanne.

He bounded off the bed, grabbed a clean shirt out of the bureau drawer, splashed water on his face and combed his tumbled hair off his face with his fingers. The mirror over the chest reminded him he hadn't shaved in two days; today would make it three. Couldn't be helped; he was in a hurry. He wanted to see Jeanne more than he wanted to spend time scraping off his whiskers.

He reached the staircase before he finished tucking in his shirt, clattered down the steps and strode into the dining room.

No Jeanne. Not at the breakfast table. Not out on the front porch. He gobbled down his eggs and toast and marched down to the livery stable. Her gray horse was gone. He'd missed her. Disappointment eroded a twisting path through his belly, but he had a job to do out at Green Valley. He saddled up his horse and headed out to the site.

Rooney was already there, his sleeves rolled up, stacking wood for the Chinese cook. "Sky looks bad," he said. "Storm comin'."

Wash studied the lowering black clouds overhead. Tinged with a dark purple-gray, they pressed down on the land like the miasma of heavy smoke he'd seen on battlefields.

"Think the Cut you're blastin' will wash out?" Rooney queried.

"Not if the rain holds off awhile and we can get it shored up." He glanced again at the sky with a sinking feeling.

The first splatter of rain came just before noon.

"*Maman,* why are you frowning?" Manette patted Jeanne's forearm with her small, sticky hand. "It makes your face look all wrinkled up, like Rooney's."

Jeanne stabbed another lavender stem into the wreath growing under her unsteady hands. It was good to be home, even if it was just a bunkhouse.

Why was she frowning? Because of that maddening man, Wash Halliday. She knew he cared about her; a man like Wash did not seduce women just for diversion.

She knew other things about him, as well. He was stubborn. He was wary of involvement. And stubborn.

Wash was a wounded bear who had unexpectedly stumbled into her life. He was the most stubborn man she had ever encountered.

What was she to do about him?

*"Maman?"*

"Oh! I am sorry, *chou-chou*. My thoughts were wandering."

Jeanne started an imaginary list. *What to do about Wash.*

First, she could forget about him. That would be like ripping her heart out, but she could try.

Second, she could pursue him. *Jamais!* A well-brought-up woman never pursued a man. Yes, she wanted Wash. But not if he was hesitant or unsure about what *he* wanted.

Third—

*"Maman!* You are wandering again." She pointed at the wreath.

"Ah, you are right. What was it you asked me?"

But Manette had been patient long enough. She dropped the fronds of lavender she had been weaving, stomped up the step into the bunkhouse and slammed the flimsy door behind her.

Jeanne sighed and snatched up her half-woven wreath. She wished Rooney had not ridden out to Green Valley this morning. He'd mumbled something about saving Wash from himself and then sauntered off to the livery for his horse.

What did that mean, "saving Wash from himself"? Her heart skipped. *Mon Dieu,* was he doing something dangerous? *Bon.* Another reason to forget about him—he could get himself killed.

"Third," she said aloud, adding to her list. "Third, I could…" Ah, no. She could not do that, even if she wanted to. Move back to New Orleans and forget she'd ever met Wash Halliday? *Never.* It had cost her too much to come out here to Oregon in the first place.

Besides, she did not want to go back to New Orleans. She found she liked Oregon. The townspeople had been slow to warm up, but that had been mostly her own fault. She had preferred to keep to herself. Ah, back to her list!

Fourth, she could marry someone else. Manette needed a father, it was true; but this was not about Manette, was it?

This was about the longing Jeanne felt whenever she thought about life with that unreachable man. Her very bones ached for him, but she could not wait for him to declare himself. Her life must move on.

Fifth, what if she decided never to marry anyone? She, too, had struggled to survive a crippling relationship before she had come to Smoke River. *But I will pine for this man, Wash Halliday, for the rest of my life. Never once have I pined for Henri.* Still, it was not enough to want a man, to hunger to be part of his life. Either she was part of it, or she was not.

And with Wash, she was not.

She must move on, in spite of him.

Automatically she wound the lavender fronds in and out, tighter and tighter; when she glanced down at her apron-covered lap, she was surprised to find the wreath was completely finished. More than finished, it was overstuffed!

She grabbed a handful of lavender stalks and started on another wreath because she needed to keep her hands busy. *Wash Halliday, you are responsible for my frown and for my flittering thoughts and for the ache in my heart.*

She was trying hard to understand, and perhaps she did, at least a little. A hurt bear looked first to his wounds; he did not join with others until he started to heal.

*Did bears stay with each other after they mated?* The thought made her laugh aloud. Of course they did not. Bears were animals; it was human beings who made commitments.

But not a man like Wash Halliday. She bit her lip. Wash was using his job as a shield.

Sixth, she could wait. She could wait until this man, whom she had accepted into her body, had healed his wounds and rejoined life.

*Non,* she could not just wait. She must move on, for herself and for Manette.

Ah, another list: Things Wash needed to learn.

First, he needed to learn that he was not alone in having suffered wounds of the heart.

He needed to learn that life would always have risks; that is what life *was*. Some risks turned out to be devastating; some were pain-filled; and some were glorious while they lasted. She had known all three: her marriage to Henri had been bitter. Birthing Manette had been so agonizing she had wished to die. But her few nights with Wash had been filled with wonder and joy and…

She jerked her mind back to the list.

He needed to learn that it took strength to be happy. He did not lack strength; the man was simply reluctant to reach out his paw—ah, no, his hand—again.

*What should I do?*

She bent her head over a spray of lavender as the truth dawned.

Nothing. She would do nothing. A man captured against his will was not what she wanted. She wished for a man who wanted to join his life with hers; a man who was willing to fight for that.

*Voila!* Another wreath completed! At this rate she should start looking for a suitable farmstead to purchase.

"Manette?" Jeanne jumped to her feet, scattering bits of stems onto the ground. "Come out, *chou-chou.* My frown is gone! I have decided something."


"You say you want to buy a farm, Miz Nicolet?" The banker, Will Rasmussen, looked at Jeanne doubtfully. "Well, yes, there's a couple of places up for sale, but…" He coughed and cleared his throat. "How do you plan to pay for it?"

Jeanne jolted upright. "With money, of course. I have now money of my own."

Rasmussen scratched his chin. "How much money?"

"How much is the farm?" she snapped.

The banker raised both hands and took a step backward. "You want to ride out and see the place?"

"But of course," she said stiffly. "I do not intend to purchase a pig in a pot."

"Poke," he muttered under his breath, trying to squash a smile. "Pig in a poke."

He cast a wary look out of the bank window where dark clouds roiled overhead. "Better hurry, then. Looks like there's a storm on the way."

It was a quick trip. Jeanne saw all she needed to see in an hour and she and Manette and Mr. Rasmussen headed back to town in the banker's horse-drawn buggy. Before they reached Smoke River, it began to rain. Not just rain, Jeanne noticed. Fat drops as big as rosebuds pelted down. Water sluiced out of the purple-black sky as if dumped from a washtub, drenching both her and Manette before Mr. Rasmussen could reach the stable.

When she climbed down from the buggy, she had to wring out the hem of her bombazine skirt. The knitted wool shawl she wore over her head and shoulders dripped water down the back of her neck and smelled like a wet sheep. And Manette's poor bonnet and the new red coat Verena Forester had sewed for her last week were sopping wet.

"It will dry out," Jeanne assured her daughter. "We will hang it near the stove in the bunkhouse."

"Why don't we go see Uncle Rooney at Mrs. Rose's house?"

"Because Rooney is not there, *chou-chou*. He is helping Wash build his railroad. Besides, I left my wreaths and my lavender and my ribbons and thread at the bunkhouse. We will be quite warm and dry, you will see."

The bunkhouse was dry. The roof did not leak, but

the place was not warm. She stirred the fire and added more wood, but the small pine logs were damp and the flames sputtered and died.

For hours the rain slashed down onto the roof without letup and a rising wind drove it sideways against the walls. It sounded like the *rat-tat-tatting* of a Gatling gun. The memory of a battle near New Orleans sent a shiver up her spine.

How would the storm affect Wash's blasted-out railroad bed through Green Valley? Rooney had explained what he was trying to do at the site; Jeanne found it unbelievable. Just imagine, cutting through solid rock at the end of the valley! She could not bear to envision what her little farm must look like now with a huge black steam engine puffing its way through her ravaged lavender field.

Oh, everything was all wrong now! When Wash had tramped into her life, her world had turned upside down.

Jeanne bit the inside of her cheek and raised her head. Everything was *not* all wrong. She must put all her efforts now toward the new farm she had bought just three hours ago. Life must go forward.

With or without Wash Halliday.

Wash studied the horizon, then lifted his gaze to the sky, which was growing blacker by the minute. The wind picked up, lifting the edge of his saddle blanket and beginning to moan through the tall pines. Sam, standing a few feet away, threw his arms over his head at the noise. "Demons come," he quavered. Still, he refused to leave with the others when Wash sent the crew back to their rolling bunkhouse.

"Only see'd a sky like that once before, when we was at Fort Kearney," Rooney said. "Remember?"

Wash gave a short nod. He'd never forget it. The rain had thundered down on their camp, the river had flooded and swept away the tents, the cook's stove and half the horses in its churning brown waters. When the water had receded, they'd dug eighteen horses and seven mules out of the mud. He suppressed a shudder. A rainstorm could be deadly.

There was no stream in Green Valley, so no danger of the tracks washing out. But at the Cut...

They rode down to inspect the area they had blasted through the day before, Sam riding double behind Rooney. The horses picked their way down following the newly laid iron tracks until they came to the Cut. Water poured over the rock from above, making a roaring noise.

"Sounds like a buffalo stampede," Rooney shouted. "Don't look good."

"Sam." Wash spoke to the Chinese man clutching Rooney's middle. "You get all the explosive covered up?"

Sam's crooked white teeth flashed in a grin. "Yes, boss. Up early. All covered."

Wash chuckled. The first thing the Orientals would think to save would be the explosives; like the fireworks they loved, setting off charges was high entertainment for the Chinese men.

"What else?" Wash inquired.

"Cook's stove. Roof leak in bunkhouse kitchen. And new shipment of logs for railroad ties."

Again Wash laughed. First priority was explosives; food came second. Well, he acknowledged, he'd have done the same. He relaxed his tense shoulders.

"Good work, Sam. Doesn't look to me like the Cut site is threatened. We'll take the rest of the day off."

The headman clapped his hands like a boy presented with a new horse. "Okay, boss. Now I finish fan tan game."

Back on the rim of the valley Sam slipped off the horse and scurried to the shelter of the bunkhouse where a comforting stream of gray smoke drifted from one of the metal chimneys. Rooney slapped his hat against his thigh, and the rainwater that had collected around the brim splooshed onto the muddy ground. He cocked his head, shielded his eyes with his hands and studied the sky.

"Let's make tracks, Wash. This ain't no summer shower."

Without another word, the two men turned their mounts toward town and spurred them to a gallop. The wind through the treetops sounded like a woman screaming, and the rain came at them sideways. Wash could scarcely see through the thickening mist. Rooney's strawberry roan was just a shadowy blur on his left.

He pulled his hat down low to protect his cheeks and chin from the slashing rain. Water blew in under the brim. He kept his head down and watched what he could see of the terrain ahead. Rooney must have done likewise, because the man's mount never wavered or slackened its pace. Good man, Rooney. Sometimes his friend seemed more than half Comanche. He prayed neither of their horses would stumble or step in a prairie-dog hole.

It took an extra hour to reach the outskirts of Smoke River. "I want a shot of Red Eye," Rooney yelled over the wind. Wash wanted a shot of Red Eye, a hot bath and a warm fire at his feet, in that order.

The honeysuckle vine on Mrs. Rose's boardinghouse fence was getting beat all to hell by the downpour. The fence itself was half tipped over from the blasts of wind that ripped across it. Wash would not ask Mrs. Rose's grandson—what was the blue-eyed kid's name, Mark?—to take General on down to the livery stable. No sense getting the youngster soaked and his grandmama upset.

Getting from the stable back up the street to the boardinghouse turned out to be a struggle. The wind buffeted them from the front, the rain hissed into their ears and up their noses.

"Gonna forget the Red Eye," Rooney yelled over to Wash. "Don't wanna swim to the saloon."

On the wide boardinghouse porch, they stomped around to dislodge the mud caked on their boots, then shucked them, stuffed the toes with pages from the *Oregonian,* and set them just inside the front hallway to dry.

A rush of warm, cinnamon-scented air met them. "Sarah," Rooney crooned at the dining-room entrance. "You makin' cookies for a weary man?"

"Gingerbread," a female voice answered.

"Gingerbread," he said in a dreamy voice. "I'll just bet Little Miss likes gingerbread. That ain't French, is it?"

"Nope." Wash took one look around the empty dining table.

"Is Jeanne upstairs?"

"No, Colonel. She's still out at MacAllister's place, working on her lavender wreaths."

An icy fist slammed into Wash's chest.

Mrs. Rose appeared in the kitchen doorway, wiping her hands on a towel stuck in her apron waistband. "Jeanne left early this morning…took Manette and rode out before breakfast."

"You mean she's been out there all this time, during the storm?"

"Sure has. I must say, that girl is no stranger to hard work."

Wash exchanged a look with Rooney. "Want me to go with you?" the older man asked.

"No. Like you said, she's my responsibility."

Mrs. Rose fluttered her hands in Wash's direction. "You're not going out in this wild storm again, are you?"

Wash didn't answer. Rooney nodded. The woman bit her lip but said nothing.

Rooney pounded up the stairs and returned with both his own black rain poncho and Wash's olive-green one. "Yer gonna need these."

Wash sought the man's eyes. "Thanks, Rooney. You're a good friend. And," he added, "you deserve a double helping of gingerbread."

The last thing Wash heard before he closed the front door behind him was Rooney's gravelly voice and Sarah Rose's laughter.

# Chapter Twenty-Four

Wash slogged his way down the street to the livery stable, an inexplicable feeling of dread burrowing into his stomach. Even with his rain poncho covering him from head to hip, water blew at him sideways until he could feel the cold drops sliding down the back of his neck. He pulled the poncho tighter.

Tom Roper met him at the stable, banged the door shut after him and faced him with hands propped on his hips. "You crazy, Colonel? Yer horse just got settled down and now you wanna take him out again in this muck?"

"Have to, Tom. Mrs. Nicolet and her daughter went out to MacAllister's early this morning. They're not back yet."

"You know Swine Creek's rising? A fella rode in 'bout an hour ago and said he had a devil of a time swimmin' his horse across."

"I know a shallow spot to cross."

He would never forget the winter the Platte had flooded—all those dead horses. He shook his head to dispel the memory and threw a dry saddle blanket onto General's back, hefted his saddle into place, and tightened the cinch. Jamming his wet boots into the stirrups, he signaled Tom to swing the door open just wide enough to let him through.

Rain hit his hat so hard it felt like he was standing under a waterfall. The livery yard was now a sea of mud. He spurred General into a canter until he had squished through it and was on the road leading west out of town.

"Okay, boy, let's go!" The animal lurched into a hard gallop. Wash hoped the horse could see through the sheets of rain, because he sure as hell couldn't.

Sure enough, the creek bordering MacAllister's property was raging over its banks. Wash reined up and stared at the raging water. Small trees carried by the yellow-brown torrent swept past like ghostly many-armed figures. He urged General into what looked like a shallows, laid his head alongside the animal's neck and tried to pray.

MacAllister's bunkhouse was faintly lit, but Wash noted that no smoke came from the stone chimney. That meant there was no heat inside; Jeanne and Manette must be freezing.

Jeanne's gray mare was sandwiched between the wagon and the bunkhouse wall for protection. He maneuvered General as close as he could get to the single step at the bunkhouse doorway and yelled to warn her he was here.

"Jeanne!" Probably couldn't hear him over the storm. He shouted her name again, then dismounted, grabbed the extra poncho, and burst through the door without stopping to knock.

Jeanne looked up from the chair by the hissing pot-bellied stove, her face pale, her nose red from the cold. Manette huddled on her lap, bundled up in a quilt.

"Wash! What are you doing here?"

"Came to take you into town. To the boarding-house."

"But why?"

A gust of wind shook the bunkhouse walls and Manette squirmed deeper into Jeanne's blanketed lap.

"The creek's rising. You're going to be flooded out."

Her face turned white.

"Water's already so deep you can't wade across it. Come on, we're going into town." He lifted Manette off her lap and set the girl on her feet.

"Got any extra blankets?"

Jeanne rose unsteadily. "Y-yes. On my bed."

"Get your wraps on," he ordered. He stripped another quilt off the lower bunk and bundled it under his arm.

"Jeanne, General is strong and steady. I want you to ride him, and I'll take your gray. I'll seat Manette in front of you. Ready?"

He was herding them toward the door when Manette let out a squeal of protest. "My coat! My new coat. She pointed to a red garment draped over the back of the other chair.

Jeanne rolled her eyes. Wash grabbed the coat and jostled Manette's thin arms into the sleeves.

"You have a coat, Jeanne?"

"*Non.* I wear my shawl."

"Not enough," he snapped. He shrugged off his dripping poncho, then the deerskin jacket he wore underneath and hung it around her shoulders. With shaking fingers, she buttoned it up to her neck, then pulled the wool shawl over her hair.

"We are ready," she announced.

Wash dropped the extra poncho over her head and slipped into his own. Before he opened the door, he snagged a rope and bridle from the hook on the wall.

He took Jeanne out first. Sloshing through a sheet of muddy water, he lifted her into General's saddle, then went back for Manette. When the girl was securely settled in front of her mother, he guided her small hands to the pommel. "Hold on to this, honey. Hold very tight so you won't fall off."

Jeanne lifted the front of her poncho to cover her daughter and wrapped one arm over Manette's body to keep her in place. Wash watched her bend forward to speak to her daughter.

"Do not be frightened, *chou-chou*. We have been wet and cold before, remember?"

A little mewing sound came from under the layers of garments.

Wash led the gray mare out, slipped the bridle on her and folded the extra quilt onto her broad back. Then he mounted, clicked his tongue and the two horses began to slog over the watersoaked ground. Wash took the lead on the gray. He couldn't set too fast a pace because of the pummeling rain and because he worried Manette could lose her grip and tumble off.

By now it was growing dark. The only sounds were the squishy clopping of horses' hooves and the endless drumming of the rain. When they reached the creek, Wash groaned. The water was even higher than before and he followed it for a good mile before he found a place still shallow enough to ford.

He reined in and waited for Jeanne. "We'll go across side by side."

Jeanne bit her lip and nodded.

"I'll be on your downstream side, so if anything happens—" He couldn't finish the thought. *Nothing* would happen. He would not *let* anything happen.

"Stay close. Ready?"

Again she nodded and they urged their mounts into the tumbling water. He heard no moans of fright, no weeping, not even from little Manette. Sure had to admire their grit under pressure.

The two horses struggled on through the raging creek, dodging the small logs and upended shrubs that rushed past. The water rose to Wash's thighs. He kept his eyes on Jeanne's skirts; the fabric was sodden with dirty flood water and the weight of her petticoats dragged at her. Still he heard not one word of complaint.

In fact, he heard no word at all. For a split-second his heart stopped.

"Jeanne? Are you all right?"

"I am all right, yes. And Manette, too."

A warm glow spread through him. They were going to make it just fine. They were over halfway to town and the worst—fording the creek—was almost over.

General struggled up the oozy bank on the opposite side of the creek while Wash hung back on the gray until he knew they were safe. Then he dug in his spurs. The mare jolted up the muddy incline to the top, where Jeanne quietly waited with General. Again, admiration filled him.

They plodded on, Wash leading, Jeanne and Manette behind him. The road widened when they neared town and Wash slowed to let her catch up. Side by side, they walked their mounts against a wind so blustery Jeanne's heavy, wet skirts were tossed up around her knees. All three of them would be waterlogged before they reached the boardinghouse.

They moved forward, their heads down against the wind, hands aching from the stinging rain. For the second time that day Wash began thinking about some whiskey, a hot bath and a warm fire.

And Jeanne.

Suddenly he was happier than he could ever remember. Here, out in the middle of the worst storm he'd seen in years, so wet his underdrawers squished against his skin with every motion the horse made, cold and hungry... But hell, he felt like singing!

Just then Jeanne's voice floated to him, crooning some kind of lullaby in French. His throat tightened.

It took another hour until he could see the blurry lights of the town through the rain; it felt like yet another hour of carefully picking their way around street-wide brown mud puddles before they rode up to the boardinghouse.

Wash leaned sideways so Jeanne could hear him. "I'll bring the horses back to the stable later."

She turned toward him, but it was too dark to see her face.

"Wash?"

"Don't argue, honey. Ask Mrs. Rose to start some bathwater heating."

Her horse swerved into his and both animals halted. Jeanne reached her hand out, grasped his and squeezed. Tears burned under his eyelids.

The two-story yellow clapboard boardinghouse loomed ahead. Wash dismounted outside the picket fence, now flattened by the wind, and lifted Manette from her mother's lap. He had to pry the child's stiff fingers off the saddle horn.

Rooney appeared in the open doorway. Manette darted up the steps and he swung her up into his arms. "Why, yer soakin' wet, Little Miss. What you been doin', swimmin' in the creek?"

The girl giggled and threw her arms about his neck.

"Jehoshaphat, yer nose is colder'n a snowball!"

Jeanne could not dismount she was so exhausted; could not swing her leg over the horse's rump with the weight of her sodden skirts pulling against her ankles. She watched numbly as Wash strode toward her, his tall form slick with mud and rainwater. He reached up, pressed both hands against the poncho that covered her and grasped her around the waist.

He lifted her out of the saddle, steadied her feet on the ground and unexpectedly folded her into his arms. Their wet ponchos brushed together with a whispery sound and all at once he was chuckling near her ear.

"Wh-what is s-so funny?" Her body shook from the bite of the freezing wind on her wet legs. She could not stop her teeth from chattering.

"Nothing is funny," he said, sucking in a gulp of air. "I'm just happy that we got here."

"You—" she tried to keep her voice steady "—are easily p-pleased." It was just a jest, but she heard his voice change with his reply.

"The hell I am."

She had said exactly the wrong thing. But it did not seem to matter because he scooped her up, poncho and all, and tramped up the porch steps with her in his arms.

Rooney, with Manette hanging about his neck, ushered them through the front door with a shout. "Sarah, they're here!"

Wash set Jeanne down and lifted off the poncho and her rain-soaked shawl, then wrestled Manette's arms out of her red coat.

He rolled all the wet garments together in one bundle and looked at Jeanne. "You want to add your wet skirt and petti—?"

"Certainly not!" A bubble of laughter escaped, and the next thing she knew he was down on one knee, unlacing her boots.

Opening the door briefly, he tossed her shoes and his own boots and the pile of wet garments out of the front door onto the lawn swing.

Mrs. Rose had the dining table set with flowered china bowls of warm bread and milk at each place. One bowl had what looked like gingerbread floating in it; Rooney plunked Manette down in front of it. "You like gingerbread, don'tcha, Little Miss?"

Manette did not answer because her mouth was already full.

"Well," Rooney said. "Turned out to be a nice day for a ride, huh?"

Wash snorted. Hiding her smile, Jeanne dropped her head to concentrate on the bowl in front of her. Wash clanked his spoon back into his bowl and eyed Rooney. "Worst damn picnic I've ever been on."

"Yeah?" Rooney eyed him with a perfectly straight face. "What was wrong with it?"

"Ants," Wash said.

At that, Jeanne laughed aloud. She felt giddy, as if the last few hours had been just a bad dream. But it was over now. She and Manette were safe and dry. While Mrs. Rose fluttered in and out of the kitchen, replenishing their supper bowls, and Wash got the horses warm and dry in the livery, Jeanne's spirits rose until she felt like dancing. Heaven help her, she could not live without this man!

Oh, yes, she could. She would soon have her own farm, her own house. Her heart might shrivel up, but she could go on and make a new life for herself. *Vraiment,* she had no choice. Even if she wanted it to be different, she could not rope and tie the man down; it would kill him.

Rooney stood up suddenly, scrabbled at the sideboard and produced a bottle of amber liquor and two shot glasses. "Sarah musta forgot this when she dusted this mornin'."

He poured both glasses full. Before Jeanne could stop herself, she reached over and claimed one.

Rooney's thick eyebrows shot up. "Didn't know you was a drinkin' woman, Jeanne."

"But I am not," she confessed. "It is an American custom I am just learning."

Both men chuckled.

"But it is true," she insisted. "I have never tasted spirits or whiskey or whatever it is called."

Rooney poured a third glass and shoved it in front of Wash. "Down the hatch." His head tipped back and he downed the liquid in one gulp.

Wash raised his brimming glass. "Down the hatch," he echoed. He gulped it all down, then sat back in his chair waiting to see what she would do.

"Oh, very well," she said. "I will do it just to prove that I can." She lifted the liquid to her lips. "Damn the match," she announced. She held her breath, poured the whiskey into her mouth and swallowed.

*Sacre bleu!* Her throat burned as if she had eaten a red-hot coal! She couldn't take a breath, couldn't talk. Her eyes watered. And both Wash and Rooney were guffawing!

Manette stared at her with widening blue eyes.

She waved her hands in front of her, trying to draw

in some air, but nothing helped. Finally Wash stopped laughing, leaned close and pounded her back with the flat of his hand.

She coughed, then choked. At last she could speak.

"Gentlemen," she announced in a raspy voice. "I have now damned the match." Both men stopped laughing.

"Is that not what one says?" she asked.

That set them off again. Jeanne ignored them, finished her bowl of bread and milk and waited for Wash and Rooney to stop chortling. Rooney exchanged a look with Wash, then solemnly poured another shot of liquor for each of them.

Both men raised their glasses in a salute to her. "Damn the match," they said in unison.

# Chapter Twenty-Five

"Bathwater's hot," Mrs. Rose called from the kitchen. "Who's first?"

Jeanne could not wait to escape the laughter around the dining table. She grabbed Manette and marched out to the back porch where the landlady had filled the tin bathtub. She had scented the water with a sprinkling of lavender leaves, and Jeanne smiled at the gesture.

She sponged off Manette and wrapped her sleepy daughter up in a towel Mrs. Rose had heated in the oven. Manette curled up on a wood bench beside a stack of wicker laundry baskets, pulled her head down inside the warm towel like a turtle and nodded off to sleep.

The door into the kitchen stood open, but the door leading to the dining room was closed; even so, Jeanne could hear Rooney and Wash talking in low tones. Quickly she unbuttoned her wet skirt and petticoat, dropped them onto the floor, and cocked her head to be sure the men were still occupied. Satisfied, she stripped off her chemise and pantalettes and stepped into the tub.

The water barely covered her nipples, but oh, how wonderful it felt, easing the ache in her thighs and soothing her frayed nerves. How, she wondered, did men manage to ride horses all day long, day after day?

Wash's tall form loomed in the kitchen doorway, and with a squeak of surprise, Jeanne clasped her hands over her breasts. "I have not finished bathing!" She thought she shouted the words, but ever since that glass of spirits she'd downed, her head had felt funny and her mind kept circling in a dreamy haze. Perhaps she had only whispered.

"Got mighty quiet in here all of a sudden," he said. "Wanted to be sure you hadn't drowned."

"I am not drowned," she said, praying her voice sounded matter-of-fact. "I am dreaming of floating down the Garonne in a little boat on a warm summer afternoon, and the lavender fields—"

She gave a cry and jolted upright. "My lavender! The flood will sweep it away into the creek!" Suddenly frantic, she stood up in the tub, realized she was naked and sat back down with a sploosh.

"What are you looking at?"

Wash took his time in answering. He walked on into the kitchen, shut the door and returned to crouch beside the tub. "What I'm looking at," he said with a hint of laughter in his voice, "is you, Jeanne. Not touching, just looking."

"What right have you—?"

"None at all," he said quietly. "Just feeling grateful for two good horses, and for two shots of good whiskey, and for Mrs. Rose and her milk cow. And…" He held her gaze. "I'm grateful for a woman who doesn't scare easy."

She gave him the oddest look, and his belly did a slow somersault.

"And…" He did not finish the thought because Jeanne was pressing her lips to his.

"Oh, Jeanne," he said when their lips parted. "Could we…?"

*"Non."* She said the word so decisively he knew he couldn't push her. He wouldn't anyway. Given the damage he'd already done to the bond between them, one more misstep and she'd likely shoot him with that derringer she carried.

But to his surprise what she said was, "And I am grateful for you."

Wash tried not to grin.

The following morning dawned so clear and bright it was hard to look at the sky. When Wash rode out to Green Valley, the endless expanse of blue arched overhead all the way to the distant mountains. Yesterday's rainwater had soaked into the parched ground so completely the layer of mud was already starting to dry up in a tracery of cracks.

Rooney had stayed behind this morning to repair the fence blown down by the storm winds. He'd volunteered his services at breakfast "as long as Little Miss and Sarah's grandson Mark would be his helpers." Wash had to smile at the thought of little Manette wielding a hammer.

Today should be an easy day laying the iron track the rest of the way through the Cut; he hoped the storm hadn't washed out the smoothed bed his crew had labored over. As soon as the tracks reached the level ground outside Green Valley, Rooney would take over supervising the Chinese crew and Wash would move on to Gillette Springs as Sykes had ordered.

He gazed up into the hot sunshine and closed his eyes. Usually he looked forward to readying a new site, bossing the survey crew, organizing the graders and powder monkeys. This morning a pang of regret nibbled at him; he wanted to spend another night with Jeanne.

When she had kissed him on the back porch last night, his brain had gone into another crazy spin. She'd looked so enticing, even wrapped up in an old plaid bathrobe Mrs. Rose had lent her. But when he'd made a move toward her she had pressed her arms over her rib cage.

"*Non.* There is Manette to think of. She is well now, and she…she sleeps lightly."

Devil take it! He liked Manette—quite a lot, in fact; he wouldn't want to disturb her. But dammit, he couldn't take Jeanne to his own room upstairs because Rooney was already snoring like a crosscut saw in the one bed. The night before, Wash had slept on a pallet on the hard floor.

He yanked his thoughts back to what faced him today. The site was wet, and the railbed the crew had graded had washed out in a few places. But by midmorning,

Sam and his crew had the damage repaired, and by noon shiny silver rails ran the entire length of the valley and through the Green Valley Cut onto level ground. His job at the valley site was finished.

He should celebrate. Instead he stacked wood for the Chinese cook's stove and walked the entire length of track, checking whether the spikes were pounded in level with the metal rails. He then reversed his direction to double-check each joint bar. Hell and damn, the truth was he wanted to delay his leaving as long as possible.

When the silver-and-black locomotive engine fired up its boilers and chuffed through the Green Valley Cut, pushing the three-tier bunkhouse and the cars of railroad ties and rails ahead of it, Wash knew his time in Smoke River was over.

What he didn't know was how to say goodbye to Jeanne.

After the lunch break, Sam shouldered him toward his horse. "Job finished here, boss. You go to next place."

Wash took a last look at what had once been Jeanne's lavender farm and kicked General into a canter. On his way through town, he stopped in at the Golden Partridge. The redheaded bartender poured a shot of his favorite whiskey and slid it down the length of polished mahogany. He sipped it in silence and was grateful the barkeep wasn't in a talking mood.

With each passing minute he thought more and more about Jeanne, and his throat grew tighter and tighter. Finally he drained his glass, signaled a goodbye to the barman and headed for the boardinghouse to say goodbye. He felt worse with every step he took, as if a black mist was settling over his heart.

Jeanne was out in the front yard, hunched over a section of fence with a hammer in her hand, pounding nails while Rooney and Manette and Mrs. Rose's grandson propped up the collapsed slats.

He felt like he always did when he first saw her, like a horse had kicked him in the chest with all four hooves. The sensation increased to agony when he realized he'd be leaving within an hour.

Jeanne looked up, her lips closed around a mouthful of nails. She tried to smile, then clapped her hand over the nails to keep them in place. He wanted to laugh but he didn't have the energy.

While Jeanne watched, her face white and pinched, he dragged the saddlebag off his horse and forced himself to turn away from her and mount the porch steps. Mrs. Rose was in the kitchen, peeling a sinkful of potatoes. He paid Jeanne's board for the next six months.

"Chances are she won't be here that long, Colonel. She won't say why, neither."

Wash stepped back. He guessed Jeanne had some sort of plan up her sleeve. He didn't want to know what it might be. At least he knew she had money, and beyond that he couldn't let himself think.

With slow steps he hefted his saddlebag up to his room and began packing his things. When he finished, he walked across the hall and laid on Jeanne's bed a small engraved medal he'd carried with him since the War.

Rooney spied him coming out of the front door, his

bulging saddlebag over his shoulder. "Leavin' now, are ya?"

Jeanne dropped her hammer with a clunk and turned toward him. She wasn't smiling.

Wash shook hands with Rooney, then with Sarah's grandson Mark, then with Rooney again. "Pick us a place that serves pancakes for breakfast," his partner ordered.

Manette sprinted across the yard and flung both her arms around Wash's knees. He ruffled her flyaway hair and she hugged his legs even tighter. Wash swallowed hard. He would remember this moment for the rest of his life.

Jeanne stood watching him in silence, her eyes anguished. He slung the saddlebag onto his horse and turned to her.

"Jeanne." He stepped toward her just as she moved forward toward him. "I'll take a week off come Christmas," he murmured. "I'll come to see you then."

She raised her head to look into his eyes. "Do not," she whispered. "This is difficult enough."

"I want to come. I'll want to see you."

"Do not," she repeated. "Please do not." Her voice broke.

She cleared her throat and looked up at him. "Besides, I have…I am buying a farm, Wash. My life will go on."

She stepped into his arms and lifted her face to his. "Kiss me," she whispered.

She could feel the trembling of his tall frame even before his mouth touched hers. She gave herself up to his lips, his scent, his strength, his being. She knew what his leaving meant; she would never see him again.

And in a flash of clarity she also knew that she loved him.

Without speaking, he kissed her again, then deliberately set her apart from him. When she glanced up she saw that his eyes were wet.

She carried the image of his face throughout the remainder of the day while she hammered nails into the broken fence. That night she found the silver medal Wash had left on her bed. On one side was engraved "To George Washington Halliday." She turned it over. "For Valor."

She didn't stop crying until breakfast the next morning.


It was forty miles to Gillette Springs, a ten-hour ride. After saying goodbye to Jeanne, Wash didn't have the stomach to push hard, so he camped out under a stand of cottonwoods near the Santiam River. The next morning he rode on into the town.

He remembered Gillette Springs as a pretty little place, with whitewashed storefronts and wide, clean-swept boardwalks on both sides of the main street. Sure didn't look that way now. The false building fronts looked weathered and gray even in the hot midday sunshine, the noon whistle at the sawmill had a gritty sound and the yellow roses that used to ramble over the lattice in the town square were withered and dry.

He ate a lunch of ham and fried potatoes in the Gillette Hotel dining room and inquired about boarding-houses.

"Got three," the shiny-faced young waitress told him. "One takes in ladies only. One has a—" she blushed all the way up to her hairline "—shady reputation. And one's all right except the landlady is crabby. Which one do you fancy?"

"Crabby," Wash said. "If she can cook."

"Oh, Mrs. Zwenk can cook, all right. Third house from the corner."

The place looked immaculate—matching curtains in every window, two bright redbrick chimneys, even the orange zinnias along the front walk were identical to each other. He knocked at the glass-paned door.

A tall, angular woman with her gray hair caught in a bun and wearing a stiff-starched white apron jerked open the door.

"Mrs. Zwenk?"

"I am Eleanora Zwenk, yes. What do you want?"

"I'm Wash Halliday. I work for the Oregon Central Railroad, and my partner and I will be spending a month here in Gillette Springs. We'd like to rent a couple of rooms."

"Railroad, eh? Gonna run it right down Main Street?"

"No, ma'am. The railroad doesn't own that land. Most likely the tracks will run alongside the river.

She firmed her mouth. She didn't look welcoming, but the longer Wash stood there on her tidy front porch the less he cared. Might as well get down to essentials.

"Do you serve pancakes for breakfast? My partner is partial to pancakes."

"Who's your partner?" she snapped.

"His name's Rooney Cloudman." He didn't think it prudent to mention Rooney's half-Comanche heritage.

Mrs. Zwenk looked him up and down with narrowed gray eyes. "Got a jail record? I don't rent to outlaws—" she studied him again "—no matter how tall and handsome they are."

"We're both working men, Mrs. Zwenk." He tried not to let his exasperation show, but he was developing a powerful thirst for a shot of whiskey. "Ma'am? About the room?" He peeled a bill out of his wallet and thrust it into the woman's knob-fingered hand.

Mrs. Zwenk's eyebrows went up and she blinked at the money.

"Dollar a day. Each. No breakfast on Sundays."

"Deal. I'll bring my things over later." He grasped her dry hand, shook it and headed for the saloon across from the hotel.

Polly's Cage. Funny name, but it didn't matter. He felt miserable. He ached all over, especially when he thought of Jeanne.

The barkeep was even more crabby than Mrs. Zwenk. "Make up your mind, mister. I've got other customers."

Wash was beginning to feel out of place. And running out of patience. He didn't much like the town anymore. He felt something inside him ignite, and if he didn't do something about it, he was going to explode. It was like a short fuse was smoldering in his gut and if he stood still for very long it would detonate.

He'd never felt this unsettled, not even after Laura. Maybe he was getting old. Burned-out. Maybe he was tired of moving on every month or so. A brimming shot glass slid in front of him, and Wash hunkered over it. Then he shoved it out of the way with his elbow and dropped his head in his hands. He needed to think.

Everything had changed and he had no idea why. Yeah, the town was older and more run-down than the last time he'd ridden through. Mrs. Zwenk was more than crabby. And his survey crew, which was just now stumbling into the saloon, looked like they were already drunk. He recognized three of them; the fourth was even younger than Lacey, the blond kid from Minnesota.

He nodded at the men and felt duty tug at him. He shrugged the feeling away. None of those things—the crabby landlady, the weathered town—had mattered before. Why did they matter now?

He needed his work for the railroad; it kept him steady. It helped him heal from the scars of the War. And Laura. It felt good to fire black powder charges drilled into a hill of rocks instead of cannons aimed at ragged reb soldiers.

The railroad was a clean thing. It was building civilization, not destroying it.

In a strange way it felt like it wasn't enough anymore.

His head spun. He hadn't downed a drop of the whiskey sitting in the glass at the edge of the bartop, but it sure felt like he had. And then a thought blazed into his mind. The simplicity of it, the clarity, was almost blinding.

There had to be more to life than a job well done. More to life than the railroad.

He was drunk all right, but it wasn't on whiskey. Even his shirt felt different—too tight, as if he'd chosen the wrong size. He pulled the constricting collar away from his neck.

What was wrong?

*Nothing is wrong,* a voice inside his head hammered. *This is what life is, some good, a lot bad.*

He'd lived through Antietam and Bull Run and more Indian skirmishes than he could count. He'd survived. He was thirty-eight years old and he was whole and strong.

He gazed through the streaked front window at the empty street outside. The door of the mercantile was shut, its front blinds rolled down. Only three horses were tied up in front of Polly's Cage; not even enough men for Rooney's nightly poker game.

Is this what he wanted for the rest of his years on earth? Hotel breakfasts and crabby landladies?

Something tightened inside him, like he was pulling on muscles he hadn't used in a long time. It felt a lot like the growing pains he'd had as a kid. He'd hated the feeling then, and he hated it now.

## Chapter Twenty-Six

For the next three days Jeanne kept herself so busy she could not stop and let the wrenching emptiness inside consume her. She scrubbed the filthy plank floor of the farmhouse she'd bought; dusted down the bare ceiling beams; scoured the battered old Windsor kitchen range until the nickel trim gleamed; and washed all the windows, upstairs and down, with hot water and vinegar.

Her hands were red and swollen, her back stiff and her neck and shoulders ached, but not one inch of her new farmhouse—right down to the wide front porch—had escaped her broom and brush. This afternoon she'd even dragged an old, rickety ladder she'd found in the barn and teetered on it long enough to mount a swing for Manette in the pepper tree in the front yard. Her daughter spent most of the afternoon dangling her feet on the ground, begging Jeanne to come and push her.

But Jeanne was busy boiling sheets and pillowcases in

the big tin washtub and sewing curtains for the upstairs bedroom windows—yellow gingham for Manette's cozy room, blue gingham for her own. How Wash would have teased her about all that gingham! Her heart constricted as if a claw were closing around it.

Now Manette was collecting bugs from the dry grass in the yard, and Jeanne sat exhausted on the porch steps, her head in her hands, trying hard not to think of Wash Halliday. He cared about her; she knew he did. He'd shown it in a dozen ways, including making it possible for her to purchase this place and move on with her life.

But move on into a life without Wash. Her throat closed. He would have liked this farmhouse. He would tease her about the gingham napkins and her gingham work dresses, about the milk cow she'd bought from Thad MacAllister, about the lopsided swing under the tree.

She must stop imagining him in her life! He would never see her new farm.

She hated the word *never*. She liked words like *forever*. And *always*.

Manette climbed the wood porch steps, plopped herself down beside her and patted her hair. "Don't cry, *Maman*."

She lifted her head to hear her daughter ask a question: "Will Wash come back?"

Jeanne choked on an unexpected sob. "*Non, chouchou*. I think not."

Manette rolled her lower lip under her small baby teeth. "Does he not like us anymore?"

Jeanne blinked away the stinging in her eyes. "He does like us, Manette. He likes us very much." *He likes us too much, and it makes him afraid.*

He was a fool. A coward. A heartless man.

*Non,* that was not true. Wash had plenty of heart. He had plenty of courage, too. He was neither a fool nor a coward, he was…simply a man. A scarred, wounded man.

Her pulse leaped at the sound of hoofbeats, but it was Rooney who cantered his strawberry roan down the lane from the town road. With a sinking sensation, Jeanne noted the bulging saddlebags behind the saddle. Rooney, too, was moving on.

He dismounted and she stood to greet him, but found she could not speak. He tramped up the two steps to the porch and lifted both her hands in his great paws.

"I'm leavin', Jeanne." His voice went hoarse. "Sure is hard."

She could only nod. He folded her against his beefy chest and pressed his lips against her forehead. "Damn," he said. He released her, blew his nose into a large white handkerchief and bent to pat Manette.

"Well, Little Miss…" It was all he could get out before his voice cracked.

Manette flung her arms around his legs and spoke a single word in her decisive child's voice. "No."

Rooney went down on one knee and wrapped her in his arms. "I have to go, honey."

"No!" She clung to him, her small arms tight around his neck, her head burrowing between his jaw and his shoulder. He held her without moving for a long, anguished minute; when he raised his head at last, his lips formed a grim line and his eyes glittered with tears.

Jeanne clamped one hand over her mouth and with the other wrapped her fingers around the medal Wash had left for her. *For Valor.* She wore it on a chain, next to her skin.

*Oh, why did valor have to hurt so much!*

Rooney cleared his throat. "Well then, how 'bout I adopt you, Little Miss? Would you like me to be yer grandfather?"

Manette clung to his hand. "Forever and ever? You promise?"

"Forever and ever. You have my word." He blew into his handkerchief again.

Manette's face shone. "Will you teach me how to cook a rattlesnake?"

"I sure will, honey. You got one waitin' to be sliced up for the fryin' pan?"

The girl giggled. "First we have to catch it. You promised to show me how to hunt, remember?"

Rooney blinked and made a show of folding his damp handkerchief and stuffing it into his trouser pocket. "Well, now, Little Miss, huntin' is a real art, 'specially the Comanche way. Takes time to learn, and it takes practice, too. How 'bout we practice huntin' when I come back to visit?"

Manette nodded but her head stayed down in a drooped position. "Would you push me in the swing?" Her voice was almost inaudible and she did not look up.

"You got a swing?"

Jeanne caught his eye and pointed to the pepper tree in the yard.

"Oh, yeah, I see it." He sent Jeanne a grin. "Mighty fine swing. You ready?"

Manette darted away to the swing. Rooney clumped a few paces behind her, lifted her into the contraption and gave the wooden seat a shove. He'd never in his life pushed a swing. *Jes' goes to show ya, it's never too late to learn somethin' new.*

Manette sailed away from him, then swung back and Rooney reached out to push her once more.

"Higher!" she called in her determined voice.

Rooney decided he kinda liked her determined voice. He pushed the swing while the girl yelped in delight. He could have continued for hours, but suddenly he remembered where he had been heading when he'd ridden out and why he'd come in the first place.

To say goodbye.

He lifted Manette out of the swing, strode over to the porch and kissed them both once more. "I'll be back," he managed over the lump in his throat.

Jeanne watched him mount and ride away down the dusty lane. She knew she and Manette would see Rooney again. Not Wash, maybe, but certainly Rooney. After all, Rooney Cloudman had just adopted a granddaughter!

Jeanne tugged one of Manette's braids. "Do you not think it is time for our afternoon café?" She knew how much her daughter loved their grown-up "teatime talks." Today they would probably talk about Rooney. Manette did not answer. She was gazing down the lane after Rooney.

Jeanne took her hand. "Come, *chou-chou*. I will race you to the kitchen."

Rooney looked back to see Jeanne and Little Miss waving from the porch. Abruptly they pivoted, raced for the screen door and clattered into the house. By jingo, he hoped Jeanne had some good whiskey stashed in her pantry so she could "damn the match."

He twisted in the saddle one more time, and with a long sigh dug out his damp handkerchief again.

Inside Polly's Cage, Wash sat hunched over the bar, his elbows resting on the smooth mahogany. A full shot glass perched on the far edge of the bartop. Rooney settled himself into the adjacent space and signaled to the barkeep.

"Congratulate me, Wash." He grinned and followed with a wink.

"What for, Rooney? You get married?"

Rooney's eyebrows danced up and down. "Now, it's interestin' you thought of gettin' married right off. Isn't it? Huh?"

Wash ignored the innuendo. "Win a big pot in a poker game?"

"Naw. I got somethin' I never had before."

Wash glanced slantwise at his partner. "New horse? Fancy dress-up suit? Chinese girlfriend?"

"Naw—" He broke off to order a double shot of whiskey from the barkeep. "Ya know there's no women in that Celestial bunkhouse on wheels. Not sure I'd care if there was."

"Well, what, then?" It wasn't like Rooney to be

secretive—or, come to think of it, to smile like a barn cat with a mouse cowering under its paw.

Rooney gurgled down a swallow of his whiskey and turned his beaming face full on Wash. "Got me a granddaughter!"

Wash knew his jaw dropped open, but for a few seconds he couldn't seem to close his mouth. "Don't you have to have a wife first, and then a daughter who grows up and gives you a—"

"Granddaughter!" Rooney chortled. "Little Miss and me, we adopted each other." He downed another slug of spirits.

Wash stared at his friend. A happier man he'd rarely seen unless he was drunk or simple-minded. Rooney was neither.

"Before I left Smoke River I rode out to see Jeanne and Little Miss. Nice little town, Smoke River. And Sarah Rose—by Jupiter, that woman's a real prize. Anyway…" He stopped long enough to swallow his remaining whiskey. "So I'm sayin' goodbye an' Little Miss, she—"

Rooney stopped and swallowed hard. "She wouldn't let go of me till I promised I'd be her grandfather. Forever and ever. Now, ya gonna congratulate me or not?" He looked pointedly at Wash's untouched glass of whiskey.

Wash felt an awful jolt inside, as if somebody had fired a shotgun just past his ear. So Rooney had a granddaughter. That was the last word he thought he'd ever hear out of his partner's mouth, *granddaughter*. Things were sure changing.

*And what about you?* a voice nagged.

He was glad for Rooney. He grabbed his drink, clinked the shot glass against his partner's. "Damn the match!" he choked out.

The two men laughed, drained their glasses, pounded each other on the back and laughed some more.

"Jeanne, now…" Rooney began.

Instantly Wash sobered. "Yeah? What about Jeanne?"

Rooney gave him a sly look. "Why, she's doin' right fine. Moved out to that farm she wanted to buy—place about a mile outta town and pretty as a painting. She has a milk cow penned up next to the barn and a whole mess of chickens in that coop she nailed together. She's tradin' eggs and lavender wreaths and smelly silk pouches for food and supplies at the mercantile. Real enterprisin' woman."

He sneaked another glance at Wash. "Kinda surprises ya, don't it?"

Wash waited for the stab of longing in his gut to ease. "Yeah. Enterprising." Dammit to hell, he didn't want Jeanne to thrive so easily without him! Of course he wanted her to have food and shelter but…

*Doesn't she need you at all?* A woman who could do just fine without him sure was a blow to a man's pride.

Rooney finished the last of his whiskey. "You all right? Look kinda gob-smacked."

"I'm fine."

Rooney leaned closer. "No, yer not. Don't waste yer

time lyin' to me, son. My Comanche half can read yer mind without even tryin'."

"I'm fine," Wash repeated. But he knew he wasn't fine. Wasn't even close. He was barely functioning. Sooner or later he'd have to face up to it.

"Lemme tell you somethin'," Rooney muttered. "It's an old Indian saying. 'Those who have one foot in the canoe and one foot on the dock will fall into the river.'"

"You don't say," Wash snapped. He slipped off the bar stool and felt the gnawing ache in his hip. Unconsciously he straightened his leg.

Rooney eyed his friend as he hitched up his belt and strode through the saloon doors. Then he laughed out loud and ordered another whiskey.

"Here's to Wash and Jeanne," he said to the swinging doors. "One in the canoe and the other one on the dock."


"Survey crew's ready," Wash announced that evening after supper. "Going to send them out tomorrow morning."

Beside him on the front porch step of Mrs. Zwenk's boardinghouse, Rooney nodded. "Did Sykes replace Montez? Or do I hafta slog around all day with a measuring rod?"

"Nope. You get to deal with our landlady, Mrs. Zwenk. See if you can get her to lighten up on her fried eggs—they're like sun-dried cow-patties with yolks."

Rooney spit out the grass stem he was chewing. "Why me?"

Wash clapped his partner on the shoulder. "Because you're so good-looking," he said with a straight face. "Plus you said yourself you 'have a way with the ladies.'"

"It's a 'way' I'm fast growin' out of it," Rooney muttered.

Wash thought about the phrase "growing out of it" and something in his belly began to unravel. He figured he didn't need to grow *out* of anything. What he needed was to grow *into* something.

He bid Rooney good-night and limped out to the stable. Rooney had found some kind of center for himself, a lodestone that would draw him, anchor him for the rest of his life. A granddaughter.

It stirred the gnawing hunger in Wash's gut. Rooney was connected in a way Wash had never been. Rooney had found a place where he belonged.

He filled General's feedbag, then dug in his vest pocket for the apple he'd spirited away from under Mrs. Zwenk's long nose. He watched the animal crunch the fruit down, thinking about Rooney and canoes and docks…*and falling into the river.*

Dammit.

Upstairs in his room an hour later, Wash lifted his head from his hands and composed a letter to Grant Sykes. For fast delivery he would send it by rail from Smoke River all the way to Portland.

Tomorrow he'd get it to the train.

# Chapter Twenty-Seven

Jeanne jolted wide-awake from a dreamless sleep, jerked upright on the simple mattress she'd stuffed with pine boughs, and concentrated on listening. There was no sound other than the soft rustling of her pallet.

A half-moon had risen, casting silvery light through the window. Making no noise, she stood up and peered outside. The barn stood silent, and in the adjacent cow pen, Bessie was folded up under the yellowing maple tree placidly chewing her cud. Jeanne watched a long time, but nothing else moved.

Uneasy, she tiptoed across the hall to check on Manette. Her daughter slept soundly, her arms hugging the pillow squashed against her stomach. She often slept that way, as if cuddling an imaginary pet. Perhaps Manette should have a puppy!

Frowning, Jeanne rubbed her right shoulder and closed the bedroom door without a sound. After an exhausting day cleaning out the barn she should be tired enough to sleep until lunchtime, but instead, she wandered down the half-lit stairs to the kitchen. Coals still glowed in the stove firebox. She stirred up the embers and added two small chunks of wood she'd chopped from deadfall near the creek.

The fire sparked and she flinched as if it were a gunshot. *Mon Dieu*, she was jumpy as a cat. The flames began to eat into the wood and the light from the stove cast shadowy figures that danced and flickered against the wall. It reminded her of something.

Her breathing stopped and a thumping began in her ear. It reminded her of making love with Wash. In her mind's eye she saw the two of them together that first time, melding into one another like two restless shadows, touching each other and becoming one.

All at once she knew why she could not sleep. And she knew what she must do to fix it. How simple it seemed.

*Simple?* Then why was her heart leaping and fluttering like a caged bird's?

"*Chou-chou*, would you like to visit Mrs. Rose in town? Perhaps you could play with her grandson?"

Manette stood straight up in the box bed Jeanne had cobbled together until she could afford a real one with a bedstead. "Oh, *Maman*, could I really? Mark knows lots and lots about spiders!"

Jeanne shivered under her man's shirt and vest. Spiders again. *Alors*, she would let Mrs. Rose deal with it this time; Jeanne had something else on her mind.

When they arrived, riding double on the dappled gray mare, Mrs. Rose took a horrified look at Jeanne. "Child, whatever are you doing in that getup?"

Jeanne calmly helped Manette off the horse and when her daughter skipped off through the gate to find Mark, she faced a concerned Sarah Rose.

"I am doing what I must do," she said, her voice quiet.

"Harumph!" The landlady looked her up and down. "Don't tuck your shirt in, honey. Look too much like a woman. Where'd you get those duds, anyway?"

Jeanne gulped. "From Mr. Ness, at the mercantile."

The older woman narrowed her eyes. "You're riding to Gillette Springs." It wasn't a question.

Jeanne looked her straight in the eye. "I will be away for perhaps four nights. Would you—?"

"'Course I will," the landlady interjected. "Don't you worry, I'll take real good care of her."

Jeanne handed down a home-made gingham duffel bag with a fresh change of clothes for Manette. Mrs. Rose caught her hand and held it tight. "Be careful."

Jeanne nodded and patted her vest pocket. "I will. And I have my derringer."

Mrs. Rose's eyes went wide, but before she could say anything more, Jeanne flapped the reins and set off down the street, heading east.

The early morning sun in the eastern sky was blinding. She tipped her hat down to shade her eyes and for the tenth time in the last hour slowed her mare and wondered whether she was doing the right thing.

It was forty miles to Gillette Springs—too far to ride in a single day. *"Alors,"* she said aloud, "I have only to cover half that distance today. I will camp out overnight in some protected place, and ride on tomorrow morning."

Her thighs felt the burn of five unbroken hours on horseback. She kept her focus on the road far ahead, watching for a puff of dust that would indicate a rider coming toward her. So far she had seen no one on the road except for the new young doctor in town, Nathaniel Dougherty, who had barreled past her in his buggy. "Baby coming," he had shouted. "Sorry for my dust."

She had drawn rein and turned the mare away from the flurry of grit and dirt, then resumed her pace.

By noon the sun rode over her head like a huge gold plate and the heat pounded down on her head and shoulders. The scant breeze died; the dust coated her skin and made her already dry throat raw. By dusk, she was fighting to keep her drooping eyelids open.

She scanned ahead for a stand of trees or large boulders where she could roll out her woolen blanket and be screened from the road. She would not risk a fire; smoke would draw attention. Perhaps unwanted attention. A shiver went up her spine and she smoothed her hand over her vest pocket where the derringer lay.

Just ahead, off the road to the left, she spotted a clump of trees. They were lush and green and would provide good cover for herself and the mare. She pulled the mare to a halt and squinted into the haze.

A single rider was moving toward her, the horse kicking up puffs of dust. She was too far away to clearly see either the rider or the horse, but she was sure it was a man. Most women rode sidesaddle.

He was coming fast. She kicked the mare and galloped off the road, headlong into the sheltering copse of leafy cottonwoods and green pines. And a spring! Was she dreaming? Water bubbled lazily into an inviting pool. Her body felt parched from her forehead to her toes.

Quickly she slid off the mare and parted the lush branches until she could see the road. The rider had not altered his pace but was still not close enough to her thicket to be a danger. She grasped the mare's bridle, held its head down close to her shoulder and smoothed her hand over its nose. Standing motionless, afraid to breathe, she listened for hoofbeats. *Holy Father, please, do not let the mare whinny.*

The horseman drew closer. Close enough to see her if she pulled aside some branches, but she dared not; he might notice the motion of the trees.

The sound of hoofbeats grew louder, and still louder…and then passed on. She waited until the pounding hooves faded into silence and all she could hear was her mare's soft breathing and air being pulled into her own lungs.

She was safe! She cast a glance at the tumble of flat stones someone had used as a campfire. "*Non.* No fire. I will eat cold beans and apples."

She waited until full dark to sponge off the dirt in the small pool and lay out her bedroll. She dribbled a handful of oats into the mare's nosebag, then wrapped herself up in the warm wool blankets and forked the cold beans straight out of the can. She felt for the derringer, drew it out and laid it within easy reach. She closed her eyes.

An incessant question hammered in her brain: what would Wash say to her?

A dry leaf crackled and her lids snapped open. A moment later a twig snapped. Very slowly Jeanne sat up and reached for the gun.

The sporadic rustling continued, not loud, and not often—just enough to let her know she was not alone. Probably just a deer, she thought. Or a squirrel or a rabbit or...

If it was a deer or a rabbit, she could make a noise and scare it off. Carefully she scooped up a handful of leaves and crackled them into her palm.

Nothing moved.

The derringer in her right hand began to wobble. She wrapped her other hand over the grip to steady it and tried hard to keep her breathing slow and even. Surely whatever, or whoever, it was could hear her heart thudding against her ribs.

*Would he spy her mare?*

Ah, no, he would not. She had tied the animal in a thick copse that was screened from view on all sides.

Sweat dripped off her forehead. Her nose itched, but she dared not lift her hand to scratch it. She waited.

And waited.

She thought she would scream, but she waited.

It was dark and quiet in the small grove of trees Wash had used as a camp before. Unnaturally quiet. No evening sparrow trilled from the cottonwoods; no small animals rustled in the undergrowth. Reminded him of how night noises went suddenly still when Indians lay waiting in an ambush.

He had purposely ridden past the campsite, then circled around and approached from the opposite direction. He dismounted quietly, slid an oat-filled feedbag over General's muzzle, and made his way to the campfire site he remembered. Whatever noise the horse made would draw the attention of whoever was hiding among the thick growth of trees.

Sure enough, a twig cracked where he'd left the horse. General was growing restless.

Wash himself jumped at a different sound, a sharp noise that rose over the gentle gurgling of the spring. He listened for a long time, holding his body absolutely still. There it was again! A chattery noise, like stepping on dry leaves.

Whoever was hiding in the shadows was taking his sweet time making his presence known. Now that he thought about it, he had to ask himself why. An outlaw? Somebody on the run?

The back of his neck got that crawly feeling he remembered from Indian ambushes. Very deliberately he fished a small stone out of his shirt pocket and tossed it into a clump of weeds. The slight rattle faded into silence. He tried another, larger stone.

Same thing. With caution, he edged one foot forward, settled it on the ground without breaking the quiet, and only then rocked his weight onto it. Indians walked silent like that; Rooney had taught him. He lifted the other boot and set it down the same way. One more step and he'd—

"Stand where you are or I will shoot." A kid's voice, pitched low to sound like a man.

Wash peered in the direction of the voice but could see only the outline of shaggy pine trees. "Who's there?"

"None of your business." Real young kid. Voice was shaky.

"Okay if I picket my horse here?"

A pause. "Okay."

"Thought I might get some shut-eye. Okay with you?"

A longer pause. "Perhaps."

*Perhaps!* A kid who used formal English?

"I'm not coming anywhere near you, boy. Just don't shoot if you hear some noise."

No answer. Did the kid really have a gun trained on him? Maybe he was just bluffing.

"Hey, kid? I'd appreciate it if you put your sidearm away."

"No." Something about that word sounded odd. In fact, something about the kid himself didn't make sense.

"How old are you, boy?"

"None of your business."

This time Wash heard a soft sound, maybe a body rolling up in a blanket. Good. He guessed the boy's gun was no longer pointed at him. He tramped noisily over to his horse, rummaged in his saddlebag for a couple of biscuits he'd swiped from Mrs. Zwenk's breakfast platter and grabbed his water canteen. Then he loosened the saddle cinch, kicked away any stone he felt under his boots and rolled out the blanket.

He lay in the dark trying to visualize his unfriendly companion and chewed a single bite of Mrs. Zwenk's iron biscuit until his belly stopped growling. He had to laugh. The kid's voice had hardly reached a man's lower register. Kinda throaty and with a funny—

He yelped as the knowledge hit him. Somewhere near him a gun went off with a sharp snap, and a bullet zinged into the tree behind him.

Wash scrambled toward the sound. "Don't shoot!" he shouted. "Dammit, Jeanne, don't shoot!"

A stifled cry came from the cottonwoods. He crawled toward it.

"Jeanne? I know it's you." His knee landed on a rock and he groaned with frustration. "For Heaven's sake, don't pull the trigger!"

"Why should I not?" came the wavery voice.

"Because if you kill me, we'll have to have a wake instead of a wedding!"

He heard a gasp and inched blindly forward until he stumbled over a warm lump huddled near the spring.

"Wash?" came a small, distinctly female voice. "Did you say *wedding?*"

"I did." He spoke before he could stop himself.

The warm lump uncurled and reached for him. "Wash," she breathed near his ear. "How did you know it was me?"

He kissed her, and took his time with it. "Doesn't

matter," he murmured after a while. He kissed her again. "You're damn lucky I'm not armed."

"Oh," she sighed. "I am damn lucky anyway. Kiss me again."

## Chapter Twenty-Eight

He held her close for a long time while she confessed why she was on the road heading to Gillette Springs. "I decided that we should not be apart. We should be together."

"Yeah?" Wash tightened his arms about her.

"It felt good when we were together, even when we were fighting. And," she added with a catch in her voice, "I have been alone for too long. I was never lonely until you came into my life, and then I began to feel what I had been missing."

She fell silent, and Wash rose, built a fire between three of the flat rocks and retrieved a tin shaving basin from his saddlebag. He filled it with water from the spring and set it over the flames. Then he tugged the wool blanket out from under her, added his saddle blanket and tossed the double roll close to the fire.

Without speaking, they perched close together on

the bedroll, toasting their feet so close to the flames the leather soles of their boots began to smoke.

"Feet warm enough?" Wash joked. Hurriedly she pulled off her riding boots; he added his and then lined them up in front of the fire like four soldiers at attention.

He tested the heated water with his forefinger. "Try it," he invited. "You can have a whole bath just by rubbing your wet hands over your skin. 'Course," he said with a grin, "you have to take off your clothes."

Jeanne began to unbutton her vest and then the boy's striped muslin shirt she wore. When she had splashed water over herself down to her waist, she hesitated. Wash drew off her denim trousers and her lacy pantalettes and finished the job for her, running his hands over her bare skin until she began to tremble.

Then he stood, stripped and poured the remaining water over his torso and waited. Jeanne took the hint.

When they had both dried off and stopped shivering, he pulled her down beside him on the blankets. Watching the flames burn down to coals, they began to talk. It was the first time Wash had ever put into words what had been growing in his heart.

"Rooney was right about me. All these years I've been driven by fear, so scared of getting hurt again that I forgot how to live."

Jeanne reached for his hand and laced her fingers with his, suddenly very close to tears. "Do you want to remember how to live?"

"I'm not sure I can," he admitted honestly. "How I spent the years after Laura wasn't exactly living, it was more like dying. And living—real living, with you and Manette—still scares me some."

Jeanne leaned over to brush her lips against his cheek.

"I think that it scares you *a lot*." She rested her head on his shoulder. "But you kept trying, that was the important thing. Courage is not walking into battle with no fear—you should know this as a soldier. Courage is feeling great fear, but walking forward anyway."

"Jeanne," he said in a low voice. "I don't want to be away from you. Don't want to spend my nights wondering if you are aching for me the same way I'm aching for you. I love you. I want us to get married."

"Ah, that is what I hoped you would want! That is why I was coming to see you."

"Jeanne…" he said when he finally lifted his mouth from hers. "Now that Manette has a grandfather, do you think she might like to adopt a father, as well?"

"I am quite sure of it. And if she does not, I will take away her spider box."

Their laughter rose into the quiet.


Dr. Nathaniel Dougherty drove his buggy slowly along the road back to Smoke River. Twins, he mused. He'd delivered twins tonight. Twice the labor, but twice the joy.

The horses were tired. He was tired. Suddenly he pulled up. Laughter floated on the warm night air, a man's deep tones and a woman's lighter ones. It came from the grove of cottonwoods up ahead.

Well, well, well. He couldn't help smiling.

He would not interrupt. Maybe nine months from now there would be another set of twins for him to deliver.

"You *own* the Double H?" Wash stared at her, scarcely able to believe what she had said.

"I do," Jeanne admitted. "It is a nice farm, is it not? I like it very much."

"Did you know this was my father's place? Before he died he turned the Bar H into the Double H, hoping I'd come home to stay after the War."

Jeanne just looked at him, her blue-green eyes widening.

"No, I did not know. That is perfect, then!" She admired the gold band on her finger. "You are Wash Halliday. And I am now Jeanne Halliday. Does that not make a Double H?"

Wash could not answer. The joy he felt made everything glow with an extra-bright luster.

For a long moment they simply stood together on a hill overlooking their farm. Then Wash and Jeanne Halliday, married that morning in the Smoke River Catholic Church, joined hands and bent to admire their daughter Manette's new collection of spiders.

\* \* \* \* \*

## COMING NEXT MONTH FROM

# HARLEQUIN®
# HISTORICAL

## Available February 22, 2011

- **THE WIDOWED BRIDE**
  by **Elizabeth Lane**
  **(Western)**

- **THE SHY DUCHESS**
  by **Amanda McCabe**
  **(Regency)**
  spin-off from *The Diamonds of Welbourne Manor* anthology

- **BOUGHT: THE PENNILESS LADY**
  by **Deborah Hale**
  **(Regency)**
  *Gentlemen of Fortune*

- **HIS ENEMY'S DAUGHTER**
  by **Terri Brisbin**
  **(Medieval)**
  *The Knights of Brittany*

# REQUEST YOUR FREE BOOKS!

 HARLEQUIN® HISTORICAL:
Where love is timeless

## 2 FREE NOVELS PLUS 2 FREE GIFTS!

**YES!** Please send me 2 FREE Harlequin® Historical novels and my 2 FREE gifts (gifts are worth about $10). After receiving them, if I don't wish to receive any more books, I can return the shipping statement marked "cancel." If I don't cancel, I will receive 6 brand-new novels every month and be billed just $4.94 per book in the U.S. or $5.49 per book in Canada. That's a savings of at least 18% off the cover price! It's quite a bargain! Shipping and handling is just 50¢ per book in the U.S. and 75¢ per book in Canada.* I understand that accepting the 2 free books and gifts places me under no obligation to buy anything. I can always return a shipment and cancel at any time. Even if I never buy another book from the Reader Service, the two free books and gifts are mine to keep forever.

246/349 HDN FC45

Name _____ (PLEASE PRINT) _____

Address _____ Apt. # _____

City _____ State/Prov. _____ Zip/Postal Code _____

Signature (if under 18, a parent or guardian must sign) _____

Mail to the **Reader Service:**
**IN U.S.A.:** P.O. Box 1867, Buffalo, NY 14240-1867
**IN CANADA:** P.O. Box 609, Fort Erie, Ontario L2A 5X3

Not valid for current subscribers to Harlequin Historical books.

**Want to try two free books from another line?**
**Call 1-800-873-8635 or visit www.ReaderService.com.**

\* Terms and prices subject to change without notice. Prices do not include applicable taxes. N.Y. residents add applicable sales tax. Canadian residents will be charged applicable taxes. Offer not valid in Quebec. This offer is limited to one order per household. All orders subject to credit approval. Credit or debit balances in a customer's account(s) may be offset by any other outstanding balance owed by or to the customer. Please allow 4 to 6 weeks for delivery. Offer available while quantities last.

**Your Privacy**—The Reader Service is committed to protecting your privacy. Our Privacy Policy is available online at www.ReaderService.com or upon request from the Reader Service.

We make a portion of our mailing list available to reputable third parties that offer products we believe may interest you. If you prefer that we not exchange your name with third parties, or if you wish to clarify or modify your communication preferences, please visit us at www.ReaderService.com/consumerschoice or write to us at Reader Service Preference Service, P.O. Box 9062, Buffalo, NY 14269. Include your complete name and address.

USA TODAY *bestselling author Lynne Graham*
*is back with a thrilling new trilogy*
SECRETLY PREGNANT, CONVENIENTLY WED

*Three heroines must marry alpha males to keep*
*their dreams…but Alejandro, Angelo and Cesario*
*are not about to be tamed!*

*Book 1—JEMIMA'S SECRET*
*Available March 2011 from Harlequin Presents®.*

JEMIMA yanked open a drawer in the sideboard to find Alfie's birth certificate. Her son was her husband's child. It was a question of telling the truth whether she liked it or not. She extended the certificate to Alejandro.

"This has to be nonsense," Alejandro asserted.

"Well, if you can find some other way of explaining how I managed to give birth by that date and Alfie not be yours, I'd like to hear it," Jemima challenged.

Alejandro glanced up, golden eyes bright as blades and as dangerous. "All this proves is that you must still have been pregnant when you walked out on our marriage. It does not automatically follow that the child is mine."

"'I know it doesn't suit you to hear this news now and I really didn't want to tell you. But I can't lie to you about it. Someday Alfie may want to look you up and get acquainted."

"If what you have just told me is the truth, if that little boy does prove to be mine, it was vindictive and extremely selfish of you to leave me in ignorance!"

Jemima paled. "When I left you, I had no idea that I was still pregnant."

"Two years is a long period of time, yet you made no attempt to inform me that I might be a father. I will want DNA tests to confirm your claim before I make any decision about what I want to do."

"Do as you like," she told him curtly. "*I* know who Alfie's father is and there has never been any doubt of his identity."

"I will make arrangements for the tests to be carried out and I will see you again when the result is available," Alejandro drawled with lashings of dark Spanish masculine reserve.

"I'll contact a solicitor and start the divorce," Jemima proffered in turn.

Alejandro's eyes narrowed in a piercing scrutiny that made her uncomfortable. "It would be foolish to do anything before we have that DNA result."

"I disagree," Jemima flashed back. "I should have applied for a divorce the minute I left you!"

Alejandro quirked an ebony brow. "And why didn't you?"

Jemima dealt him a fulminating glance but said nothing, merely moving past him to open her front door in a blunt invitation for him to leave.

"I'll be in touch," he delivered on the doorstep.

*What is Alejandro's next move? Perhaps rekindling their marriage is the only solution! But will Jemima agree?*

*Find out in Lynne Graham's
exciting new romance
JEMIMA'S SECRET*

*Available March 2011
from Harlequin Presents®.*

# Start your Best Body today with these top 3 nutrition tips!

1. **SHOP THE PERIMETER OF THE GROCERY STORE:** The good stuff—fruits, veggies, lean proteins and dairy—always line the outer edges of the store. When you veer into the center aisles, you enter the temptation zone, where the unhealthy foods live.

2. **WATCH PORTION SIZES:** Most portion sizes in restaurants are nearly twice the size of a true serving and at home, it's easy to "clean your plate." Use these easy serving guidelines:
   - Protein: the palm of your hand
   - Grains or Fruit: a cup of your hand
   - Veggies: the palm of two open hands

3. **USE THE RAINBOW RULE FOR PRODUCE:** Your produce drawers should be filled with every color of fruits and vegetables. The greater the variety, the more vitamins and other nutrients you add to your diet.

Find these and many more helpful tips in

## YOUR BEST BODY NOW

by

## TOSCA RENO

**WITH STACY BAKER**

Bestselling Author of
**THE EAT-CLEAN DIET®**

*Available wherever books are sold!*

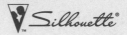

HARLEQUIN*
*Super Romance*

Top *author*
# Janice Kay Johnson

*brings readers a riveting new romance*
*with*
# Bone Deep

Kathryn Riley is the prime suspect in
the case of her husband's disappearance
four years ago—that is, until someone tries
to make her disappear…forever. Now
handsome police chief Grant Haller must
stop suspecting Kathryn and instead begin
to protect her. But can Grant put aside the
growing feelings for Kathryn long enough
to catch the real criminal?

**Find out in March.**

*Available wherever*
*books are sold.*

HSR71692

HARLEQUIN® *Presents*®

USA TODAY *Bestselling Author*

# Lynne Graham

*is back with her most exciting trilogy yet!*

## SECRETLY PREGNANT CONVENIENTLY WED

Jemima, Flora and Jess aren't looking for love,
but all have babies very much in mind...and they may
just get their wish and more with the wealthiest, most
handsome and impossibly arrogant men in Europe!

Coming March 2011

# JEMIMA'S SECRET

Alejandro Navarro Vasquez has long desired vengeance after
his wife, Jemima, betrayed him. When he discovers the
whereabouts of his runaway wife—and that she has a two-
year-old son—Alejandro is determined to settle the score....

## FLORA'S DEFIANCE (April 2011)
## JESS'S PROMISE (May 2011)

Available exclusively from Harlequin Presents.